MAINELY MAYHEM

Novels by Matt Cost
aka Matthew Langdon Cost

The Goff Langdon Mainely Mysteries
Mainely Power
Mainely Fear
Mainely Money
Mainely Angst
Mainely Wicked
Mainely Mayhem

The Clay Wolfe / Port Essex Mysteries
Wolfe Trap
Mind Trap
Mouse Trap
Cosmic Trap
Pirate Trap

The Brooklyn 8 Ballo Mysteries
Velma Gone Awry
City Gone Askew

Historical Fiction Novels
I Am Cuba: Fidel Castro and the Cuban Revolution
At Every Hazard: Joshua Chamberlain and the Civil War
Love in a Time of Hate

MAINELY MAYHEM

A Goff Langdon Mainely Mystery

MATT COST

Encircle Publications
Farmington, Maine, U.S.A.

MAINELY MAYHEM Copyright © 2024 Matt Cost

Paperback ISBN 13: 978-1-64599-578-4
Hardcover ISBN 13: 978-1-64599-579-1
Ebook ISBN 13: 978-1-64599-580-7

Library of Congress Control Number: 2024948884

ALL RIGHTS RESERVED. In accordance with the U.S. Copyright Act of 1976, no part of this publication may be reproduced, distributed, or transmitted in any form or by any means, or stored in a database or retrieval system, without prior written permission of the publisher, Encircle Publications, Farmington, ME.

This book is a work of fiction. All names, characters, places and events are either products of the author's imagination or are used fictitiously.

Encircle Editor: Cynthia Brackett-Vincent

Cover design and digital illustration by Deirdre Wait
Cover photographs © Getty Images

Published by:

Encircle Publications
PO Box 187
Farmington, ME 04938

info@encirclepub.com
http://encirclepub.com

To the checks and balances that keep our nation great.

Three weeks earlier...

As if in slow motion, he saw the man pull the gun from the duffel bag as lethargically as rush hour traffic on the beltway. It was a stunning July day, 80° with no trace of humidity in the capital city. A perfect day for a baseball game. A wonderful day to be with your son, grandson, and granddaughter. The Nats were hosting the Cincinnati Reds in an early afternoon game. Not that the Nats were having a good season, but a game was a game. There'd be hot dogs, pretzels, ice cream, and maybe a beer.

The gun came sweeping up, not twenty feet from where he walked with his family and the two U.S. Marshals. Somebody yelled. Ben Till of his security detail stepped toward him with a hand raised. It was all too late. They were in the process of bypassing the line that was waiting to enter the game, ready to flash their credentials and go to their special box seats. The day went from idyllic to surreal to horrific in a snap of the fingers.

He could see the blue of the Anacostia River in front of him, the Supreme Court building was less than two miles behind him, his home for the past few years, and the gunman stood to his right. Several pigeons startled from their roost fluttered into the air. As the gun swept up, Ben Till attempted to step in front of him as a shield, but he was already moving to push his grandchildren to the ground. Till's partner pulled his weapon from the holster.

People in the crowd opened their mouths to yell, to scream, but he heard nothing. One step, a thrust of his arm, toppling little Jimmy to the ground with one shove, reaching for Katie when he felt the impact. One. Two. Three. There was no pain. It was as if he'd been hit with a padded baseball bat. His breath was gone.

It wasn't his time. He had so much to do. But it was his time.

Chapter 1

Langdon winced inwardly at the dinginess of his office. Most times he embraced this shabby back room to his mystery bookshop. This is where he entertained clients of his private investigator business. But usually, the men and women who hired him were locals who did not look as if they'd stepped straight from the pages of *GQ* magazine, as did the man and woman presently across from him.

Cooper Walker wore a dark blue suit with a stiffly pressed white shirt and a muted red tie. His shoes were shined like black mirrors and his hair was carefully coiffed and parted to the side. He was thin but athletic and his blue and piercing eyes blazed keenly forth. His handshake had been firm and his manner matter of fact. He was the assistant to the chief of staff to the president of the United States.

Zara Farhat was equally thin and athletic, wore a gray pantsuit, had straight black hair and brown eyes that bespoke a fierceness of temperament. She sat down in the L.L.Bean chair, which was part of a pair that perhaps were the only classy items in the office, as Cooper sat down next to her. She slid a folder onto the desk. Zara was a junior member of the office of the White House counsel.

Dog, a chocolate Lab simply named dog, small d, sat between them, turning his head, first to one, and then the other for head rubs. They didn't seem to fear getting dog hair on their fine clothes. Langdon chalked that up in the plus column of their character assessment that he was building, a necessity whenever entertaining a potential client. Dog was Langdon's trusted sidekick.

"What can I do for you?" Langdon asked after a pause indicating the ball was in his court to begin the proceedings. The meeting had been set yesterday with no details. "Is the president paying a visit to Brunswick?"

Cooper grinned. He had an easygoing and likeable face. "No, that is not the purpose of our visit."

"Think the last president to come to town was Bill Clinton back in '94. Didn't see him, but I did work out in the gym right back there," Langdon nodded his head to indicate behind the two clients, through the Coffee Dog Bookstore, and out the back of the building, "alongside of George Stephanopoulos, his senior advisor on policy and strategy. Terrible form on the stair climber. Surprised the man can still walk."

"That was before you became a PI and opened up the mystery bookstore?" It seemed that Cooper would be running the initial part of the conversation.

"Around about the same time."

"It would be safe to say that you know Brunswick as well as anybody. Born, raised, local businessman, private investigator—you'd be the resident expert."

"I know a few secrets, for sure, as well as all the surface stuff."

"Such as?"

It was Langdon's turn to grin. "Wouldn't be secrets if I told you, now, would it? Ben Franklin said that three men," he looked at Zara, "people, can keep a secret just fine if two of them are dead."

"You have quite an impressive resumé. Including, but not restricted to, toppling a sitting governor, getting shot in the head, being used as a dartboard, saving a U.S. Senator from blackmail, finding that boy, and uncovering that wendigo cult of cannibals last year."

"You seem to have done your own investigation of me. Am I in some sort of trouble?"

"Not in the slightest, Mr. Langdon—"

"Just Langdon will do fine."

"Not in the slightest, Langdon. But perhaps you could fill in some details about yourself that is not of the… public record."

Langdon leaned backward in his desk chair and surveyed the man, barely of shaving age, probably recently out of law school, but on a fast track to success. He shrugged. "Getting shot in the head was great for business. Tipped the scales and turned the mystery bookshop profitable and kept my investigation firm busy for several years."

Cooper chuckled. "Hadn't thought about that. Your file suggests that you vote independent, often meaning democrat, but almost never republican. Yet, you exposed the villainy of an independent governor and aided a republican senator."

Langdon wondered if there was a question. Dog, as if growing impatient, wandered over to the leather sofa, worn and comfortable, and hoisted himself up for a nap.

"How is your wife? Chabal."

"Perhaps we can stop beating around the bush and get to the point of this meeting."

Zara cleared her throat. "The nature of our business demands these personal questions as well as absolute confidentiality."

Langdon shifted his gaze to her. "And do you plan on sharing the nature of your business?"

Zara tapped the folder on the desk with her finger, the short nails polished a light blue. "We need you to sign an NDA before entering that level of mutual sharing."

Langdon leaned forward, pulled the file closer, opened it. The document was nineteen pages long. There were tabs for him to initial, sign, and date. He did so without reading what it said.

"You don't want to read it?" Zara raised one eyebrow.

"Don't figure this is some diabolic plot by the president to con me."

"You heard about Justice Daniels' death a few weeks back?" Cooper resumed the role of speaker.

Langdon nodded. "Sure. Terrible but ironic that he was killed by a random act of gun violence after just voting that the latest gun bill was unconstitutional."

Cooper seemed to measure Langdon with his eyes. "Justice Daniels was one of the most conservative members of the Supreme Court. But now he will be replaced by a much more liberal justice. Appointed by the president."

"If the senate approves it and the republicans don't hold the nominee hostage."

Cooper nodded. "That is why the president wants his choice to be of impeccable virtue. A shining star of morality and a career filled with good deeds and important accomplishments."

"Don't tell me you're here to let me know I'm being nominated to replace Daniels on the Supreme Court?" Langdon kept his face deadpan. "Justice Langdon does have a ring to it."

Cooper's grin was a bit more tight-lipped this time, and then realizing the sarcasm, filled his face with teeth as he emitted a small guffaw. "Close. But the president has selected another prominent Brunswick resident other than yourself."

"And who would that be?"

"Judge Cornelius Remington."

This did not surprise Langdon. "I, of course, know who he is. He's even come in to buy a few mysteries, but I can't say I *know* him. I'm not sure that I'd be the best person to be a reference."

Cooper leaned forward, elbows on the desk, fingers steepled under his chin. "We, well, a pair of FBI agents will be doing a background investigation in the local area, but it was thought that a local liaison would be a good choice. A guide, if you will, for their inquiries and scrutiny."

"That would be the two people I'm meeting with this afternoon?"

"Yes."

"What is your role in being here?"

"The president wants to make sure that there are no snakes in the closet of Judge Remington. We can't risk a debacle like what occurred with the nomination from the last administration. It all has to go squeaky clean. That said, Zara, me, and the two agents will be working together to make certain that there are no snakes in the closet."

"Skeletons," Langdon said. "I believe the adage is no skeletons in the closet."

~ ~ ~ ~ ~

Chabal poured her second glass of Chardonnay of the day. It was almost noon, and she hadn't showered or brushed her teeth yet. Didn't look like she was going to. She had on a pair of loose and comfortable shorts and a T-shirt with no bra. She settled back onto the couch as the commercials ended and the game show she was watching resumed. She wasn't even sure what the program was, even though she watched it Monday through Friday. Her thoughts were elsewhere.

It was usually the third glass of wine that chased the horror of the wendigo from the marrow of her mind. The routine was to accomplish that feat by high noon. Then it was a balancing act of priming the pump without overdoing it and entering oblivion. Not that mental blankness was worse than sobriety. It had been 407 days since the wendigo and the wiccans had abducted her, stripped her naked, and tortured her in preparation for a ritual slaying with plans of eating her.

Self-medication was the second thought of everyday. The first was to ascertain that she was still alive. Langdon was usually gone off by that time and she'd go straight to the fridge for a green-skinned grape breakfast. It had been 408 days since she'd made love to her husband, and this pinched the guilt sensors in her body, but the thought of sexual intercourse made her body go dry and tight.

There was some satisfaction that the wendigo had been merely a man, even if deeply warped and perverted. And that he'd been convicted to multiple life sentences, living out the rest of his life without a nose or a penis. Chabal cackled with grim amusement at the dismemberment of the beast. She'd tried to throw herself into working the bookstore, helping with the PI business, doing household improvements, and even exercise, before tailing off into her present state of crapulence.

It was usually now, on the second glass of wine of the morning, that Chabal would vow that this was the last day of drunkenness. Tomorrow she would put her life back together. Perhaps she'd wake the following dawn with the cockcrow in time to climb astride Langdon and connect physically and mentally with her husband as she hadn't for far too long. She'd go to the gym along with Langdon, shower afterward and put on a sun dress. Put on a bra and walk over and into the bookshop. She would just have to get over the wendigo.

That vision would dull with the third glass. Fade with the fourth. And then would come the welcome embrace of oblivion. A place where the wendigo did not exist.

Chapter 2

Langdon walked Cooper and Zara of the White House staff to their car in the back parking lot. Once they drove off, he looked at the time on his phone. He had an hour to kill before the phase two team arrived. Just enough time to pop out and get a bite to eat.

He ducked back inside to make sure that everything was running smoothly. Jonathan Starling was waiting on a customer at the counter and a few others browsed the shelves.

One had the look of an out-of-stater vacationing in the area, probably out to Harpswell or Bailey Island. Another was the owner of Lenin Stop Coffee Shop just across the street. The third looked familiar but he couldn't quite place them. He approached the tourist woman first to see if he could help her find anything. She asked if the store carried anything other than *just* mysteries. He told her no, that was why it was called the Coffee Dog *Mystery* Bookstore.

His tone must have reeked of sarcasm for she apparently took offense and stormed out the door. One down, he thought, a grin creasing his face, a rare occurrence over the last year, since his wife had failed to emerge from the ordeal with the wendigo as anything but a husk of her formal self. Nightmares, day drinking, and apathy ruled their home and there didn't seem to be anything he could do to fix it. Offending a pretentious tourist was about all he had to look forward to these days.

That sort of person didn't belong here, anyway, Langdon mused. Not with the jazz music drizzling forth from the Sonos Era 300 speakers, the wide variety of coffee set up in the urns, and the all-around chill vibe that he'd worked so hard to create for the past twenty-five years. There was currently on display artwork by high school students, including an array of photographs, paintings, and sculptures. And, of course, the welcoming presence of the host, dog, who greeted most customers with an unbridled enthusiasm.

"What'd you say to Miss Priss?" Starling asked having completed the transaction for a trio of Portland based mysteries by Bruce Robert Coffin, Kate Flora, and Jule Selbo.

"Told her Walmart sells books, too."

Starling grinned. He'd looked to be in his eighties the entire twenty-five years Langdon had known him. His face was lined and cracked from a younger bout with alcohol, a drug that he'd steered clear of for quite some time now. Langdon had been plying this former lawyer, now turned bookstore clerk, with questions on how he'd achieved sobriety for the past year, but the only magic seemed to be that if one wanted to quit badly enough, then one had a chance. And then it was still one day at a time.

"You're getting just as crusty as me," Starling said.

Langdon felt as old as Starling looked. It'd been a tough year. "Guilty pleasures."

"The best kind."

"You be okay here at the store if I run out and get some lunch?"

"Not that you do anything around here, but yes, I'll be fine. Plus, Raven is coming in at noon."

"Don't do anything?" Langdon raised an eyebrow in disgust. "Didn't you just take notice of how I dispatched that lady from away?"

"Where you getting food?"

"Wretched Lobster. You want something?"

"Fish and chips if you're coming back this way."

"Got a meeting with the FBI at one."

Starling whistled. "What'd you do?"

"I, being a local legend, have been retained by the White House."

"President's wife cheating on him? You supposed to snoop and take pictures?"

Langdon chuckled. "I'll have you know that those two who just left are inner circle."

"Looked young enough that the circle might be story time at preschool."

"I've been retained to investigate the background of Judge Cornelius Remington as his name has been proffered to be a Supreme Court justice." It, Langdon thought, hadn't taken him long to break the NDA.

"Wow. A member of SCOTUS from right here in little ole Brunswick."

"That's what a lawyer with ambition can achieve."

"That and a boatload of stress. No thank you."

"I'll be back by one with fish and chips." Langdon waved his hand, whistled for dog, and went into the hallway.

The Coffee Dog Bookstore was in an old department store building that now housed various businesses, offices, and was connected to a gym via an underground tunnel that had once been the way goods were moved from the warehouse out back into the store. Langdon and dog breezed out the front door onto the only Maine Street in the state. There were wide sidewalks, four lanes of traffic, raised crosswalks, and small trees providing shade.

To the right, up the hill, was the First Parish Church and behind it, Bowdoin College. Straight ahead led up the coast to popular tourist destinations such as Damariscotta, Boothbay Harbor, Camden, and Bar Harbor. Behind them was L.L.Bean, Portland, a series of upscale towns, and then the exit from Maine and the rest of the country. Langdon and dog turned left, toward the Androscoggin River and the Green Bridge which separated Brunswick from Topsham.

Brunswick had avoided the path that much of the rest of America had followed, that is, turning downtowns into strip malls and chains. Here, in town, owner-operated shops sold a variety of items from organic foods to furniture, and diverse restaurants offered anything one could want from steak to sushi and an ethnic array of possibilities for every palette. Galleries displayed and sold artwork, breweries and wine bars offered beverages, and a green area called the Mall had a farmers' market, music, and food trucks.

All of this was pressed together into less than a one-mile span, stretching from Bowdoin College on the hill to the old Fort Andross Mill building on the river. This was his town. A place he'd been born and raised and raised his own daughter in. Been married, divorced, remarried. He owned a bookshop, ran a PI business, had coached sports, and embedded himself into the very cracks of the brick sidewalks of this town. He was Brunswick and Brunswick was him.

The Wretched Lobster was just a couple blocks down on the left. Langdon greeted several people by name as he walked, simple hellos for those he knew but couldn't remember their moniker, but dog said hello to friends and strangers alike.

The first-floor restaurant was the kind of place that had lace tablecloths and classical music playing in the background. Everybody spoke in muted tones and candles adorned the tables. It hadn't always been this elegant, a gradual change over the years to meet the upscale clientele of Brunswick. This shift toward the more highbrow customer was one that Langdon mocked his friend, Richam, the owner, about on a regular basis.

Langdon took the stairs down to the basement tavern where he knew he'd find Richam and a much more inviting and comfortable atmosphere. The bar itself was made of Brazilian cherry, polished to a fine sheen with plush padded stools and shelves crowded with every liquor imaginable. Postcards sent from patrons on vacation around the world were pinned, taped, and tacked to every inch of available wall space. Lanterns with brass bases bolstered dim, recessed lighting along the bar, with smaller lanterns deployed on the seven or eight high tables scattered across the room. A dartboard took up one corner, while two pool tables sat on display, silent and inviting at this time of day.

Richam was a slim man with a military bearing even though he'd never served. He'd moved to Brunswick with his pregnant wife twenty-five years earlier from a South American island nation when the politics of the country overflowed into violence. He wore thick-framed black glasses, had a narrow mustache, and was always impeccably dressed. Even though the owner of the establishment, he preferred working as the bartender downstairs, a place where he'd gotten his start.

Dog bounded over to the man, his butt wiggling, following the motion of his tail, his head gyrating with the rest of his body. Richam was his friend and, more importantly, had access to unlimited food. As if on cue, Richam pulled part of a sandwich that was sitting on a deserted plate that hadn't yet been bussed and tossed it to the canine.

"Long time, no see, my friend," Richam said.

"Been too long," Langdon said.

"How's Chabal doing?"

Langdon shrugged. "Not real good."

"Jewell has been trying to get her to come over to the house just to hang out, but so far, no luck."

"Tell her I appreciate that. Hopefully, given time, the mental scars will heal."

"You eating lunch?"

"Reuben. Fish and chips to go for Star."

"Something to drink?"

"Lemonade." Watching Chabal deteriorate into the bottom of a wine bottle had dried up Langdon's own proclivities with alcohol and he'd been totally dry for some months now.

Richam tapped out the order on the computer screen, poured the lemonade, and set it on the counter. "How you holding up?"

"High season for book selling."

"Not what I mean."

"Looks like I'm getting hired in a high-profile case." Langdon looked left and right, leaned forward, and spoke in his best whisper. "Working for the White House."

"Still not what I mean."

Langdon shrugged.

"How about you invite us over? Me and Jewell. Heck, gather the whole gang. It's been too long."

Langdon's eyes burned into the countertop.

~ ~ ~ ~ ~

The Coffee Dog Bookstore was devoid of customers when Langdon returned with the take-out bag.

"Couple of modern Boy Scouts waiting for you in the office," Starling said.

"Modern Boy Scouts?"

"FBI 2023. Seems the government doesn't just hire white pretty boys who look like Tom Cruise in that *Top Gun* thingy."

"Don't believe that was about FBI agents," Langdon said.

"You get the point, Ghost Rider."

"Sure. I guess." Langdon nodded. "All good here?"

"You think to get anything for Raven?"

Langdon looked to where Raven was straightening books. "Her dad thought she might like the Greek Salad. That's for her if she wants it."

"How's Richam doing?"

"Prying into things as always." Langdon started to walk away, paused, and looked back. "Thinking about having a barbecue at my place Saturday night. You got any plans?"

Starling scoffed. "You know better than that. I imagine that my Derry Girls will do fine without me for one night."

Langdon raised an eyebrow.

"Thing on Netflix."

"Gotcha."

Langdon gave a wave to Raven as he passed by. She'd arrived in America two years back to inform Richam Denevieux that she was the daughter he didn't know about. This had been shocking to him but even more so to his wife Jewell. Last year, Langdon had hired her on part-time at the bookshop, hours that had become full-time as Chabal ceased coming into work.

As Langdon entered his office, two figures rose from the chairs in front of his desk and turned toward him.

The first to reach out his hand was in his mid-thirties, had skin like a caramel candy, and a thin-and-tight mustache under his hawk-like nose. "Royal Delgado, sir, good to meet you."

"Goff Langdon. Just Langdon will do fine." The handshake was firm and brief.

The second agent stepped up, a square-faced woman with blonde hair cropped on the side and a crease in her forehead. "Parker Thomas, sir."

Langdon wanted to see if saying 'at ease' would be helpful but refrained. Instead, he shook her hand. "Sit. And call me Langdon." He walked around and took his seat, noting the empty chair next to him, the one that had been forlorn for a year now. "I understand that I am to help the two of you with the background investigation of Judge Remington."

"Yes, sir, I mean, Mr. Lang… Langdon." Parker flushed slightly.

"We would like to stress that there is no reason to believe that anything will turn up that will be a problem," Royal said. "We would just be performing our due diligence."

"Yes. Our due diligence." Langdon narrowed his eyes at the man. "And what, exactly, would that look like?"

"CARLA F. BAD is what it would look like," Royal said.

"It's a mnemonic," Parker said.

"Character, Associates, Reputation, Loyalty, Ability, Finances, Bias, Alcohol/Addictions, and Drugs."

Langdon tried not to grin and was only partly successful. These were not the FBI agents of the movies. Stern faced men with closely clipped short hair, cleanly shaven, and sparse on conversation. This is what Starling had meant by FBI 2023. Diverse and green behind the ears, not yet seasoned. Perhaps the movie-type agents were infiltrating drug cartels, running down serial killers, and investigating fraud.

"Where do we start?" he asked.

Chapter 3

Royal and Parker had given Langdon the names of three people whose last known address was in the local area, but who had not yet been found. They all had some sort of relationship to Judge Remington. The mission confused him slightly—if the FBI couldn't find somebody, what was he to do? It wouldn't do any good to get his cop friend, Bart, Sergeant Jeremiah Bartholomew, to run the names through the system. That would usually be his first choice, but now he'd been asked to find people who the FBI couldn't.

Langdon grinned thinly at the notion that he'd been tasked with an undertaking that the Feds had failed to accomplish. Then his bared teeth turned to a sneer and then a snarl before wiping clear of his face entirely. Typically, his next choice after Bart in something like this would've been to pay a visit to Danny T. The man knew every inch of Brunswick, each and every buzz, chatter, hearsay, slander, scandal, or bit of gossip that even slightly passed fleetingly through the dullest dimwit in Brunswick.

But that ship had sailed. Danny T. no longer existed.

This left Langdon with a dilemma on where to start his search. The computer was useless. Anything that he could find would've been already found. It was time for old fashioned detective work. Stomping the streets. Gabbing with the people. Following tendrils of rumor and searching in the cracks of the sidewalks and the tiniest of spaces.

There was no place like here, he thought. Langdon had modified

Dorothy's mantra from *The Wizard of Oz* to his own particular application. There was no place like here. There was no time like now.

He peeked his head out of his office. The store was empty but for Starling and Raven. He called to Starling and waved him back. The here and now.

"Did you friend them?" Starling asked sinking into a chair across from Langdon.

"Friend them?"

"Isn't that how it works now? With the young people anyway. You hold up your smart phone and connect on FaceSnapChat or something like that so that you can then know everything there is about each other right down to what you eat for dinner and when you poop."

Langdon chuckled. Shook his head. But figured that his own social media presence, what little there was of it, had been completely scoured. It wasn't his own postings he worried about. It was people like Delilah Friday and others that may've taken pictures of Langdon in embarrassing predicaments. Things he might not want his daughter to see or his customers to know about.

But that is what he'd been asked to do regarding Judge Remington. Ferret out any illegal, unethical, or embarrassing incidents of his life, past or present, and expose them to the world. It was not the first time Langdon had wondered about this conundrum of his life. He was, after all, a PI, who made his living by exposing cheating spouses, revealing false workplace injuries, uncovering lies, and exposing employee theft. What if the tables were turned? If the chessboard were reversed so that now he was the one being investigated? How would he like that?

What things did he, Goff Langdon, have to hide? Through the course of his life, he'd drank too much, which sometimes had led to things he certainly wasn't proud of. Would he like it if his depressed wife, Chabal, were dragged into the spotlight? Because a clinically depressed spouse was certainly something the White House would be concerned about before selecting a Supreme Court justice. Especially a wife who began the day drinking and proceeded to do so all day long while never leaving the house.

Langdon decided that if the president ever came knocking, he'd most certainly turn down the nomination for the highest court in the land.

"What are you smirking at?" Starling asked.

Langdon broke from his thoughts with a start. Inside his own mind was a journey he'd been traversing more and more lately. "Just thinking I wouldn't be happy about a background check done on myself. Especially as exhaustive as one for a Supreme Court justice."

"I got a better chance than you of being chosen on account of me having been an attorney at one point in my life. And while I don't think that anything in this here life is zero chance, I'd say that would be pretty darn close to zero."

"Just saying I wouldn't want some of the stupid stuff I've done being snooped into."

"You ever roll under a car to get out of the rain because you're homeless and so dead drunk you can't think of anything else to do? Not that I even cared about getting wet, but it was more like hail, and the temperature was cold as a witch's tit."

Langdon shook his head. "I suppose taking cover under a parked car when you're homeless and drunk isn't the most idiotic thing anybody could do."

Starling snorted. "It is if the car is just parked at a stoplight. That little move gave me a roof over my head and three squares a day for almost a week."

"Arrested?"

"Hospital. Redington-Fairview. I'd show you the scars but I'm kind of embarrassed."

It wasn't an even playing field, Langdon surmised, this not being the first time his employee with a brilliant mind, but also a recovering alcoholic, had shared sage advice with him in the form of a riddle. There were different standards for a homeless person, a bookshop owner, and a Supreme Court justice.

"What they want you to do for them?" Starling asked.

Langdon also knew that this uneducated speech of the man was on purpose, not that he knew exactly what image he was trying to affect. "They got me looking for three people who are most likely long gone. And two, they want me to poke around town to see if I can upend any naughtiness in the life of Cornelius Remington."

"What three names are you looking for?"

Langdon looked at the pad on is desk. "Tara James, Chris Taylor, and Michael Levy."

"Michael Levy used to come in here and buy books, but I haven't seen him in some time, if it's the one I'm thinking of."

"Same age as Remington. Fifty-six. Classmate of his at Bowdoin." Langdon pulled a photo from a folder and pushed it across the desk. "Photo is from five years ago."

Starling nodded. "That's him. He used to like to read everything by Grisham. Think he might've been a lawyer."

"How about the other two?"

"Names don't ring any bells. Not that they would."

Langdon slid the photo of Tara James across the desk. When Starling shook his head, he did the same with the picture of Chris Taylor.

"Nope. Can't say either one looks familiar."

"I'll send these to your phone. Maybe you could ask around about them on the down low. Poor people disappear. Bowdoin College graduates leave a trail. Keep your ears peeled."

Starling chuckled. "I believe it's eyes peeled."

"That doesn't make any sense." Langdon raised his eyebrows. "Sounds painful."

"I think it just means keep your eyes open, you know, peel your eyelids open."

"Whatever. Keep your eyes and ears uncovered."

"Gotcha, boss. Anything else?"

"What do you know about Judge Remington."

Starling shrugged. "Been in a few times. Keeps to himself. Good looking feller. Well dressed. Don't guess I've heard much about him one way or another."

"Okay. Well, ask around about him. See if anything pops up."

"What sort of things we looking for?"

Langdon picked a piece of paper from the folder. Read it aloud. "CARLA F. BAD."

"She an old flame? Sounds like a broad from some pulp noir mystery."

Langdon held up the paper to read from it. "It's mnemonic. C is for character. Does anybody have anything bad to say about the man? Was he a player back in the day, shoot squirrels with a BB gun, that sort of thing? A is for associates. Who did the judge hang out with? Lenny and Squiggy? R is for reputation. I think this is different than character in that it focuses on how people who *don't* know him think of him. Is he fair from the bench or a real prick? L is for Loyalty. Not sure what that's all about. Maybe, is he a good son, husband, and friend? A is for ability. Not really up to us to decide. I think the American Bar Association rates him on that. F is for finances. Does he owe money? I think that last fellow to the bench mysteriously paid off a bunch of credit card debt right after he was nominated."

"Lenny and Squiggy?" Starling's face might've creased into a grin but there were so many thick lines traversing it that it was tough to be certain. "Wouldn't have taken you for a *Laverne & Shirley* fan."

"Gotta love their spirit."

"We're gonna make it," Starling quoted their theme song.

"Doing it our way."

"Make all our dreams come true."

"Role models for us all."

After a moment of silence, Starling cleared his throat. "That covers CARLA F. Now let's get to the BAD."

"Bias. Alcohol and Addiction. Drugs."

"The good stuff."

"Bias is a tricky one. Alcohol and drug addiction should be easy enough."

Langdon winced inwardly. He'd struggled most of his life with alcohol addiction, staying just above the bubble of it becoming a real problem. Starling had not fared so well but had persevered and seemed firmly in control for the past twenty-five years. Chabal? She was drowning.

Starling smiled gently. "Easy enough to get hooked on, boss, easy enough to get caught in that riptide, sure enough."

~ ~ ~ ~ ~

After their conversation, Starling went home, or wherever he went after work. Langdon was closing the bookshop along with Raven. They were open until six, giving Langdon a chance to quiz her regarding what she might know about Remington, Tara James, Chris Taylor, or Michael Levy, but she didn't know any of them by name or picture.

Two years prior, Raven Burke had hired Langdon to investigate her boss for sexual harassment. She'd recently immigrated to the U.S. from the Dominican Republic. He'd been suspicious that this young woman was having an affair with his friend Richam after spotting them in several clandestine meetings, that is, until it came out that she was his daughter, one that Richam didn't know he had.

Being the child of Richam allowed Raven to bypass the tedious route of applying for a Green Card, and then waiting three to five years before becoming a citizen. It also was helpful that Jewell, Richam's wife, not Raven's mother, worked for a nonprofit in Portland who aided immigrants in Maine. There'd still been a few hoops to jump through, but she now had dual citizenship with the Dominican Republic and the U.S. She was taking classes down at USM in Portland and worked full time for the Coffee Dog Bookstore.

They closed the shop right at six o'clock and were out the door fifteen minutes later. Langdon asked Raven to keep her ears open, he refrained from saying peeled, regarding the judge, checked to see if she'd be interested in some overtime over the next few weeks, which she was, and they parted ways. Raven out the front door, most likely to her in-town apartment just across Maine Street and down a couple of blocks, and Langdon and dog out the back to the parking lot.

It'd been a wet June and Langdon hadn't taken the top off his Jeep until just a few weeks back, and he and dog were still in full appreciation of the natural air conditioning of the Maine coast. He stopped at Hannaford for some hamburger and a bag salad and then they went home, both with a fair bit of anxiety. Langdon worried about what shape Chabal would be in and dog concerned about when he might get to eat.

They lived just outside of town in a neighborhood where the houses weren't too scrunched on top of each other and had the added benefit that their backyard opened onto the Town Commons. It was a nice blend of in-town and country living.

Chabal didn't budge from the sofa in the living room as they came in. Her eyes were slightly glossed over, some comedy was on the television, and Langdon wasn't sure if she was awake or asleep. He went on the back deck and poured the charcoal into the cone on the grill, crumpled a sheet of newspaper, and lit the bottom. He and dog had twenty to thirty minutes for a walk while the briquettes simmered to a blistering and fiery orange in preparation for searing the patties to the perfect crisp exterior and partially rare interior.

There was a trail out back that led to a larger loop, but they didn't have time for that. There'd been a day when dog would've been severely disappointed to miss out on the larger hike, but now, at eleven years of age, his joints no longer quite kept up with his personal canine belief that he was still just a puppy. Langdon knew the feeling. Cutting way back on the booze had been extremely beneficial, but his workouts at the gym were more difficult every day. Time, age, and life had a way of interfering with the best of intentions.

When they got back, Langdon poured the scorching red-hot cubes into the bottom of the grill, spread them, put the grates back over the coals, and closed the lid, giving it five minutes to heat up.

In the kitchen, Chabal was struggling to open a bottle of wine with the corkscrew.

"I'm making some burgers," Langdon said.

"Okay."

Langdon slapped the hamburger into two-and-a-half patties, not to leave dog out, who'd already eaten his dinner but wouldn't mind a bite, or rather, a swallow of a burger.

"How about a glass of water?" he asked.

"I don't want any water. Goddammit. Why won't this thing work?"

Langdon took the bottle from her and turned the twist-off cap. He poured her goblet three-quarters full and went out back to put the burgers on. When he came back in, Chabal was at the island, hands on the counter, wobbling. Before he could react, she lurched, knocking her wine glass to the floor and shattering it.

"Goddammit."

Langdon righted her wobble with a hand on her elbow. "Why don't you go sit down on the sofa and I'll clean this up."

"I can clean up my own mess."

He could see the mixture of embarrassment, drunkenness, anger, and fear contorting her face in efforts to gain supremacy.

"I got it," he said.

She pulled her arm free, stumbled, and then tumbled into a heap in the middle of the spilt wine and shattered glass. "Shit."

Langdon knelt next to her. A large, jagged piece of glass jutted from the palm of her hand. He pulled it free, grabbed a dish towel, and wrapped it around her hand. He pulled his wife to her feet and led her to the bathroom with her mumbling apologies. Luckily, that was the only embedded glass. He cleaned and bandaged the wound before leading her to the bedroom. He helped her get out of her clothes, draped one of his T-shirts over her naked body, and tucked her into bed.

Then, he went back, grabbed his burger, burnt on one side, raw on the other, and sat on the back deck with dog listening to the night.

It was just another night in the house of Langdon.

Chapter 4

Langdon opened the Coffee Dog in the morning, but when Starling came in at noontime, he skedaddled out the door to meet his cop buddy, Bart, for lunch. The day was overcast, clouds with silver linings mottling the sky, looking like a school of haddock racing to the shore to spawn, providing a nice relief from the summer sun. This made Hog Heaven the perfect place to eat, as sitting in an open Jeep at a drive-in restaurant in oppressive heat was no fun, nor was sitting in a running car to gain the benefit from the AC.

Hog Heaven was a Brunswick establishment. You pulled into a parking spot and turned your lights on when you were ready to order. They were known for their McDonny burger, but the fried seafood baskets were pretty fabulous, as were the fresh-cut French fries and onion rings. There'd been a day when he and Bart would meet for lunch and bring a six-pack to polish off while eating, but that had been some time ago. Now, Langdon reached into the back and pulled out a bottled water.

Bart came lumbering over, a huge bear of a man at seven inches over six feet and approaching 400 pounds. Langdon knew from experience that he'd parked his cruiser out back to be out of sight. There was always a busybody who'd complain that the police were hanging around eating burgers or donuts instead of doing their jobs.

Lieutenant Jeremiah Bartholomew (having been once again promoted), ping-ponged back and forth between sergeant and lieutenant because of merit and insubordination. He had just the smallest cowlick of hair left on his head. Bart had grown up dirt poor in The County, which was how the northern most region of Maine was locally referenced. He'd actually been born in Brunswick, but soon after birth, his mother had brought him up to Aroostook County following a man, a relationship that had lasted less time than the trip north.

For some reason, perhaps because she didn't have enough money to move back to Brunswick, they'd stayed, and their only income other than welfare was during the potato harvest that lasted most of the months of August and September, and partway into early October. Aroostook County schools used to start in early August, so they could close during the harvest to allow students to work the fields in this crucial period when every hand and every hour was turned to unearthing and storing the "black gold" that much of the population depended on.

Bart was one of the few to escape the crushing poverty of this rural area of Maine, going to the academy when he was eighteen, and then returning to Brunswick.

"Where the hell you been?" Bart asked as he wrestled his bulk into the Jeep.

He was a well-known grump, bringing fear of recrimination to most people who encountered him, but Langdon had realized early on that the man had a heart of gold. And a penchant for poetry. Two things that the rest of the world would never guess.

Langdon looked at the clock. He was, actually, right on time. "Been sitting here for the past ten minutes wondering where you were."

Bart snorted. "The hell you have. I watched you pull in. I thought I might have to get an appetizer and put it on my own tab."

"Who says I'm buying you lunch?"

"The fact that you want to meet up in the middle of day means one thing, my friend, and that is that you want something from me. So, it would be you that says you are buying me lunch."

Langdon winced. By lunch, he meant a buffet meal that could satisfy an entire high school football team.

"Hello, Goff. What can I get for you?"

Langdon turned his head to see Susie, the waitress, with order pad in hand.

"Hi Susie, How've you been?"

"Ah, you know. Time freaking flies by when you're having fun."

She was a few years younger than Langdon, a two-pack-a-day smoker, and he suspected some sort of opiate addict, relegated to menial summer employment, who went from man to man, but there was still a fire in her dark eyes that smoldered with an enjoyment of life.

Langdon suspected she was being sarcastic. "McDonny Burger for me and dog will take some fries."

"Anything for the cop?"

Bart glared at her. "Police officer. Know your place little lady."

"That mean you don't want nothing?"

"Yes, that means I don't want nothing. I want something. How about two of those McDonnys, a basket of fried clams, a lobster roll, some onion rings, and a chocolate shake."

"Oh, where do you put it all?" She walked off.

Langdon suspected she was being sarcastic. He turned his face away from Bart to hide the grin and chuckle that he couldn't quite suppress. "You best have some valuable information for what it's going to cost me to feed you."

"A fellow has to eat."

"What can you tell me about Judge Cornelius Remington?"

"His wife divorcing him?"

"What? No."

"What for you wanna know about Judge Remington then?"

"I'm a private investigator and can't reveal the cases I'm working on."

Bart guffawed. "No, really. What do you got going?"

"He's being vetted for Supreme Court justice. The White House and FBI have retained me to investigated him."

Bart snorted. "Yeah, and I'm…." He paused and looked hard at Langdon. "You're being real. The White House? You sure you don't mean the Blaine House?"

"Yep. Not the governor, but the President of the United States."

Susie came out with a tray and set it on Langdon's window. "That's for you and dog. I gotta go back and get a pack mule to carry the stuff out for the copper."

"You watch your mouth, girl. You still staying out at Blueberry Estates? Maybe I'll come by and make sure you ain't getting into no trouble."

Susie walked off.

"Cut the girl some slack," Langdon said. "She did me a real solid a couple years back when she got me the license plate number of those mercs who were trying to kill me."

"That ain't none of my concern. What is of my concern is the smart mouth on her."

"She's going to spit in your food for sure." Langdon chuckled. "And you'll deserve it."

"Nothing wrong with a little spit, now is there. Kind of like making out with a chick, am I right?"

Langdon shook his head. He wasn't sure if Bart had ever even kissed a girl. "There's something wrong with you."

Bart guffawed. "You got that right."

"How 'bout we get back to Remington?"

"He's a world class arrogant prick, but aren't all judges?"

Susie walked back out with a tray overflowing with food and set it on Bart's window. "I'm sorry if I upset you, officer. I sometimes act a bit strange when I am incredibly attracted to a man." She smiled coyly and walked away.

Langdon suspected she was being sarcastic. "How would you rate him on the CARLA F. BAD scale?"

"You mean that FBI investigative shit?" Bart shrugged, stuffed half of a McDonny Burger in his mouth, and continued as he chomped. "Never heard of him being anything but an upstanding member of the community and a beacon of justice on the bench. Tough, but fair."

"Can you poke around a bit and see what you can find out?"

Dog leaned forward from the back of the Jeep and lay his head on Bart's shoulder, his eyes wide, sad, and imploring a little bit of mercy in the form of sharing some food.

"Oh, don't you start on me, too, my furry friend," Bart said. But he did slide a fried clam into the wide trap of a mouth, almost losing a finger in the process. Dog had a cast iron stomach and could eat just about anything.

"Just keep your ears open and your fingers intact," Langdon said with a grin.

"I imagine your FBI friends have already interviewed the chief. Don't imagine I can provide anything more, but if I hear something, I'll be sure to meet you for lunch. On you."

"Thanks. I appreciate it. I'll just invoice the White House for your meals. That should pretty much match the defense budget in spending."

Bart guffawed. "Money better spent. I hear you're going to be feeding me again tomorrow night?"

"What's that?"

"Richam told me you're having a barbecue. Were you not planning on inviting me?"

Langdon inwardly cursed. Dang Richam. Pushing for a social event meaning to be supportive, but not understanding that it was likely that Chabal would be blackout drunk by the time the crew showed up.

"It'll be fine," Bart said gently. "It will be good for Chabal. Don't worry, bud. The demons are going to pass."

Sure, Langdon thought, except for the simple fact that nobody except him knew how bad things had gotten. "I got three other names I was hoping you could run through the system and get me their contact information. Doubt it'll help, as the FBI has come up empty on their end, but let me know." He handed Bart a piece of paper with the names Tara James, Chris Taylor, and Michael Levy.

Bart looked briefly at the list and stuffed it in his shirt pocket. "Got you bud. Anything else?"

"The big one is whatever you can find out about Judge Remington."

"Judge Remington?" Susie was at the window to retrieve the tray. "That guy's a perv."

"What?" Langdon swiveled to face her.

"Yeah. He used to come by here with his wife. One day he came alone. Ogled me up and down and made lewd comments."

"Like what?"

"He asked if I came with a side of fries and a shake, for one."

"He ever proposition you?"

"Not in so many words. It was just that once, but he made it clear that if I was interested, that he was too. I was hoping he'd come back here with his wife. Then I would've confronted the prick." She shrugged. "But I haven't seen him since."

"Anything else you know or have heard about the judge?"

Susie shook her head.

Langdon had the fleeting thought that she might just fill the shoes of Danny T. on the local knowledge base. Susie was down on ground level with those scraping by each and every day, struggling with mental issues, drug dependencies, alcohol addiction, or lack of education. The central gossip exchange of any community.

"You let me know if you hear anything about the judge," Langdon said. He handed her the bill with cash to pay for it, giving her an extra twenty on top of the tip. "Anything at all."

~ ~ ~ ~ ~

The next stop was the law office of Jimmy 4 by Four in the Fort Andross building, an old mill perched on the Androscoggin River. Large windows faced out toward the Green Bridge separating Brunswick from Topsham, the river below high and angry for this time of the year, a result of the extremely rainy summer.

In another life, 4 by Four had been Jim Angstrom, born poor in the Bronx, but with a driving ambition that sent him to Rutgers University and then Yale Law. Upon graduation, he was courted by several firms and ended up accepting the offer of Wachtler, Bilgewasser, and Tompkins, one of the more prestigious law firms in New York City.

He worked fifteen hours a day, seven days a week, and billed for all of them. He was a legal genius driven by his desire for wealth and power, but he smoked four packs of cigarettes a day, drank twelve cups of coffee, and lived in a high-rise he never saw in the light of day.

One morning, he woke up and said 'enough'. By 11:30 a.m., he was driving north in his BMW. At 2:00 p.m., somewhere between Hartford and Boston, he traded the car straight up for a Volkswagen bus that sat in the furthest corner of the lot. The dealer thought he was taking a real chance with what he assumed was a stolen car, but his greed got the better of him. The bus maxed out at fifty-six miles-an-hour, which was just fine with Jimmy.

He broke down on 295 North, the Volkswagen just able to limp off the exit into Bowdoinham, Maine, and he'd never left. It wasn't the deep woods he'd been shooting for, his goal having been Dexter, but he was able to rent a house without plumbing, have a garden where he could grow plenty of pot, entertain a revolving door of girlfriends, and plenty of time to just contemplate life.

Slowly he'd reemerged from his cocoon, took and passed the Maine Bar exam, and begun practicing in Brunswick, but no longer was he a slave to the work. He was good at two things in life. The first was law, and the second was the seduction of women.

Over the past twenty years, 4 by Four had transformed from hippie to hipster. His long hair was piled into a bun that appeared casual, but Langdon was well aware of the careful construction of this topknot hairstyle. His thick and carefully manicured beard perched on his face as if false, and his left ear had a meticulously polished gold stud. His tailored blazer hugged his wiry frame with a Burberry silk pocket square that matched the Archival Collection silk tie from Brooks Brothers. The white collar of his striped shirt was crisp, as was the crease in the jeans he wore. He did retain his fondness for weed, though.

"You here to personally invite me to your barbecue tomorrow night?" Jimmy asked by way of greeting.

Darn Richam, Langdon thought. "Nope."

"You need me to bring something?"

"Nope."

"Okay if I bring a date? I was supposed to go out with a smoking hot gal who's the chef at that hotel restaurant up on Maine Street."

Langdon didn't bother to answer. But, more and more, it looked as if he were hosting a barbecue Saturday night.

"Want a drink?" Jimmy asked as Langdon sat down across from him.

Langdon shook his head. "Trying to lay off the hooch these days."

Jimmy nodded. "Fair enough. What brings you to visit me on a weekday if not for libation?"

"Got a new case. The White House hired me to investigate Judge Cornelius Remington. Seems the president is considering nominating him to be a Supreme Court Justice."

Jimmy whistled. "Doesn't the FBI handle that sort of stuff?"

"I'll be working in correlation with them." This was certainly a stretch, Langdon knew, but he couldn't come right out and say he was their lackey, now, could he?

"Want me to look over the NDA?"

"Nah. I just signed it."

Jimmy shook his head wearily. "Chances are that you are in breach of contract and could face federal charges just for speaking with me."

Langdon grinned. "You wouldn't tell, would you?"

"Under oath on the stand with the White House as the prosecution? You bet your ass I will. But I *will* visit you in prison."

"Fair enough."

"So, if not legal counsel, what can I do for you?"

Langdon took a dollar out of his money clip and laid it on the desk. "I guess I'd like to retain your services. Now, if pushed, you can keep your mouth shut."

Jimmy shrugged. Took the dollar. "Might share that with a lady down to Exit 48."

"Might want to bring yourself a bigger bankroll than that."

"A single dollar gets you in the door, my friend. Well, no, usually the cover is more than that, but a single dollar is all I need with the ladies to make a connection."

Langdon chuckled. "Whatever you want to tell yourself."

"Okay, okay, enough of insulting me. What is it you want to know?"

"I've been tasked with finding the whereabouts of three individuals, and in an informal manner, investigating whether there are any flaws in the character of the judge."

Jimmy nodded. "CARLA F. BAD. Character, associates, reputation, loyalty, ability, finances, bias, alcohol/addictions and drugs."

"You being a lawyer and all, let's start with ability."

"Judge Remington has a very firm grasp of the Constitution and makes fair judgments." Jimmy shrugged. "I guess you think about a Supreme Court justice, and you think superhero, but really, they're just people. I'm sure the ABA will fully scrutinize every case he has ever ruled on.

"You don't know of any blunders or aberrations that he has made from the bench?"

Jimmy shook his head. "Nope. Unless you consider the amusement in his eyes when he refers to me as Counselor 4 by Four."

"How about the rest of it? Have you heard any scuttlebutt about his character?"

"Not I, but you know what? I went out with a woman once who mentioned that she knew him in college. Graduated same year from Bowdoin as he did." Jimmy picked up his phone and scrolled through it. "There, I just texted you her name and number. Marsha Verhoeven."

"Can you give her a call now and put in a good word for me? See if she'll talk to me?"

Jimmy snickered. "I don't think that would be of any help. As a matter of fact, it's probably best to not mention me."

Chapter 5

Mayhem. That was what they had decided their super-villain nickname would be. They, as in the new pronoun for ungendered, rather than referring to multiple people.

Because Mayhem had decided that they no longer wanted to be tied to a particular gender. That was not what defined them. For so long, Mayhem had been bound to a singular role, a stereotypical role, a role that did not truly represent who they were. Thank goodness for this new generation in realizing that two chromosomes, two possible pairings, two choices—was so goddamn limiting.

But that had all changed when Mayhem had killed Michael Levy. Zip-zap and the man was twitching and convulsing on the ground. That had been a real shocker. Mayhem giggled a bit to themself as they realized their funny. Shocking. It had been shocking.

The man deserved it. He had a big mouth. Couldn't keep a secret. Was going to spill the beans. Thought his poop didn't stink. Mayhem giggled again. Because they had seen to it that Michael Levy had been found dead on his toilet as if he'd electrocuted himself while taking a number two.

Mayhem had been impressed with how well they had handled the situation. It was just supposed to be a warning, a cautionary threat to keep his goddamn mouth shut. How were they supposed to know the man had a bad ticker? But it had worked out perfectly in the long run. The problem was eliminated. The police thought it was a terrible accident. Michael Levy's goddamn mouth was shut permanently. Win-win-win.

Now the FBI was in town. But that shouldn't be a problem. There were no loose ends. Mayhem had made sure of that. But there was some concern over that local fellow. Goff Langdon. Mayhem was no longer a weak and sniveling mortal but was now a criminal mastermind. The elimination of a problem as simple as that was but child's play.

Sometimes, they thought, you gotta just grab the bull by the horns and hang on, and sometimes you gotta wrestle the goddamn thing to the ground. This was one of the latter times.

It was an instance when they had to step to the plate and hit the ball out of the goddamn park. Oh, they'd had to watch far too many baseball games in their time, but that was the least of the things that Mayhem had had to abide by in their existence on the face of this earth.

It wasn't the first time they'd taken things into their own hands, and it wouldn't be the last. Blue jeans. Yuck. A T-shirt. Yuck. Garden shoes. A baseball cap pulled low over their eyes. Mayhem knew they looked like a yokel. This had to be face to face. Not a text message. Not an email. Not a phone call. Nothing that could be monitored by the government.

They knew that he'd be drinking a cup of coffee and gabbing with his buddies at the Community Market in Harpswell. Mayhem's car was too conspicuous, so they parked down the street and walked over and climbed into the passenger seat of his truck. Fifteen minutes later he came out and opened the door, started to get in, and then froze, his eyes indicating he was considering running.

"Get in," Mayhem said.

He did. "What do you want?"

"We got a problem."

"I don't got no problem."

"Yes, yes you do. Or have you forgotten?"

He was quiet for a long time. "What is it?"

"There's a man causing trouble."

"What kind of trouble?"

"Is there more than one kind of trouble?"

He squirmed in his seat. "What do you want us to do?"

Chapter 6

Langdon met Marsha Verhoeven at the Lenin Stop Coffee Shop at two in the afternoon on Saturday. He was there early, sitting at an outdoor table, and waved to her as she walked toward the front door. He had, indeed, stalked her on the internet that morning after she called him back and agreed to meet with him.

Marsha had voluminous red hair, probably dyed he surmised, a pretty face with a few wrinkles etching her forehead as well as the corners of her eyes and mouth. He guessed that she was five inches over five feet. She was dressed comfortably in Capris, a white T-shirt, and an aqua-colored scarf.

Marsha had grown up in Mount Joy, Pennsylvania, before attending Bowdoin College and graduating in 1989 along with Cornelius Remington. She'd begun her career with Unum, down in Portland and worked in management positions in finance, marketing, and sales before leaving the company to earn her master's in business administration from Harvard Business School. Upon graduation, she'd returned to Unum and rose through the ranks to vice-president of operations. She'd retired a few years back and had moved back to Brunswick.

"Goff Langdon?" Her voice was firm and gentle.

He stood up and extended his hand. "Yes. Marsha Verhoeven?"

She took his hand. "You waved to me, so I assume you know that I am Marsha."

"Can I buy you a coffee?"

"Sure. Caramel mocha latte."

Marsha sat down while Langdon went in to get her latte and a coffee for himself. When he came back out, she was scrolling on her phone.

"Thank you for meeting with me," he said.

"Well worth it for a caramel mocha latte."

"As said, my name is Goff Langdon. People call me just Langdon. I own the Coffee Dog Bookstore across the street and I'm also a private investigator."

She smiled. "Quite famous, actually. You're the one who tracked down that sick wendigo creature last spring. And a few other things over the years have made the news."

Langdon wondered if he'd also been stalked by Marsha Verhoeven or if she had indeed read about it in the newspapers and connected the dots. "He was a twisted human being, that's for sure."

"You said you wanted to ask me some questions about Cornelius Remington."

"Yes."

"Why?"

"He's being vetted for an important government job that requires a background check. I have been retained to do that."

"That bastard is going to be nominated for a Supreme Court justice, isn't he?"

"I can't say."

"You don't have to. Goddamn. Go figure. Supreme Court."

"It sounds like you dislike Judge Remington?"

Marsha laughed coarsely. "Not so much. I've run across my share of pricks in my life, but he is *high* on my list of arrogant assholes."

"That is the sort of thing I'm looking into. His character, amongst other things. What don't you like about him?"

"Didn't. I haven't spoken with him since college."

"But you've seen him around?"

"On the news. In the paper. A few times around town since I

moved back to Brunswick. But never to speak to."

Langdon nodded. "So, your… assessment of Cornelius Remington is based upon him as a student at Bowdoin."

"Yes."

Langdon leaned forward across the table. He didn't have much of a whisper and realized that this conversation shouldn't be broadcast. "Why was Cornelius Remington a… bastard?"

Marsha placed her elbows on the table and tilted her face closer to his. "Him and his friends were pranksters. Loved to create mischief. Often at the embarrassment or chagrin of other, less popular, students."

Langdon could see why Jimmy had been taken by Marsha Verhoeven. Her lips were full, as was her body in a healthy way, and her eyes were an alluring violet color. "Did he ever pull a prank on you?"

"No." The violet eyes flashed violently. "Not directly. But my sophomore year, he and his buddies filled a trashcan with some kind of fishy water, I heard they got it from a lobster pound or someplace like that and leaned it against a good friend of mine's dorm room door. Then they knocked and ran away. When she opened the door, the can fell over, and the smelly water doused her and flooded her entire single. It took months to get the smell out."

"Was this reported to the administration?"

Marsha shook her head no. "No, of course not."

"How do you know it was Remington and his buddies?"

"Everybody knew. I don't think they tried to hide the fact. As a matter of fact, I'm sure they walked around gloating about it."

"What other sorts of things would they do?"

Marsha sighed. "I don't know. I believe they wiped some sort of hot pepper on the doorknobs at a hall party one time. Sooner or later, it seems, everybody wipes their eyes. That put a damper on that party. Things like that."

"They ever get in trouble for any of their pranks?"

"Not that I know of. Nobody wanted to be a rat. I think that Neely and his cronies just thought they were being funny. That it was cute, or some such thing."

Langdon thought of some of the stupid things he'd done over the years and was again glad that he wasn't about to be cast into the public spotlight and exposed for some of his more asinine doings. "So, it was just pranks, but with a bit of a mean edge to them."

"They even had a name they called themselves. I think there were five of them, and they were all from Maine, so they referred to their gang as The Maine Men of Mayhem."

Chapter 7

When Langdon got home with food for the barbecue that night, he found his wife smoking a cigarette in the backyard. Smoking was another development of the past year. Chabal sat at the table he'd set up in the yard with chairs for the night's activities. At least it looked as if she'd showered and dressed for company, meaning a bra under her T-shirt.

The descending sun had turned the sky to burnt-orange fiery embers glowing in spliced pieces between the trees. The moon would not rise for another hour, just a few days short of being full, a phase that Langdon was very well attuned with and Chabal even more so. It was the people eating people moon, she now called it.

"How you doing today?" he asked.

"You been at the bookstore?"

"Earlier. Just had a cup of coffee with a lady regarding that case I told you about."

"Lady, huh? She pretty?"

Langdon chuckled. "She used to date 4 by Four."

"You want to fill my wine glass?"

He took the proffered glass and went inside, returning with it half-filled and the charcoal for the grill. "Be good if you went easy tonight."

"Need any help?"

"Nope. I made pasta salad this morning before I went out. Got burgers, including vegan, and dogs. KISS. Keep it simple stupid, like my mother always told me."

"I'll prepare the chips when it's time." Chabal smiled, a hint of her wicked mischievous self leaking out past the despair. "Who's coming?"

"The usual. Jimmy asked to bring a date, no surprise there, but get this, Bart just called to let me know that *he* is bringing someone."

"Bart? Bringing a date?"

"I asked who, but he only said it was somebody I knew, and hung up on me."

"Well, that's a fascinating nugget of information."

Langdon poured the charcoal into the cylinder, shoved a crumpled page of the morning newspaper underneath, and lit it. Chabal walked past him on the deck, her glass empty in hand. Dog went racing around the corner from back to front, suggesting that perhaps the first arrival had come. Sure enough, he returned with Richam and Jewell.

They were a striking couple. He was slim, had thick-framed black glasses, a narrow mustache, and was always impeccably dressed. She was tall and fit, had strong angular features, and an Afro exploding from her head in natural waves.

"Great idea to have a barbecue." Richam smiled broadly.

"I made brownies for dessert," Jewell said. "Chabal inside?"

Langdon nodded and she went on past him and in through the sliding door.

Richam stepped up close and whispered, "Hey, should we not be drinking tonight?"

"Chabal is well into her cups of wine already."

"That doesn't really answer the question."

"I might have a glass of brown liquor."

"I got a bottle in the car. An eighteen-year-old Macallan. Let me grab it."

Langdon poured the charcoal from the cylinder into the bottom of the grill, spreading the briquettes evenly around. He figured it couldn't hurt to have one glass of scotch. Abstaining while his wife imbibed didn't seem to make a lot of sense, and with everything going on, it sure would be nice to let a few trickles of fine-tasting brown liquor course down his throat.

Richam came back around the corner with not only a fine bottle of scotch, but with Jimmy 4 by Four and his date in tow. Langdon did a double take. It was Marsha Verhoeven.

"Hello, again," she said.

"Hello, to you."

"We brought a potato salad from the Park Street Market." Marsha held up the container.

"I have to go inside for glasses and ice," Richam said. "Come on in and I'll show you the fridge and introduce you to our wives who are probably in there bad mouthing us."

As the door slid shut, Langdon looked at Jimmy with a raised eyebrow.

Jimmy shrugged. "My date canceled, I thought, what the heck, let's see if Marsha is still holding a grudge for me standing her up, and, *voila*, here we are."

"Or you used me to break the ice."

"Maybe a little bit of both."

"I thought Bart bringing a date was going to be the biggest surprise of the night." Langdon started popping burgers onto the grill. "You still eating vegan?"

"Vegetarian. I do eggs and dairy… Wait… you said Bart is bringing a date?"

"That's what he said?"

"That should be interesting."

"I'll put a piece of cheese on your Beyond burger. How about Marsha?"

"She likes her beef bloody. But what the heck is this about Bart bringing a date. You mean, a real woman? Not a blow-up doll or some such thing?"

Jewell came back out the door with a glass of red wine in hand. "Chabal is deep into the sauce," she whispered in Langdon's ear.

No shit, he thought, that's why he didn't want to have this barbecue that Richam and Jewell had foisted upon him. "She's still working through some things."

Dog leaped off the deck and went around the corner, soon returning with Bart and Susie. The Susie from Hog Heaven that Bart had been quarreling with just the day before. The woman who bounced around boyfriends, smoked heavily, and probably did some form of drugs, be it heroin or meth or opiates, Langdon couldn't be sure. And Bart was a cop, even if an incredibly heavy drinker.

"Langdon, you know Susie. Susie, this is Jewell and Jimmy."

"Are you two together?" Susie held out her hand to Jewell.

Jewell laughed loudly. "No. My husband is inside."

"You work at Hog Heaven, don't you?" Jimmy asked.

Langdon didn't think that there was any vegetarian food to be had at Hog Heaven. Heck, probably even the fries were cooked in beef grease. But, he mused with a smile, trust Jimmy to know all the single ladies in the area.

The eight of them ate and chatted and laughed. Dog mostly just ate, working the crowd. Langdon noted that Chabal refilled her wine glass three times during dinner. Where some people got louder when drunk, she got quieter, drawing into herself, putting on layers like a Russian babushka doll between her and the world. Marsha and Susie seemed to hit it off, a strange pairing, Langdon thought. One, a retired chief executive officer of a large company, and the other a struggling waitress at a seasonal job.

After dinner, Langdon built a fire in the pit, and they sat around it with drinks in hand as the day melted into night.

Langdon might've just poured his third glass of brown liquor when things went to hell.

"How can you know how I feel?"

Langdon looked across the fire where Chabal had suddenly

screamed. Her face was flushed and her eyes glowed hot in anger.

Jewell put her hand on Chabal's arm. "I'm sorry. I just worry—"

Chabal knocked her hand from her shoulder. "You want to know how I feel?"

Even dog looked concerned. Not a sound could be heard except the crackle of the fire.

"Everybody tells me how to deal with it. My husband. My shrink. Strangers in the grocery store. You. Everybody. But nobody knows." Chabal stood up and threw her glass into the fire, the residue of wine flaring briefly in the dark night.

Langdon stood up. "Hey, babe, let's—"

"Sit the fuck down."

Langdon sat.

"Everybody wants to know why I drink all day. How I feel. What my thoughts are. Okay, I'm going to tell you." Chabal looked up in the sky. "First of all, the moon was full, bigger than I've ever seen it. Not like that puny ball up there now. I woke up groggy from being drugged as they stripped me naked. Naked."

Chabal pulled her shirt over her head. Langdon went to stand. "Sit the fuck down. I'm doing this my way." He sat.

Chabal kicked her shoes off. Pulled her shorts off. Reached behind and undid her bra. Slid her panties to the ground. She stood stark naked in front of them all, the fire creasing shadows into her bare skin, crevices and cracks across her stomach—creating an opacity of her body that matched her tortured soul.

"Then they strapped me to a cross like Jesus Christ and cut me, sliced into my body, to use my own fucking blood to tattoo me with strange symbols—hieroglyphs to draw Satan to the task at hand. His bitches with breath so vile and odious it made me wish they'd just stick the knife in my heart and end the whole thing."

Langdon was glad to see she didn't have a knife. He saw Jewell looking at him, imploring him to stop this insanity. He raised a hand to her, lowered it, gave a slight nod to the negative. The message was clear. Let it play out. As far as he knew, this was the first time Chabal had spoken openly about that night. Sure, she often woke up screaming in the night. But this was no nightmare. Maybe the real-life when awake kind.

"Then they carried me out of this cottage and hung me, cross and all, from some rope by a bonfire. Not some little dinky thing like this fire, but a blazing inferno, a conflagration that was meant to welcome the Devil, old Beelzebub himself."

Chabal raised her hands over her head, the flickering flames of the fire dancing across her body and began to chant nonsense.

Langdon caught Susie staring at him. He shrugged. Pursed his lips.

"Then the king fucking bastard, the Wendigo himself, came and told me what he was going to do to me. How he was going to gut me and bleed me out, my life leaking from my still breathing body, and how he was going to make a fucking stew of me. And then he was going to eat me, and we would be one and the same and together for all of time."

Chabal looked around the circle, her eyes feverish, pausing on each one of them. "And I'm not sure that he didn't eat me and that we *are* the Wendigo."

Chapter 8

When Langdon woke in the morning, dog was not on the bed as was his normal morning wont. That was strange, Langdon though, wondering if the canine had finally discovered how to feed himself.

There was a noise from down the hallway in the kitchen. A slight clatter of a pan, the rustle of feet, the fridge door opening and shutting. Langdon looked next to him where Chabal slept, tiny snores rippling from her mouth like waves lapping the sand.

Langdon slid his legs to the floor, pulled on a pair of shorts and a T-shirt, and eased out the door, pulling it silently shut behind. It was just a few steps to the kitchen. Jack, Chabal's oldest son, was cooking bacon.

"Morning."

Last night, once everybody had left and his wife had fallen into a fitful sleep, Langdon had texted all three of Chabal's kids, as well as his own daughter. Jack lived just down in Portland, so he was the first to arrive.

Jack turned and grinned. Then his face grew somber. "Hey. How is she?"

Langdon shrugged. "Slept through the night. That's a good sign."

"She lost her shit last night?"

Langdon gave Jack the details of the night before. "She's been, uh, drinking very heavily. To cope with all of this, I guess."

"I'd be more than drinking heavy if that sick psycho dude had done that to me."

"You know if your brother and sister are going to make it up?" Langdon's phone was plugged in at his desk as he didn't want to wake Chabal during the night with incoming messages.

"Darcy was visiting Gary in Boston already. Work related, I think, but they're on their way. Should be here before noon."

"I think last night was what your mother needed. To get it off her chest, expel it from her mind, and now, maybe, she can truly start to heal. It'll be really important to have you all around to give her some emotional support. How long can you stay?"

"Me? You know I work remote. I'm here as long as you need me. Can't say for Darcy and Gary. You want a waffle?"

"Sure. I gotta grab a shower first. Be right back."

As Langdon eased into the shower, his thoughts were on his heroes who had driven him to becoming a PI and opening a mystery bookstore. Sam Spade. Phillip Marlowe. Sherlock Holmes. Hercule Poirot. Later on, Jack Reacher. Unlike all of them, he was *not* a loner. No matter how much he admired these literary legends, he was not them. On the contrary, Langdon had a wife, a family, friends, and was a business and social pillar in his community.

And he wouldn't change it for anything in the world.

~ ~ ~ ~ ~

Langdon had managed to polish off a waffle and three pieces of bacon before getting downtown and opening the Coffee Dog up about five minutes late. It was a dreary day, the kind meant for indoor reading, and there were already several people waiting as he unlocked the door. He was flat out busy selling books right up until Starling and Raven arrived at noontime.

They jumped into the fray and helped clear the customers through the queue. It was almost one before the deluge of customers let up. Langdon liked to say that the best advertising he'd ever done was getting shot in the head some twenty-five years ago. Something about that incident had drawn readers to the mystery bookstore like moths to a flame. The incident with the wendigo last year had again proven that point, and book sales had literally jumped off the shelves for the past year.

"Missed you both last night." Langdon decided to confront the elephant before it took over the room.

"Sorry, something came up," Starling said. What he didn't say spoke louder than what he did say. "Thought I texted you, but I guess I never hit send."

Langdon nodded. Looked at Raven. "Your dad said you had a date?"

"I went out with a male friend for dinner. I'm not sure you'd call that a date."

Langdon thought it sounded very much like a date, but kept his mouth shut. "There was some drama to the night."

"Dad called me this morning and told me all about it," Raven said. "Only, he told me not to tell you that he told me."

"We ran into each other at the Lenin Stop and she filled me in on the way over here," Starling said.

So much for that elephant, Langdon thought. Somebody else had let it out of the room. "It was quite disquieting."

"Anything I can do to help, boss, you just let me know." Starling's strongest quality was his boundless loyalty to his few friends.

"Me too," Raven said.

"Thanks, guys. I'm hoping we'll start seeing her back in the shop more and more. Just be her friend." Langdon whistled and dog woke from a slumber on his bed in the corner. "In the meantime, if you two are good here running the show, I got to go knock on some doors."

~ ~ ~ ~ ~

Langdon and dog spent the next few hours knocking on doors in the neighborhoods of the three missing individuals from the FBI's list. He was recognized by a few people and treated like a Jehovah's Witness by others, even if he didn't fit the profile. He'd already been to a dozen doors, working the neighborhood of Tara James, when he got his first hit.

Langdon had been playing the game straight up, telling people that he wanted to speak with Tara regarding being a character witness for Judge Remington. This, he figured, was akin to killing two birds with one stone, as it also gave an opening as to whether or not these people had any inner knowledge of the judge.

At the lucky thirteenth door was a nice lady who could've been anywhere between fifty and seventy years of age, her face showcasing flawless skin that probably had never seen much exposure to the unvarnished sunshine, nor the dehydrating effect of too much alcohol, and was carefully but not overly touched with makeup. She had been friends, in a neighborly fashion sort of way, with Tara.

Kate told Langdon that Tara had left her a phone number, and when a package had been left on Kate's front door for Tara, she'd been given a P.O. box in Marathon, Florida, to send it to. Langdon had found for the most part that people were not that suspicious, not in Brunswick anyway, and a straightforward request was often the best approach.

He called the phone number as he climbed back into the Jeep to go on to Michael Levy's neighborhood. It went straight to voicemail. He left a message and drove off.

Finding Michael Levy was a bit quicker. The first door that he knocked on in the Woodside neighborhood of Topsham wielded an immediate result.

"Michael Levy, you say?" The man was ninety-five if he was a day, thin and crooked, but full of vim, vinegar, and a bit of bite. "They carted him away 'bout a month back. Imagine he's six feet under by now."

"What? He's dead?"

The man cackled. "Died on the shitter, I heard."

How had the FBI missed this, Langdon wondered? The man knew few details, only rumors, as the newspaper had barely covered the story. Heart attack. Pretty normal stuff. Langdon banged on several more doors and got collaborating stories from two more neighbors.

He texted Bart to find out more about the death of Michael Levy, wondering how the FBI had not been able to find a dead man.

Chris Taylor proved to be a strikeout. According to the neighbors, Taylor kept to himself, wasn't unfriendly, but didn't interact with anybody. One lady said he was divorced. That was the most Langdon gleaned, other than that the man had been there one day and gone the next. He'd been renting from a local realtor and Langdon got the name and number.

Back in the Jeep he dialed the phone number. Voice mail. He left a message.

Before he could put the Jeep in drive, his phone buzzed. The phone number he'd just entered for Tara James popped up and he answered.

"Hello, Miss James, this is Goff Langdon."

"Hello." The voice was firm but noncommittal.

"I am calling regarding Cornelius Remington."

"Who?"

"Judge Cornelius Remington. Of Brunswick. You went to college with him."

"Oh. Yes. Neely. I haven't spoken to him in ages. Is everything okay with him?"

"Yes, he's fine. As a matter of fact, I am just doing a routine background check for a new position he is seeking. Can you tell me anything about him?"

"I haven't spoken to the man in… god, I don't even know. Twenty-some years. I'm afraid I can't help you."

"What kind of person was he when you knew him?"

"I haven't really known him since Bowdoin. Thirty-four years ago, if I'm correct, as the thirty-five-year reunion that I'm going to skip is next summer."

"What was he like in college?"

There was a pause on the phone. "Just another college boy. Thought he was placed on this earth as a shining beacon of inspiration to others."

Langdon dug in to get more specifics, but Tara had little to share, and then claimed she had to go, and the line went dead.

There were several text updates from his daughter and all three step-kids that he hadn't noticed, and he read through them. It warmed his heart to know how much they cared. Not only in thought, but in action.

When he got home, his daughter, Missouri Langdon, was in the kitchen with her fiancée cooking dinner.

Jack and his siblings, Darcy and Gary, sat at the dining room table, playing cards with Chabal.

Chabal appeared to be sober.

Dog enthusiastically greeted all of them, running from one to another with his butt wiggling as they all laughed at his antics.

"How was the trip, honey?" Langdon hugged his daughter.

"We took the direct bus to Portland. Jack came down to pick us up."

Langdon turned and hugged the fiancée, Jamie. "Big day coming in October."

She smiled. "We picked out our dresses."

"Fabulous. Do we get to see them?"

She pulled out her phone and shared the two wedding dress pictures. Langdon made the appropriate, or at least he thought he did, positive comments. To him, wedding dresses were like babies, they all looked the same.

"Darcy, Gary, so glad you were able to come visit."

"We both had some time off due," Darcy said. "We'll be here all week, if that's okay."

"That's fantastic."

"Food is ready," Missouri said.

The seven of them sat down to a pasta dinner with salad, non-alcoholic drinks, updates, jokes, memories, and the strength of family bonds, blended though they might be.

Chapter 9

"I got updated addresses for two of the names on the list." Langdon sat in his dingy office opposite the two FBI agents. He wondered that they didn't beckon him to whatever posh space they were working out of. "Tara James moved to Florida this past winter. I got a phone number and called and spoke with her. She had little to say good or bad about Remington. Here is her contact information if you want to follow up." He pushed a piece of paper across the desk.

Agent Delgado picked up the piece of paper. "How about the second one?"

"Michael Levy died a month ago. He now resides in the Riverview Cemetery in Topsham. Surprised you didn't pick up on it. His house is vacant waiting for the executor of his estate to act."

Agent Delgado looked sheepish. "Dead, you say?"

"Heart attack, I heard. I'm following up on the particulars."

Agent Thomas cleared her throat. "No need for that if the man is dead. Guess we didn't look too hard. Went by and saw the *For Sale* sign and that the place was empty. Just another acquaintance from years ago."

"Well, you can cross him off the list."

"And the third person on the list?" Agent Thomas asked.

"I went knocking on doors this weekend but was unable to ferret out Chris Taylor. Waiting to hear back from his old landlord. House is deserted. Divorced. No kids. Neighbors say he was there one day and gone the next."

"Interesting."

Langdon cleared his throat. "Why is he on the list? Does he supposedly have some sort of information on the… CARLA F. BAD of Remington?"

Agent Thomas smiled thinly. "Just following up on contacts, Mr. Langdon. Nothing that concerns you."

Langdon didn't like how she said *you*. As if it was so far above his pay grade that an explanation of why he couldn't know was not deemed necessary. Then he caught himself, realizing that he was not on the hierarchy ladder at all, but had been merely hired to do a job. A mercenary following orders for a paycheck with no vested interest.

"I did come across one interesting item," Langdon said. "From a classmate of his at Bowdoin."

"Yeah? What is that?"

"The who is Marsha Verhoeven. She said that Judge Remington and his buddies used to play some pretty mean tricks directed at the unpopular crowd. Him and his pals called themselves the Maine Men of Mayhem."

Agent Thomas scoffed. "We know all about it, Langdon. Innocent pranks. College humor."

"She seemed to think that there was more of an edge to it than just having fun."

"Like what?" Agent Delgado asked.

Langdon shook his head. "Leaning a trashcan filled with fishy saltwater against a door and knocking so that when the occupant opened the door, it fell, and flooded the room. That sort of thing."

"We're looking for serious moral breaches of character, Langdon, not practical jokes." Agent Thomas snickered. "I'm sure we have all been involved in a few blameless antics that may've gone a bit too far. Like your dalliance with that woman, Delilah Friday. Or the time you were on film breaking into that vacant home."

Langdon stared at her, realizing that his background had been looked into as well, even if he wasn't nominated to be a Supreme Court justice. "Would you like me to speak with Verhoeven and see if there is anything more of substance there?"

Agent Delgado cleared his throat. "No need. We have thoroughly investigated Judge Remington's involvement with the so-called Maine Men of Mayhem."

"How about Judge Remington?"

"What about Judge Remington?" Agent Thomas narrowed her eyes.

"Do you want me to be part of an interview with him?"

Agent Thomas scoffed. "No. That's not what you have been hired to do. And I think he is in Boston, anyway."

"The appellate court was last week. He should be back home now."

"No need." Agent Delgado stood up. "Our business is tying up here. We're going back to D.C. first thing tomorrow. If you want to drop a bill by the hotel front desk by the end of the day, we will make sure you get paid."

Agent Thomas also stood. "Thank you for your service."

"Done?" Langdon couldn't have stood if he wanted. He felt as if he'd been pole-axed. "That's it? The entire investigation?"

Agent Delgado paused, with his hand on the doorknob. "Judge Remington has had two previous background checks, which he has passed with flying colors. This was more of a formality, just to ensure that no surprises jumped out of the closet. None did."

Agent Thomas smiled at him. "As long as the American Bar Association gives their approval and your Maine senators blue-slip him, the president will then nominate him and send the matter to the Senate."

"Where a Senate Judiciary Committee will review and interview Judge Remington," Agent Delgado said. "Then they will pass the matter to the Senate Floor with their recommendation for a vote."

The two agents nodded and walked out the door.

~ ~ ~ ~ ~

"That was quite the barbecue Saturday night."

Langdon looked up. Marsha Verhoeven stood over him at the outdoor table of the Lenin Stop. He was sipping a black coffee trying to untwirl his brain. A five-day investigation of Remington, suggesting he'd already been rubber-stamped, and that the White House staff and FBI had just been going through the motions. He was done. Been told to submit an invoice. And now his internal disposition came screeching back to the turbulent meltdown of Chabal.

"Sorry you had to see that," he said. "It's been a tough year. I think you probably got the gist of what happened."

"Wow. I sure did. Do you mind if I sit down for a moment?"

"Go ahead."

Marsha settled into the chair, a cup of chai tea in her hand. "The newspapers kept that part of it hush. Not often that the media does the right thing."

Langdon nodded. He wasn't sure if this woman expected him to open his emotional vault or share some inner secret, but that wasn't happening.

"How is she?"

Langdon shrugged. What could he say? Tortured? Ravaged? Or should he say that she was doing better, that the kids had circled the wagons, come home, and she'd gone an entire day without drinking and that meant everything was fucking hunky-dory again. That she was healed. No more visits to the shrink. No more nightmares. No more vacations into the wine bottle.

"Stupid question. I'm sorry. How are you?"

How was he, Langdon thought in wry amusement? He hadn't really considered that. He was just doing what he had to, moving forward, doing the best he could. Until being hired for this case, he'd been spending more time at home, but that hadn't helped. Now the case was coming to a close, without any apparent resolution, and he'd be back to despairing over how to help the woman he loved.

"I'm sorry," Marsha said. "Do you want to be alone?"

Langdon shook the cobwebs from his addled noggin. "I'm sorry. No. Stay. I just don't have a lot to say about… "

"No worries. I'm sorry for sticking my nose in where it doesn't belong." Marsha took a tiny sip of the chai. She swept her thick red hair back from her eyes. "How is your investigation of Cornelius coming?"

"The White House and FBI are wrapping things up and going back to D.C. Looks like he got a gold star."

"What? Did you tell them about the mean pranks they played? About the Maine Men of Mayhem?"

"Sure did. Said they'd looked into it, and it was all just harmless college pranks."

"Until it happens to you."

"Did it ever happen to you?"

"I told you no."

"You don't happen to know a fellow by the name of Chris Taylor, do you?"

Marsha furrowed her brow but then her eyes lightened. "Oh, you mean Chuckie. I forgot her real name was Chris. We all called her Chuck, you know, as in the sneaker, Chuck Taylor."

Langdon pursed his lips. Sure, he thought, not that it made much sense, and neither did the fact that Chris Taylor was a she. "Her?"

"Confusing, right? You never asked who the other Maine Men of Mayhem were. Well, she was one of the five."

Langdon shook his head. "I'm not sure I'm following you."

"Three years ago, Chuckie sold his house and moved down to Ogunquit. At the same time, he… she changed her name and began transitioning."

"Chuckie began transitioning from being a male to being a female?" Langdon didn't want to appear obtuse, but he thought it important to be clear.

"Yes."

"I asked around his… her neighborhood in Freeport where… she used to live, and nobody knew anything about this. As far as I know, neither did any of… her classmates at Bowdoin."

"She was extremely uncomfortable about making the conversion. Fought against it, refused it, ignored it. Was married to a woman for a bit, but that didn't take, and finally, in her fifties, she came to accept who she was." Marsha shrugged. "But I think she just wanted to start all over. You know, some place other than *Cheers*?"

"Cheers?" Langdon was feeling like the sugar muddled at the bottom of an Old Fashioned.

Marsha snickered. "You know, *Cheers, where everybody knows your name*?"

"Ah, gotcha. He… she wanted a fresh start. Let's start with the basics. You said that Chris, Chuck, Taylor, changed her name?"

"Yes. About three years back she legally changed her name to Shannon Undergrove."

"Shannon Undergrove. That's quite a name."

"I didn't ask her about it."

"But, this person, who used to be one of the Maine Men of Mayhem at Bowdoin College, who ostracized others and pulled nasty pranks—you kept up with this person. It would appear that you are the only one who knows about the change of name, address, and gender."

Marsha shifted uncomfortably. "I did not keep up with Chuckie… Shannon."

"How is it that you know all these things about her that nobody else does?"

"That one prank they played that I told you about? Where the bastards tilted a trashcan of fishy water against a door and knocked on it, so that it would spill into the room when the door was opened?"

Langdon nodded. "What about it?"

"That girl, she was… more than just a friend of mine. We weren't exactly dating but had hooked up a few times. I was furious and confronted Remington and his Maine Mayhem juveniles and told them exactly what I thought about them."

Langdon was in over his head, he knew, but did have the wherewithal to keep his mouth shut about Marsha sleeping with this woman and currently dating his friend Jimmy 4 by Four. "That doesn't answer the question of why Chuckie or Shannon came to you and shared all this personal information that she kept from everybody else in the whole world."

"I think it was an apology."

"An apology?"

"One day, I guess it was three years ago, give or take, my doorbell rang. When I opened the door, there was a woman on the steps, one that I didn't recognize. It was Shannon Undergrove, formerly Chuckie Taylor, right at the beginning of her hormonal therapy for gender affirmation."

"Go on."

"She wanted to make amends. Sort of like that stage where A.A. makes you go back to all the people you've wronged and apologize. Make it right."

Langdon breathed deeply. The White House was pulling the plug on the investigation. He was no longer being paid. But he had been tasked with finding three names, and this third one, Chris "Chuckie" Taylor, now known as Shannon Undergrove, could be a very important piece of the puzzle as to the true character of Cornelius Remington.

There was no reason to continue the investigation. As a matter of fact, it would most certainly annoy the FBI, the White House staff and counsel, hell, the president, if he did. But it would niggle at him if he did nothing.

"You said that Shannon Undergrove has moved to Ogunquit. Do you have an address for her?"

"No. But about a year ago I was down that way at a place called *The Veranda*. It's a piano bar, very queer friendly. Anyway, I saw Shannon, sitting with a few other people having a good time. She seemed like she might be a regular there. Also looked like she might've undergone top surgery. She was much more feminine looking then when she showed up on my doorstep."

Langdon had been to *The Veranda* before. It was a fun spot, and Ogunquit was a beautiful town. It looked like he might be paying it another visit soon.

Chapter 10

The two men and two women were having dinner in the enclosed patio at the hotel on top of Maine Street, just before it curled its way past Bowdoin College and off toward the Atlantic Ocean. There'd been threats of thunderstorms, but they'd apparently been pushed off to the west. The sun was out, it was about 75°, and while the humidity was bad, it didn't compare to what was going on down in D.C.

Cooper Walker, deputy chief of staff at the White House, was having the pork belly with scallion radish slaw and spicy peanuts. Zara Farhat, junior counselor for the White House, was having the spiced chickpea tacos with charred corn salsa. FBI agent Royal Delgado had a burger, complete with bacon, cheese, and bourbon-Gruyere fondue sweet potato French fries, while his partner, Parker Thomas, had a simple Greek salad.

"Any luck on finding Chris Taylor?" Walker's tone was precise, clipped. Everything about the man bespoke efficiency bordering on haste. Even if youth seeped from his eyes and from cheeks that rarely saw a razor.

Agent Thomas shook her head. "Chris 'Chuckie' Taylor seems to have dropped off the face of the earth."

"His accusation was what, like five years ago?"

"Yes. When Judge Remington was being vetted for the appellate court."

"And the investigation then found nothing of merit?"

"No, sir. Cleared of any malfeasance."

"That is outside the scope of our investigation, then, as it has already been covered once before." Walker took a sip of his bourbon. "What did you find out about Levy?"

Agent Delgado looked up with burger juice running down his chin. He wiped it away, swallowed. "Heart attack. Seems legit."

"Why didn't we know about his death?"

"I don't know. Bumfuck town like Topsham probably didn't record it properly."

Walker took a careful bite of his pork belly. Chewed thoughtfully. "Interesting that he died just a week after reporting that he had information regarding Judge Remington."

Thomas shrugged. "Shit happens."

"Did we interview the woman? Tara James?"

"I spoke with her on the phone," Delgado said. "She didn't have any idea what Levy was talking about. She had nothing negative to say about Judge Remington. She no longer keeps up with him, not since moving to Florida anyway. But…"

"But?"

"She seemed a bit odd. A little mechanical, and while she didn't besmirch the man, she also did not give him a glowing recommendation."

Walker stared at her. "Are you suggesting that we should follow up?"

"Maybe."

"POTUS wants this investigation concluded. He wants to move it along. Are you proposing that we tell him that there has been a hiccup?"

"I just—"

"Because a person who doesn't even keep up with Judge Remington was not effusive in her praise of the man?"

Farhat cleared her throat. "The American Bar Association will investigate his capacity, capability, and competence as a judge to review his qualifications. The Senate Judiciary Committee will do their own investigation. I believe that we have done our due diligence here."

"Can we agree that our investigation is concluded?" Walker asked.

Delgado set his napkin on the table. "What about the PI?"

"The PI?"

"Goff Langdon. Our local liaison."

"What about him?"

"He seems to think that there are a few loose ends yet to be followed up on."

"You told him to submit his final report and that our business was concluded?"

"Yes."

Walker pushed his chair back. "Then we are agreed that it is two resounding thumbs up for Remington. POTUS will be very happy."

Delgado and Parker nodded.

Walker stood up. "I have phone calls to make. Zara, you'll take care of the bill?"

Farhat nodded. Walker walked off.

~ ~ ~ ~ ~

Jonathan Starling sat in his living room on Boody Street in Brunswick staring at nothing. He wasn't much of a TV watcher, preferring a book, sometimes silent contemplation with jazz music drifting around him like an old friend. Tonight, he was alone with his thoughts.

Tiny tentacles of remorse, self-loathing, contrition, and regret veered from his mind connected by one singular and consuming apparition that had recently sprung from his past to his present. Tara James.

It had to be the same person. Tara James, graduate of Bowdoin College, intern to Truman & Starling Law Associates in the summer of 1988. Back before Jordan Fitzpatrick had come along and steered the practice into oblivion. Preceding the events that had turned Starling to the bottle, seeking escape from a magic lamp that contained not a genie, but demons.

Of course, perhaps Tara James had been his first step down that slippery slope that descended from the moral high ground to the land of the miscreants. Oh, Starling had been so full of vim and vigor—a newly minted attorney with a penchant to be a mouthpiece for the environment. He wanted to change the world, preserve the land, fight the rich corporations.

Starling winced, swallowed, and sighed, thinking of the young man he'd been. He thought it was Jordan Fitzpatrick who had pushed him down the mountain, but in retrospect, he'd always been a horse's ass. Cocky. Arrogant. Full of white middle-class male privilege. So sure of himself. Knowing that the world revolved around him and that he was Atlas, and that when he shrugged, the world would pause and heed his words and actions.

Youth was wasted on the young, Starling thought, a pained and wry grin creasing the weather map of his face. He had totally blocked Tara James from his memories. When Langdon had mentioned the three names he'd been tasked with finding, this one woman on the list, Tara James had made the blood of Jonathan Starling freeze in his veins.

Starling's only company, other than his searing memories, was a bottle of Macallan that sat on the coffee table in front of him. It was an eighteen-year-old. Not much younger than Tara James that day thirty-five years ago when she came into his law office in Madison. She'd just turned twenty-one, legal to buy liquor, an adult, but still a kid. She was interning for the summer. Ten weeks. Just a few years before Starling's life had been torn apart at the seams.

Over twenty-five years ago, Bart and Jimmy had retrieved him from a dive bar in Madison and brought him to Brunswick as a witness to the immoral character of the governor of Maine at the time. He'd met Langdon, a young PI stumbling his way through a case that was way over his head, and the rest of the group, and somehow this had been the boost that Starling needed to stop boozing.

He knew how long it'd been, because in his hand he clutched a bronze coin, with the Roman numerals XXV. *Unity, Service, Recovery. To thine own self be true.* It hadn't been easy. It truly took a village.

Chabal had been the first to extend a hand. Sure, Langdon had treated him like a human being and not a derelict, gave him the benefit of the doubt, counseled him. But when Langdon had been shot in the head and was in a coma, it was Chabal who'd given him a job in the bookshop, who'd sat up with him the long nights with his body wracked by chills.

It couldn't have been easy for Chabal. Her marriage was dissolving. The man she loved was in a coma. Running his business in his absence was thrust upon her. Yet, she'd found time to guide Starling through the dark recesses of recovery. And the group had embraced him. Langdon, when he woke, Richam and Jewell, Bart and Jimmy, and Danny T. Even little Missouri Langdon who called him Uncle Star had taken him under her wing and given him life again.

And Jonathan Starling had been repentant. The young firebrand so cocksure of himself had been replaced by a man whose spirit had gradually come to peace with his soul and the world in which he lived. It was a simple life. But a full life.

The bottle of fine brown liquor stared silently at him from the coffee table.

~ ~ ~ ~ ~

The two men sat on the rickety porch of the cottage in Harpswell. The tall pine trees cast even taller shadows into the cove like giant beanstalks stretching across the saltwater connecting land to land. Their chairs rocked in unison, slow and easy, in rhythm with nature, the lap of the ocean on the shore, with each other.

"S'pose we gotta do what we got to do."

"He don't seem a bad sort."

"Don't matter."

They rocked, contemplating that thought. Several winter wrens flitted and bobbed about the underbrush between them and the water. Earlier, a seal had been sunning on a rock, but had long since left looking for warmer places or food.

"We gotta do what we been told. Else we'll be exposed."

"Can't have that."

"We could just come clean. Tell our side of the story."

"People around here aren't going to understand."

"This is the last time. I was firm. We ain't going to be pulled and jerked around anymore."

"S'pose we gotta do it, then."

"Yep."

"When?"

"I'll scope it out. Find a good place for it."

"Can't be no people around."

"I look stupid?"

"Maybe a little."

There was a pause and then both men snorted, chuckled, and laughed out loud. The sounds began as a trickle and then echoed loudly on the rocky coast.

"How long we known each other?"

"Long time now."

"We're not bad people, are we?"

"A man's gotta do what a man's gotta do."

"Yep."

"Was told it should happen soon. Next couple of days."

"No reason to put off something that needs to be done."

"Get 'er done."

"Yep."

Chapter 11

Langdon was just about to lock up the bookshop when a man walked through the door. Dog, who was excited to go home and get dinner, looked disgusted. The fellow was in his mid-fifties, had a very distinctive widow's peak, his hair black and just faintly tinged with grey. He was probably just eight or nine inches over five-feet tall, and while he walked like a former athlete, he'd now rounded out a bit in the belly and face.

It was Judge Cornelius Remington.

Langdon didn't remember seeing the man in the bookshop before, but Star said that he'd seen him once or twice, a thickness to his voice when he mentioned it, like there was a bad taste coating the interior of his mouth.

"You are Goff Langdon?"

"Yep. And you are Judge Cornelius Remington."

"Do you have a few minutes?" His voice purred forth like waves lapping the beach on a lake.

"Sure. If you don't mind, I'll lock the door and we can go back to my office."

"Perfect."

Langdon locked the door. Dog looked absolutely crestfallen. "Office is back this way."

"Actually, do you mind if I purchase a book first?"

"Sure. You know what you're looking for?"

"A book by John Grisham. *An Innocent Man*. Do you have it?"

Langdon grinned. "I believe you mean *The Innocent Man*. We should have it. Right over here."

"Fantastic."

They did, indeed, have one copy of the book. Langdon pulled it from the shelf and handed it over. "Always wondered how accurate Grisham is with his books. I mean, I get that he was a lawyer and knows his stuff, but does he take liberties with things to, you know, spice things up for the reader?"

Remington laughed. "He's pretty spot on, to tell you the truth. I mean, he cuts out all the mundane crap and condenses things, but all his basis is accurate, as are the rulings. Even if he doesn't seem to care much for judges." He pulled another book from the shelf. "For instance, how about this one, where there's a serial killer who turns out to be a judge."

"I guess you judges are just people, like all the rest of us, with human weaknesses, susceptible to our emotions, and sometimes wired for badness."

"You're right, I suppose. There's always going to be a few bad apples. How much do I owe you for the book?"

"Consider it a gift."

"Not a good idea. Wouldn't want people to think I'm being bought. I'll pay you."

"Clarence Thomas can be gifted a $19,000 bible but you can't accept an $18.00 book?"

"Ah, Goff, the difference is that he's been elected for life to the Supreme Bench, whereas I do not have that same luxury, nor inclination, to be perfectly frank."

"People call me just Langdon. And you don't have that luxury, yet."

"What people? Friends?"

"Everybody. Friends and foes. Even my wife."

Remington nodded. "My friends call me Neely. How much do I owe you."

Langdon collected a twenty-dollar bill from the man, gave him his change, and they moved to the back office that would've made Sam Spade jealous in its very dinginess.

The desk was cluttered with papers and Langdon shuffled them together and put them in a drawer to be dealt with later. "When you say you don't have the inclination, does that refer to taking gifts or reporting to the Marble Palace for work each day?"

Remington smiled genially. "It would be my honor to serve at the Temple of Justice. Even if it means leaving Maine behind."

"No fun down that way in the summer, that's for sure. I think they've been measuring the humidity by the shovel full."

"I've spent my entire life in Maine. Grew up in Cape Elizabeth. Went to Bowdoin. And then stayed in the area."

"Although you did do a stint in D.C. Georgetown Law, I believe?"

The wide smile came back. "One would think that you have been investigating me… Langdon."

"I hate to assume, Neely, but I'm thinking you didn't just come in here to buy a book about an innocent man falsely accused."

"It has come to my attention that you *had* been retained by the White House to do some background research on *moi*."

Langdon was transfixed by the man's broad smile, the teeth stretching like the keys on a piano. "And?"

"And what?"

"Well," Langdon shrugged, "you are here for a purpose, again, I assume. Let's get to it."

"I understand that the White House and the FBI are flying out in the morning. It seems that they've completed their business here."

"You seem to be continuously dancing around the objective of your presence here, Neely, so why don't you just come out with it."

Remington's eyes narrowed but the smile remained plastered on his face. "I thought that as we are fellow Mainers, you might want to share with me what conclusion they came to."

Langdon pursed his lips. Shook his head. "You don't think they shared with *moi*, do you?"

The grin faltered on Remington's face when he used *moi* back at him but regained its place with some notable effort. "No, of course not. I just thought you might've gotten some indication."

"Not a hint or whiff of anything at all. They were rather brusque, actually."

"And now you have tied up your part of the investigation as well?"

Langdon leaned forward and steepled his fingers under his chin. "I'm submitting my final report to them this very evening. I did have some questions left, though."

"Perhaps I can help."

"It seems that while you were at Bowdoin, you had a group of friends, and you all called yourselves the Maine Men of Mayhem. What sort of mayhem did you get into?"

Remington cleared his throat. His gun-metal grey eyes glittered like enemy weapons, just for a split second, and then softened. "We were just a bunch of silly college boys."

"I understand that you were renowned for playing pranks."

"Like I said, just silly kid stuff."

Langdon tilted his head. "Things like dumping an entire trash can of fishy water into somebody's dorm room?"

"That was most unfortunate. I regret that. But it wasn't my idea."

"Speaking of… who were the other Maine Men of Mayhem?" Langdon knew, of course, but he wanted to get Remington's talking.

"I guess it was just the three of us. John Boyle, Fred Duffy, and me. Not that it was anything more than the fact that we were all from Maine, liked to joke around, and were all male." Remington stood up. "Either way, I'm glad that it is all wrapped up. Having people poking into my life feels very intrusive."

Langdon remained seated. "Wasn't Michael Levy one of the group?"

Remington paused, turned back to face Langdon. Shrugged. "I wasn't as close to Michael as I was with the other two."

"Did you hear that he died last month?"

"Yes."

"Do you know how he died?"

"Heart attack. Terrible for somebody so young. I must admit, though, that I didn't keep up with Mikey. Hadn't seen him in years."

"How about Chuckie Taylor?"

The gun-metal grey eyes burned brightly for a split second and then cooled. "Ha. Chuckie Taylor. I haven't heard from him in years. He doesn't attend any of the reunions. Seemed to fall right off the face of the earth. What do you know of… him?"

Langdon noticed the hesitation. "Chuckie lived right here in town. Surprised you hadn't seen him around. Brunswick not being that big of a place."

"What are you getting at, Langdon? This thing is over and done with. Submit your paperwork, take your check, and see to your personal life."

Langdon stood up abruptly and rounded his desk. "What's that supposed to mean?"

Remington held his stare. "Nothing at all. I just thought that you might have other things to occupy your time. Summer in Maine. Take the missus to the beach. Listen to some music. Eat some oysters."

Langdon thought that none of that sounded like a bad idea. But there was an underlying current that he didn't much care for. He followed Remington to the front door, unlocked it, let the man out, whistled for dog, and followed the Judge out the back of the building.

"Good luck, Neely, with your confirmation hearing," he said.

~ ~ ~ ~ ~

The Judge had made Langdon just a tad bit late getting home for supper. Darcy had grilled chicken along with green beans and garlic bread and the family was just starting to get their food and sit at the table in the yard.

Chabal was clear eyed as she waited at the grill to get food with Missouri. There was a smile on her face that had long been absent. Darcy plopped a piece of chicken on her plate, topped it with the green beans, and added a hunk of garlic bread for good measure.

Jack and Gary were already seated, talking animatedly with Jamie, the three of them waiting for the others so as to begin eating. It was an idyllic scene, perhaps taken from some family life magazine, a postcard from the '50s, a posterboard for the way life should be.

Langdon fed dog, grabbed a glass of water, and went out to join them. Dog was right behind him, having gobbled down his dinner in the time it took Langdon to get water from the faucet. His wife, his daughter, her fiancé, his step kids—all were varying shades of red. They'd gone out to Popham Beach for the day.

They sat and ate and talked of the beach. Several sand dollars had been found. A seal had been spotted. A hole dug and a castle made. His wife and adult children had had a throwback day to when they were all younger, inspired by the wonders of the beach, the ocean, and the seagulls.

After they ate and cleaned up, Langdon made popcorn, and they settled down to watch *The Truman Show*. They laughed and joked and bonded.

Partway through the film, Langdon began to grow uneasy, wondering if he and his family had been cast into a Utopian dome of falseness, and that that bubble was about to burst, allowing the real world to come flooding back into the living room with all of its ugliness.

Chapter 12

Langdon slipped out of bed in the morning quietly as to not awaken Chabal. He took a moment to appreciate her repose and beauty. Tiny snores rippled from her mouth. A lock of hair had fallen across her forehead. He put on his gym clothes, fed dog, poured a to-go mug of coffee, and went out the door with his canine companion rushing past him to see if any unwary and silly squirrels had ventured into the yard over the night. They had not.

One benefit on drinking little to no alcohol and having zero sex was that Langdon was in the best shape he'd been in some time. It seemed that pleasure came with pounds, but life with an edge brought fitness. He worked out at the Cellar of Fitness behind the bookstore six, sometimes seven days a week for close to two hours. Dog was a favorite of the early morning clientele, many of them bringing him treats from their own breakfast.

The gym had been the warehouse for the department store that once existed in the building, and that was how they moved product from one space to another. Today, Langdon went back up the stairs after showering, confusing dog, who was a creature of habit. He'd decided to swing by the diner this morning for breakfast for the first time in over a year, which required them clambering back into the Jeep for the almost mile ride.

Jimmy 4 by Four was already at the counter with a cup of coffee when Langdon and dog walked inside. Rosie, the owner, was across from him drying a mug with a towel. Her eyes lit up when she saw them come in, blazed ferociously for a moment, and then softened in understanding.

Rosie was just under five-feet-tall and almost as wide. Her hair had grayed considerably since the last time that he'd seen her, but her ruddy complexion and ready smile had not altered one single bit. Dog ran excitedly behind the counter to greet his old friend and was rewarded with a piece of bacon and a head massage followed by a butt rub.

"Good to see you, Langdon," she said.

"And you, Rosie."

Langdon, after almost forty years of eating breakfast at the diner five to six times a week, had taken to eating that meal at the Maine Street Deli. He'd rationalized that the deli was closer, just a short walk from the gym and bookshop, but knew that that was not the real reason.

Rosie poured a cup of coffee and slid it onto the counter. "I've missed you and the brown fur ball."

Langdon sat down. "Yup. As you can tell, we missed you, too." Dog was poking his nose into her ample thigh hoping for more rubs or food.

"Ha. Dog just missed the bacon." Rosie gave the canine another piece.

"And the love." Langdon took a sip of the coffee. "How've you been?"

Rosie shrugged, a surging of her thick body upward and then back down. "Ya know."

Langdon nodded. He did know. The truth was that Rosie and Langdon had been Danny T.'s closest, possibly only, friends, and now he was dead, murdered with his throat slit. This had been his hang out. A place where Langdon had often met with the man, bought him meals, and placed bad bets in exchange for information.

"The normal?" Rosie asked.

Langdon nodded. Bacon. Eggs. Home fries. Toast. An orange

juice. Forty years was a long time to eat the same thing, but he'd managed. Truth was, he'd toned this all-American breakfast back some, and had even been known to get the fruit and yogurt cup at the deli. But that would have created shock waves of unrepairable proportions if he'd suggested that to Rosie. First of all, Langdon was pretty certain there was no fruit to be had at the diner, except maybe an orange wedge, but more importantly, sometimes, routine was all that humans clung to in an effort to survive their day-to-day existence.

"You're late," Jimmy said. "I was worried that I might have to pay for my own breakfast."

Food was the currency Langdon paid for information, especially with his friends. It seemed to work for all involved in the transactions.

"That'd be a shame. What is your going rate these days? $300 an hour? I'm sure you could expense the breakfast with some bigwig *and* make a bundle. Unless you've grown morals since I last saw you."

Jimmy looked offended. "What? I am the epitome of principles and ethics. I am the nobility of the legal profession."

"Maybe so. I was referring more directly to your interaction with women you find attractive."

Rosie slid a fruit cup with powdered sugar and whipped cream, as well as a side of avocado toast in front of Jimmy.

Langdon tilted his head, corrected, as they did apparently have fruit here in the diner.

"You know that I never lie to women," Jimmy said. "I make no bones about the fact that I'm not interested in a relationship, thus, making them want to fix me—and that is how you ignite a fire, my friend."

"How about your amigos? Do you use them to kindle the flame of the affairs of your heart?"

"What are you talking about?"

Langdon chuckled. "I'm talking about you using me to get back together with Marsha Verhoeven."

Jimmy started to open his mouth as if to protest, shut it, grinned, and took a bite of sugar covered fruit. "Much like my romances, my friend, we both got what we wanted. You got information and I got—"

"I don't want to know." Langdon held up his hand to stop the man. "But maybe you can tell me what you know about Marsha."

"Like the fact that when you unhook her bra that her breasts spill—"

"Stop. Please."

Jimmy laughed. "You've been married too long, even if Chabal is a great…" Jimmy, not known for flustering, reddened and bent his head as if studying the spread of the avocado on his toast. "How is she doing?"

"Better than last time you saw her. Matter of fact, I think that was a cleansing therapy for her. First time she's spoken about that night." Langdon sighed. "Plus, the kids all came home to help out."

"Let me know if there's anything I can do. I'd love to see them all, but don't want to rock the boat. Missouri bring Jamie with her?"

"Yep. Look, I gotta go write up a report for the White House and the FBI. What can you tell me about Marsha Verhoeven?" Langdon had enjoyed family time the night before in lieu of writing up the report. Plus, he had a few more t's to cross. They could wait another day or two, or so he figured.

Rosie delivered a platter of food to Langdon. "You're right," she said. "It's weird having you here. But I'd like to get used to it." She moved off down the counter to fill coffee cups.

Langdon looked at Jimmy. "Marsha?"

Jimmy took a deep breath. "My kind of gal. She's intelligent, witty, sarcastic, and completely whackadoodle."

"What do you mean by whackadoodle?"

"She'll do anything. Yeah, in the bedroom she's pretty wild, but I'm not just talking about that."

"So, what are you talking about?"

"She loves to crash parties. If we're out and see a wedding or something like that, you can bet we're walking in and trying to bluff our way through it. A form of streaking, I suppose. Speaking of, we were in a crowded elevator going up to our hotel room once, and she took her blouse and bra off and stood there without a sign that anything was out of the ordinary. Things like that, I guess."

"Trustworthy?"

"Other than lying to parents of the bride and spending an entire day walking backward? Sure. I don't think she's ever lied to me, but I've never given her cause to, I suppose."

"What do you mean, cause to?"

"People generally lie because they're embarrassed about something, but I don't much care what shenanigans she gets up to, as long as we end up getting some horizontal refreshment."

"What are you talking about?" Langdon blew out a deep breath. "You being a lawyer know that people lie for an entire host of other reasons. They lie to get their own way, to cover up criminal behavior, or for money to name just a few."

Jimmy stood up. "She seems to be happy with her life. No kids. No alimony. Great pension. Good investments. I'd guess that she is trustworthy. I gotta get to work. Got a nine o'clock appointment this morning."

~ ~ ~ ~ ~

Langdon helped Raven get the bookstore open and then turned it over to her. Tuesday mornings were usually pretty slow, even though the horrible humidity of July had broken, turning the August weather delightful. You never knew what might bring people into the bookshop. Rain could draw shoppers and leave people home watching television, and sun might send people boating and to the beach or perusing the shops of Brunswick. Either way, he was just back in the office, on call if need be, until Starling came in at noon.

There seemed to be too many questions left to finalize his report on findings regarding Judge Cornelius Remington. As a matter of fact, there was little to put in his report, as what Langdon had mostly uncovered was tangents leading to further inquiry as opposed to any sort of substantial answers. Halfway into typing the first line of the analysis of his investigation, Langdon sighed, pushed his chair back, put his feet up on the desk, hands behind his head, and closed his eyes.

Michael Levy had a heart attack. Remington had omitted mentioning him as one of the original Maine Men of Mayhem and claimed that he didn't keep up with the man. Langdon made a mental note to check with Bart about the official autopsy report and to also give a phone call to his contact, Jackson Brooks, at the Maine State Police. It was awful coincidental that Michael Levy, who'd been part of Remington's college-day shenanigans, had suddenly died right before a background check to nominate the judge to the Supreme Court. And Langdon did not believe in coincidences.

Had the FBI looked into the other two Maine Men of Mayhem who had not been on the list given to Langdon? John Boyle and Fred Duffy. Two names given to Langdon by Remington, but most likely, not missing, or the FBI would've asked for Langdon's help looking for them. But Langdon had a searing desire to speak with them, because he wanted to know the real truth, which pretty much summed up where he was currently residing in his brain. The FBI and White House might be done with the investigation, but Langdon was not.

Why had Tara James been on his list? Perhaps her move to Florida was no coincidence. Born and raised in Maine, a Bowdoin college alum who stayed in the area after graduation for thirty years and on the eve of the nomination of Remington, she suddenly moves to Florida. Another loose string flapping in the wind. The trick was to find what that string had been attached to before being cut loose.

Marsha Verhoeven seemed to be a woman of contradictions.

A Bowdoin grad who liked to go topless in elevators, had dated the victim of Remington's pranks in college, and was now going about with Langdon's good friend, Jimmy 4 by Four. She'd been a successful businesswoman, now retired, and seemed to have an axe to grind with Remington. Thus far, she had been the main source of information for Langdon, while keeping tidbits and nuggets hidden from view.

Chris 'Chuckie' Taylor, now Shannon Undergrove, seemed to be a perfect place to begin his personal probe for the truth. One of the original Maine Men of Mayhem. Now a woman. A person who had suggested that they were interested in making amends for past transgressions. Langdon dropped his feet and sat forward, pulling up the LocateNOW software on his computer and typed in Shannon Undergrove.

Chapter 13

Ogunquit was a fabulous small town down in Southern Maine with only one serious drawback as far as Langdon was concerned. Summer traffic. The town name came from the Algonquin Indians and translated to 'Beautiful Place by the Sea'. And it was absolutely stunningly gorgeous, a four-square mile downtown on the Atlantic Ocean with scenic walking paths, small shops, a thriving theater, and lively restaurants.

Although the year-round residents only numbered about 2,000, the summer months saw that number explode with tourists and seasonal homeowners. And, Langdon mused, all of them thought it important to constantly drive up and down Route 1, creating probably the most congested roadway in all of Maine. Thus, a drive that should've taken him only about an hour more than doubled.

The Veranda was a restaurant and piano bar nestled between Route 1 and Ogunquit Beach, the back patio having spectacular views of that said beach and shimmering ocean. This is where Marsha Verhoeven had seen Shannon Undergrove, formerly Chris "Chuck" Taylor. And on LocateNOW, Langdon had discovered that The Veranda had recently hired Shannon as a bartender. He'd called and been told that her shift today was from noon to eight.

Langdon figured that the slowest time would be around two, after the lunchtime rush and before the serious drinking began. Thus, that had been his goal of an arrival time, but traffic had been worse than the GPS had suggested, and it was quarter to three before he parked the Jeep. Dog had been left at home with Chabal and the adult children, for as dog friendly a place as Ogunquit was, Langdon didn't want to keep one eye on the antics of the canine while trying to speak with Shannon.

The bar stretched across the side of the restaurant, some fifty feet long, a gleaming hardwood polished to a high sheen. High backed stools stretched down the length of it, about half of the twenty-five occupied. It looked like the serious drinkers had gotten a start. There were twenty or so round tables filling out the room, most of them occupied with people having a late lunch. It would seem in the vacation town of Ogunquit, everything happened a little bit later, starting with crawling out of bed. Except, he chuckled to himself, for the consumption of alcohol, which began a bit earlier.

Two pianos took up space in one corner of the room, and a fellow with a long face to match his fingers sat at one sliding his fingers casually across the ivories to produce a gentle backdrop of notes. Langdon had read that every night there was dueling pianos, and on the weekends that was followed by dueling drag divas.

Shannon was a light-skinned Black woman with long platinum hair that Langdon surmised was a wig, but he couldn't actually tell, suggesting that it was of very high quality. Not that he was an expert on wigs. She wore a black dress, heels that made her six-feet tall, or so he was guessing, and a floral scarf wrapped around her neck.

He'd spent an hour perusing her social media sites, primarily Facebook, but a scattering of Instagram, as well as Twitter, or X, or whatever it was called now. She was extremely anti-Republican, pro-LGBQT+, loved small dogs, and was a big Red Sox fan.

"What can I get you?" she asked as Langdon settled into a stool on the corner. There was an underlying deepness to her voice.

He looked at the dry erase board mounted on the wall with beers on draft listed. "Baxter Stowaway."

She delivered the beer and moseyed down to a couple who were eating sandwiches at the bar and refilled their wine glasses.

Langdon waited until his beer was almost gone to get to the point of his visit.

"You want another one?" Shannon asked.

"Sure. And I was wondering if you could answer a few questions for me."

She looked warily down the bridge of her nose at him. "Sure. Fire away."

"What can you tell me about Cornelius Remington?"

Her long lashes flickered violently but her face remained impassive. "Who's that?"

"Fellow you were friends with back in college." Langdon held her gaze.

"Sorry. I don't know anybody by that name." Shannon grabbed a fresh glass and began to pour a Stowaway.

"I'm thinking it'd be hard to forget one of your fellow Maine Men of Mayhem."

Her hand shook and beer slid down the exterior of the glass in a single rivulet. "I think you got me confused with somebody else, Mister."

"You might be right, there. The person who knew Remington was named Chris Taylor."

"That's not me."

"Not anymore, anyway. But I need your help, Shannon."

She moved down and checked the computer and then began filling a tray with drinks for one of the waiters. Langdon sipped his beer patiently. There was a window overlooking the beach, which was quite crowded for a Tuesday. Children played in the sand. People of all ages waded in the surf. Seagulls floated lazily in the air. Summer in Maine. A boat skipped across the waves. Eventually, Shannon had no choice but to come back.

"Who are you?" she asked.

"Name is Langdon. I'm a private investigator, as well as a bookstore owner up in Brunswick."

"The Coffee Dog Bookstore." She nodded. "I've been in. Read some about you in the newspapers as well. That whole wendigo thing was big news, even down here."

"I've been hired by the White House to do a background check on Judge Cornelius Remington." Langdon neglected to mention that the investigation was now officially over and moving onto the Senate Committee and the American Bar Association.

"What for?"

Langdon looked into her eyes and saw a dawning realization creeping forward from the depths. "The President is going to nominate him to be a Supreme Court justice. For life."

"Sweet Jesus." Shannon sighed. Muttered under her breath what sounded like a curse. "I get off at eight. I can talk then."

Langdon didn't much believe in wearing long pants in the summer, nor socks, so it was easy enough to take off his Hey Dude shoes and take a stroll down the beautiful Ogunquit Beach. Afterward, he had a very tasty dinner at a Mediterranean Bar and Grill, followed by another walk, this time along the cliff walk footpath. Just before eight, he made his way back to The Veranda, where Shannon asked him to wait outside for her.

Ten minutes later, she joined him, and led him to a bench overlooking the Atlantic Ocean. The sun had disappeared behind them, obscured by the town, but still illuminated the sky with a faint light. The beach had emptied out, the walkway was mostly barren of pedestrians, and they sat quietly for a moment enjoying the peace before the storm.

After a bit, Langdon cleared his throat. "Tell me about Cornelius Remington."

"How did you find me?"

"Marsha Verhoeven."

Shannon nodded. "I saw her down here a while back. I wondered if she recognized me."

"You'd gone and apologized to her before that. She said it was like you were making amends."

"Amends." Shannon nodded. "That'd be a good way of putting it. I wasn't proud of a lot of things I did."

"Things that involved Remington?"

"Yes. I didn't realize it at the time, but he was a bully. Made us all do things."

"Such as?"

"Corn Porn King, we called him. He loved to watch porn. Wanted all of us to watch it with him. Something strange about five guys in a dorm room watching pornographic videos, don't you think."

"The Maine Men of Mayhem. Cornelius, Michael, Fred, John, and you."

"Yes. Five guys squished in a tiny room watching people having sex."

Langdon shrugged. "Plenty of people watch porn."

"I'm no prude. But every single day got a bit old. He'd harangue us if we didn't."

"How about the pranks you played?"

"What about them?"

"Was there anything that crossed over the boundaries of unkind to… criminal?"

"No. Just mean spirited. It was always Corn Porn's idea. He targeted gay people, unpopular students—the weak." Shannon snickered. "Wonder what he'd think if he could see me now. Chuckie fully transitioned to a female. That'd blow his mind."

Langdon stared out over the Atlantic where stars were starting to pierce the night sky. Pranks and porn weren't going to give pause to the nomination process rolling forward.

"Why'd you do it?" he asked.

"Do it?"

"Why didn't you just say no?"

"I've given that a lot of thought over the past thirty-some years. Once we graduated, I did cut ties even though we both stayed in the area. Sure, I'd see him around town on occasion, but I deflected his overtures to hang out, get together, have a beer. But why'd I let him push me into being a bully in college? It was his charisma, I suppose. It was infectious. It lit up a room like a lightning storm. And his persistence. He wouldn't take no for an answer."

Langdon pondered the characteristics of charisma and persistence. They were a deadly combo in the wrong hands. "Tell me about Michael Levy."

"Mikey is the best of us. He—"

"He is dead."

"What? Mikey is… dead?"

"Yes."

"Did Corn Porn kill him? No, I guess not, or he wouldn't be nominated for the SCOTUS." Shannon looked shaken. Her face had gone ashen underneath her heavy makeup. "How'd he die?"

"Heart attack."

"Yeah, I think there was something wrong with his heart. A murmur, or something like that. Had it all his life, or at least from college on."

"Why was your first reaction wondering if Remington killed him?"

Shannon looked out over the vast ocean with eyes that looked inward rather than outward, backward rather than forward. "Mikey was the only one of us that ever tried to stand up to Corn Porn. He wasn't successful, for the most part, but somehow Neely would always lure him back in, get him back on board. But he fought it. I remember one time, Neely wanted to dump a bunch of irate bees into the computer lab and barricade the door. He even had them on order from some company. Mikey threatened to go to the president of the college if he did. It was an awful row, but eventually, for one of the only times ever, Neely backed down."

"Do you think it possible that Remington killed Michael Levy to keep his mouth shut about something?"

"He wouldn't be nominated for the Supreme Court if he killed him, now, would he?"

Langdon sighed. "He would if he got away with it. If nobody suspected him, or better yet, the official line is that Mikey died of a heart attack when he was home alone."

"You think that Neely could've killed Mikey?"

"Do you think he could've? I mean, would Remington kill somebody to keep his reputation intact?"

"Hell's bells, yes, he would," Shannon said. "In a heartbeat."

"I need something more than opinion and college pranks to stop the SCOTUS train from pulling into the station. Can you think of anything that will help?"

Shannon grunted. Shifted uncomfortably. Scratched at her throat. "Like what?"

"I think your friend is about to be rubber-stamped into the highest court in the land unless you can provide me with something more tangible to derail the process."

They sat in silence. A couple walked by holding hands. The moon sat high in the sky, just a sliver missing. The waves crashed.

"I'm not sure if this is anything, or not," Shannon said. "But something happened with his girlfriend junior year. I don't know what it was, but they broke up and he was different for some time after."

"Different?"

Shannon let the word percolate around them. "Scared. We didn't pull a prank for a month. He didn't badger us to watch porn with him. Locked himself away in his room."

"Any idea what happened?"

"No idea. He could've just been upset they broke up, but it seemed different. Worse. There was something more than just heartbreak. You could smell the fear on him."

"Do you remember her name?"

"Tara James."

Chapter 14

It'd been late the night before when he got home. After eleven, very late, but Chabal had been up watching television in bed, waiting for him. Sober. They'd talked about the case, the kids, a funny show she'd watched—until the early morning hours.

Thus, Langdon had missed his morning workout, but was still in his office an hour before the opening hour of the bookshop at nine. There was something about Judge Cornelius Remington that wouldn't release its hold on his mind. Neely. Maine Man of Mayhem. Corn Porn. SCOTUS.

Langdon put his feet up on his desk in his best thinking pose. What were the circumstances of Michael Levy's heart attack? He'd read the police report. It was concise and to the point. Levy had been reported as missing. When the police got around to checking on him, he'd been found dead. The medical examiner and coroner agreed that it was a heart attack. The Maine State Police Major Crime Unit probably barely noticed a blip on their radar. There was nothing suggesting anything other than a fellow with a bad ticker had a heart attack while alone and died.

Langdon leaned forward and pulled the keyboard onto his lap. He used the mouse to click on the Text Icon and scrolled down to click on Bart's name.

Can you check into the death of Michael Levy and fill in the lines between what was written on the police report. See what the ME has to say. Check for red flags, irregularities, any oddness at all.

It was a boon in life that Apple products could now text on the computer, the keyboard much easier on Langdon's large fingers for longer messages.

The death of Michael Levy was lead number one. Lead number two was this mysterious Tara James. Two people on his list. Two names that everything kept winding around. He'd tried calling Tara James on the way home last night. Voice mail. He tried again this morning. Straight to voicemail.

What was it that Shannon had said? Charisma and persistence. A deadly combination in the wrong hands. He called Tara James again. This time the message said, "The phone you have called has been switched off." Nothing more.

Fingers kept pointing toward Tara and she seemed to be avoiding speaking with Langdon. What were the options? The FBI had been notified of her phone number and P.O. box number. But Langdon didn't think they had any intention of following up with her. Where did that leave him?

"Got a moment, boss?" Starling stuck his head into the office.

Langdon opened his eyes. "Sure. C'mon in."

Dog yawned lazily from the couch.

Starling approached the desk, his fingers nervously twisting together.

Langdon pointed at a chair. "Sit. And spit it out."

Starling sat. "I know that woman on your list."

"What woman?"

"Tara James."

Hmm, Langdon thought, all roads keep leading to Tara James. Recently moved to Florida. Elusive. A thought began to solidify in his brain. "From here in the bookstore?" he asked.

Starling sighed. Burbled his lips. "No. Well, yes. She has been in and didn't recognize me. I wasn't always the wrinkled old fart I am now."

"When did you first know Tara James?"

"It was the summer of 1988."

Langdon digested that and let it settle a bit. "The summer before her senior year at Bowdoin."

Starling nodded. "Right after me and Harper Truman hung out our shingle up in Madison and began taking on the large paper companies who were razing our forests to the ground creating a carnage that looked like no-man's land after the Great War."

"Before Jordan Fitzpatrick came on board?"

"Yeah. Before she twisted us up in knots and sent Harper on a power-hungry trip and me diving deep into the bottle of whiskey."

"And you've seen her here in the bookshop?"

"Here and around town. Maybe a dozen times over the past twenty-five years."

"But she didn't recognize you?"

Starling spread his arms wide. "The changes I went through in the ten years after I knew her—I didn't recognize myself. Look at me. I look like an old road map drawn upon the hide of an elephant."

Langdon nodded. "I suppose I never knew you before your descent into the sauce."

"There were some dark days there."

"And why didn't you just introduce yourself to Tara James?" Langdon had an inkling of why Star had not done this. "Just say, 'hi Tara, it's Jonathan Starling. Remember me?'"

Starling burbled his lips again. Breathed in deeply through his nose. Stared down at his lap before raising his eyes to meet Langdon's. "It was the summer of 1988. As I said, me and Harper Truman had just opened our practice. I was a hotshot fresh out of law school. We both were. We were young, full of ourselves, our blood running hot. We thought we were going to change the world. Save the environment. The fallacy of youth. And we, I, was full of my virility. Testosterone coursed through my body like a pinball game when you get the bonus and play five balls at once. *Ping-ping-ping-ping-ping.*

"We hired an intern from Bowdoin College to help with some of the paperwork so we could be out in the field, in court, in meetings, whatever it took to slow the destruction of the forests. Tara James. She was a pretty girl with doe eyes and a wry smile that would twist your insides. But there was a sadness to her. A wariness. She seemed to be extremely guarded. Like something was clawing at her from the inside, trying to get out, to be released and let go.

"I took her out for a drink after work one day. Truman wasn't around. I think he'd gone down to Portland for some reason. Anyways, we went down to that bar, The Pines, where Bart and Jimmy drug me out of so many years ago. Down by the river in Madison. And after a couple of drinks, Tara, she opened up to me. Told me something terrible.

"That spring she'd been dating a fellow at Bowdoin College. I can't remember the guy's name. I've tried to dredge it up since this case began, to see if it was any of the people you're looking into, but parts of my memory have just vanished, sucked into a black hole over the years. Gone.

"Anyway, as the story that I remember goes, she had too much to drink one night. A tale as old as time. But she was with her boyfriend, so she thought she was safe. That he'd take care of her. Things got hazy and she blacked out. When she woke up, she was in her boyfriend's bed. And she was naked. And somebody was having sex with her. But it wasn't her boyfriend. It was one of his friends.

"After it was done, she fell back asleep, or passed out, and when she woke in the morning, her boyfriend was next to her. She wondered if it might've been a dream. It was all very surreal. Shadowed and filled with cobwebs. Just pieces of images and recollections and fragments of memories all rolled up and jumbled together in one big mess."

Starling closed his eyes and leaned back in his chair. His face was waxen. Grey. Perhaps more lines had creased his visage in the telling of the story. Lines upon lines.

"The boyfriend was no other than Cornelius Remington,"

Langdon said.

Starling stared blankly. "You'd think I'd remember that. You sure that's true?"

Langdon shrugged. "According to Shannon Undergrove, of the original five Maine Men of Mayhem, it is. What's more, she told me that something happened between Remington and Tara the spring of their junior year that caused a rift in the shenanigans for a bit, before they got back to their plundering ways."

"Shoot," Starling said morosely. "Another reason to never drink alcohol. Memory deterioration."

"Or obliteration."

Starling smiled wanly. "Was it this Shannon guy who was the other dude?"

"First of all, Shannon is a she who used to be a he, Chris 'Chuckie' Taylor as a matter of fact."

Starling shook his head in confusion. "Don't forget that I'm an old fart and my mind has deteriorated and been obliterated. What's that again?"

"One of the original Maine Men of Mayhem, Chuck Taylor, has recently transitioned to being a female. I spoke with her yesterday. She said that she wasn't even aware of what had thrown a wrench into Remington and closed him up like a clam for about a month, but I'm putting two and two together and thinking that it has to do with this thing you're talking about."

"Wow. It only gets worse."

"And you don't know who the other person was?"

There was a long pause. Starling finally replied without opening his eyes, the words tumbling out through a cheese grater. "She wouldn't tell me."

"Did she know?"

"I don't know. Maybe. Maybe not."

"What happened. I mean, did she confront her… boyfriend?"

"No. At first, she wasn't sure if it'd really happened, and then, when she realized it had, she was humiliated. Embarrassed. Blamed herself. A few days later she broke up with the boyfriend. Threatened to report him to the school. To the police. But after a few weeks, came to the thought process that she had been just as much at fault as he had. Put her head low and moved on in a separate direction. But it hung over her."

"Star?" Langdon waited for his friend to open his eyes before he continued. "Why didn't you tell me that you knew Tara?"

"Because I took her home and made love to her that night. I took advantage of her vulnerability and my position of authority as her boss. I, of course, didn't look on it in that fashion back then. I thought we'd shared a moment. That we'd connected on a higher plane. That we shared a love together. Of course, now, I realize how wrong I was. Every time I've seen her since, I've wanted to tell her who I was, apologize, beg her forgiveness for what I'd done. It was wrong."

"What happened?"

"We spent the summer working together during the day and making love at night. One day, I woke up, and she'd left a note on the table saying she was going home to visit with her family before school started back up in the fall. That'd it been nice—but it was over."

"And that was it?"

Starling shrugged. "I was young. There were other fish in the pond. I realized it'd been a summer fling and moved on, threw myself back into the law practice. Sometime after I lost it all—when I'd become a drunk—I came to the realization that my actions had been completely amoral."

Langdon drummed his fingers on the desk as he thought back on the actions of a young man that had tortured his friend all these years. "Maybe you should apologize to her?"

Star nodded. "I've tried. Come close. But was too weak."

"Sounds like we might need to speak with her. Find out who her boyfriend was and who was the person who took advantage of her drunkenness to molest her. And that will be your opportunity to atone. To make your amends."

"There's one more thing."

"Yes."

"There's a bottle of whiskey on my coffee table in my house. Can you dispose of that before I leave here today?"

Chapter 15

After Starling went out front to open the bookshop, Langdon checked his phone. He wondered again that the death of Michael Levy, in such close proximity to the pending nomination of Remington, was a strange coincidence indeed. Him being one of the Maine Men of Mayhem and the lynchpin that seemed to connect the man with possible nefarious behavior.

Bart had texted back to tell him he'd be happy to oblige checking in with the Medical Examiner, the responding officers, and whatnot, but it was going to cost him lunch. Langdon already figured that would be the case.

He sent a text to Tara's phone number but had little hopes of getting a reply. The phone number listed was now turned off or out of service. That was interesting. Terminated right after his phone call, it seemed.

He wondered what sort of relationship Tara had with Remington after they broke up, presumably because he'd shared her with a buddy, quite probably one of the other Maine Men of Mayhem. Was that why she had been on the list from the FBI for him to find?

Maybe Marsha Verhoeven knew more. All Langdon knew at this point was that Tara James had dated Remington, and then when drunk, had engaged in sexual relationships with somebody else. It sounded as if it was a clear case of sexual assault. If this person was also drunk, the law became grey, but if less inebriated than Tara, it could be considered rape, but only if it were reported as such. But could it be connected back to Remington?

Langdon pulled out his phone and whipped off a quick text to Bart.

Check and see if there were any rape accusations or charges filed at Bowdoin College in the winter or spring of 1988. Tara James would've been the victim.

He was betting that there'd been no report, no charges filed, no accusation. Thirty-five years ago, most college women in similar circumstances would've just bowed their heads in shame and kept their mouths shut, hoping nobody heard, blaming themselves for the assault upon their bodies.

Some things had changed, perhaps in the slightest possible increment, but most sexual assault occurrences were still unreported, especially when alcohol or drugs were involved and when the victim knew their assailant.

The fact was that Tara James was the wild card to finding out a very egregious piece of Remington's background and potentially exposing it to the world. It was very likely that that was why she'd suddenly moved as far south as she possibly could.

Who was her assailant? Michael Levy? Langdon put that on the back burner pending the findings of Bart regarding whether there'd been assault charges filed. Instead of dead and missing people, why not get started with the living? Marsha had told him that in addition to Shannon, then Chris Taylor, Remington, and Levy, that there'd been two other men in the Mayhem group. Fred Duffy and John Boyle. He hadn't looked them up yet as they hadn't been on the list given to him by the FBI.

A quick search found that the two men still lived in Brunswick. One on Bunganuc Road and the other on Federal Street. He could've walked over to the latter as it was not far, but he figured he might be continuing on afterward, so he took the Jeep. Dog was certain that it was going to be some grand adventure, and perhaps it was, as he put his paws up on the windshield of the topless Jeep and let the wind blow in his face.

There was nobody home at John Boyle's house on Federal. No newspapers piled up or signs of desolation. It seemed that the man, or somebody still lived there. No luck at Bunganuc and Fred Duffy, either. Langdon had found on LocateNOW that both men had two adult children living out of state, and both were divorced, and currently single. Two peas in a pod.

There was a walking path that led to Maquoit Bay that Langdon and dog did on occasion right off Bunganuc, and now seemed like a grand time to give dog some exercise and spend forty-five minutes in quiet contemplation.

An hour later, with very little more figured out, other than the burgeoning question of why he was still investigating a case that had ended, Langdon pulled into Hog Heaven. He was a bit early but figured that might give him some time with Susie. He didn't put his lights on requesting service until he saw her come out with a tray of food for a truck across the way. When she returned inside, he pulled the Jeep over next to the truck to ensure he was in her 'station'.

As Susie approached the Jeep a smile flashed across her face and then quickly extinguished. "Langdon. Is your wife doing okay?"

"Better. Thank you. It's been a tough row to hoe."

"Sounds like she went through some real freaky shit. Can't blame the girl. That fellow who ate those women, the pig who did all that stuff to her, they gone on trial yet? Haven't seen anything about that for quite some time."

"Nope. Not yet. Hey, I wanted to follow up with you on Judge Remington. You know anything else about him?"

Susie looked left and right before leaning closer to his open window. "I checked around after you was asking about him and just yesterday this girl, Alice, she told me that the Judge paid her five hundred bucks to bump uglies with him. Said he made her call him 'your honor' and apologize for being a lawbreaker and shit like that."

"Think she'll talk to me?"

Susie shook her head no. "Broads like me and Alice don't go on record badmouthing a judge. Not one as powerful and vengeful as Remington, that's for sure."

"Vengeful?"

"Alice, this was some years ago, had a pending court date for solicitation. He told her he was going to throw the book at her if she didn't agree to sex and role playing with him. Still gave her a pretty stiff sentence, all things considered, she said, and then threatened that she best keep her mouth shut or he'd make her life a living hell."

"It just happen the one time?"

Bart pulled in next to the Jeep and lumbered his enormous frame out of the Brunswick PD cruiser. "Hi, honey." He went to kiss Susie on the cheek.

She pulled away, his affection turning into a light brush and an air kiss. "I'll give you more time to decide what you want."

Bart watched her walk away. "Man, she's something, ain't she?"

Langdon kept his face impassive. "She seems to be good people. What's up with the two of you?"

Bart smiled broadly, his teeth about popping from the gums. "I'm not one to kiss and tell but we had a good night after we left your house. A real…" His voice trailed off and his face flushed red. "How's Chabal?"

"Better. The kids have rallied. They all cleared their schedules and came home."

"That's good. You know, if there's anything I can do, just holler."

Langdon knew. The gruff cop had a heart of gold and would do anything for him and Chabal. As far as he knew, the man had never dated a woman in his life. Now, at the age of sixty-one, he had his first girlfriend. Langdon suspected the man had hooked up before, possibly even paid for sex, but this was different. His eyes had teenage boy sparkle to them.

"Yeah, I know."

Bart walked around and squeezed into the passenger seat of the

Jeep, pushing dog to the backseat in the process. "What do you think of my Susie?"

"I never would've put you and her together."

Bart's smile breached his face again. "She's a tough cookie. Not had an easy life, but neither have I. But she's got a purity to her, don't you think?"

"Yeah. She does have a purity." Langdon wasn't quite sure what Bart meant by this but figured it best to agree with him.

Susie came back to take their orders and Langdon figured it was a tossup if Bart or dog had more drool on their face. Probably Bart, as he was just as excited about eating as dog was and had the added hunger and appetite for more than just food. For her part, she smiled coyly at Bart, but was very matter of fact in her order taking.

"She's pretty, don't you think?" Bart said.

Langdon wondered if they were back in high school and worried that he was going to be asked to pass Susie a note. "Sure. She's great. Hey, what'd you find out from the ME about Levy's heart attack?"

"I emailed you the report, but I doubt you'll understand it any better than I did. But I got the ME on the phone, and he told me that Levy had a bad ticker to begin with, but the heart attack was instigated by an electric shock. It was a freak accident. Levy was sitting on his toilet listening to music on his headphones. The ME concluded that the cord was frayed, and that it appeared that he put the wire in his mouth, possibly to peel the plastic coating, and that created a conduit from the water in the bowl, up through his piss and body, and gave him a severe jolt. Probably not enough to kill him if he didn't already have a bad heart."

Langdon stared at him wondering if the cop was pulling his leg. "Seriously?"

Bart stared him dead in the eye, a small grin creasing just the corners of his mouth. "I shit you not."

Langdon groaned. But he believed Bart was *not* pulling his leg. It was just the one-liner he'd been waiting to deliver that caused the smirk. "It could be a freak accidental jolt that caused a heart attack or—"

"It was made to look that way," Bart finished for him.

"Because Michael Levy had damaging information to share about the Judge, something bad enough to kill for. Do you think the ME would be willing to take another look at the body? See if anything sticks out as being suspicious?"

Bart shook his head. "Can't. The body was cremated two weeks ago."

"Shoot. That's too bad. I'll see what Jackson Brooks has to say about it."

"The pretty boy Statie? You'll have to catch him between pedicures."

Langdon chuckled. Bart was not a big fan of Jackson, who indeed, was very concerned and impressed at the same time about his looks. "No worries. We both use the same nail technician. I'll just catch him there."

"Just the fact that you know they're called nail technicians makes me want to vomit."

Langdon's phone buzzed. It was his daughter. He held up a finger to Bart. "Hey, Missouri Langdon, what's up?"

The answer chilled him. "It's Chabal. She's kinda freaking out, Dad. You should probably get home."

Chapter 16

The morning started out okay for Chabal even though she'd slept poorly. Several times over the course of the night she'd verged on getting out of bed and taking the car to the store to buy wine. The kids had helped her totally excise the house of alcohol, even her hidden stashes, so a run to buy a bottle or two of wine would be necessary. She'd just mentally caved into doing this when she realized that the time had passed 1:00 a.m. and her opportunity had evaporated with the closure of alcohol sales in Brunswick.

In the morning, she reasoned, she would buy a bottle of wine just to take the edge off and allow her to relax. When the sunlight seeped through the window bringing another rotation of the earth to the calendar, Chabal shrugged off this weakness of mind and realized that she did not need the wine. Langdon had already left when she wandered into the kitchen for a cup of joe to clear the cobwebs.

When Jack came wandering down the stairs, the bacon was sizzling on the griddle, and when Missouri and Jamie stumbled bleary-eyed in for their morning coffee, she dipped the first stack of bread and began the first batch of French toast. The tantalizing smell of breakfast brought Darcy and Gary down and the six of them sat down to eat breakfast at the table together. Family was good.

But now, as the morning waned and the afternoon loomed, Chabal was feeling a strange mixture of anxiety and fatigue. There was a tremor in her hand and a crushing stuffiness in her head. Chills overlapped sweat, even though she had no temperature. It had been eighty-two hours since her last drink. The first three days had not been bad. A myriad of activities with her adult children had kept her mind occupied.

Now, Missouri was in the living room doing remote work on her laptop, as most likely the others were also doing in their rooms, and Chabal sat at the island in the kitchen scrolling social media on her phone. She knew that a physical activity would be good for her, but she was too tired. A part of her suggested a nap, but she wasn't that kind of tired. A diversion was needed. She was a walking conundrum and was lost in a maze devised by her mind to trick her into slipping back into drinking.

She grabbed her keys and went to her car and drove down to the 7-Eleven in the center of town. The Chardonnay was not chilled. She grabbed two bottles from the rack, paid for them, and drove home.

Jack was waiting for her when she came through the door. He looked at her, his eyes flickering to the bag of wine in her hand, and then back to her face. She said nothing, brushing by to put one bottle in the freezer and the other in the fridge. She wasn't an animal. She wasn't addicted. It wasn't like she was going to drink cough syrup, for Chrissake. Chabal could wait for it to grow cold.

"What's up, Mom?"

Chabal breathed deeply through her nose. She could feel her cells opening in anticipation of the soon-to-be wine coursing down her throat. Warming and melting the icy embrace of the wendigo. The being who'd inhabited her and become one with her just as he'd promised.

"Mom, are you okay?"

"I'm good. Why?"

Missouri came into the kitchen. "What's going on?"

"Mom went out and bought alcohol."

"Since when did you become my keeper, Jack Daniels?" Chabal snorted, thinking of the name she and her dad had bestowed upon the boy. "I just need a glass to shake the cobwebs and calm my nerves."

"Maybe we can go for a walk?" Missouri said. "Get some fresh air?"

Chabal looked from her son Jack to her stepdaughter Missouri, her eyes flickering from one to the other. "Sure. Just give me a few minutes." She pulled the wine bottle out of the freezer. It'd been all of two minutes and was barely cool to the touch.

"It's okay, Mom. We're here for you."

Chabal twisted off the cap and grabbed a glass from the cupboard.

"Does it really help?" Missouri asked. "Or does it make it worse?"

Chabal poured the glass to the rim. "Both. It helps at first and then gets worse when I stop. That's why stopping is not a good idea."

"I love you, Mom." Jack stood silent and sad in the middle of the kitchen.

"What can I do?" Chabal wanted to cry, to sob, to scream, but you didn't do that in front of your children. She realized that Darcy, Gary, and Jamie now stood in the large arched opening into the living room. "He's in me."

"Who?"

"The wendigo."

"He's not, Chabal." Missouri stepped closer. "He's in jail awaiting trial before he goes away to rot in prison."

"Just one glass. Then we can walk."

Missouri shrugged. "It's your decision. Not mine. You do as you want."

Chabal dropped the glass of wine on the tile floor where it shattered. She looked at the bottle, still in her hand, and threw it through the window, smashing the glass and tearing through the screen. She screamed, unintelligible words—guttural yells of pain and anger and sorrow and suffering.

Jack stepped forward to hug her and she pushed him back and swept the Keurig and assorted items from the island to the floor in a crescendo of sound and a clamoring of commotion.

Chabal realized she was still yelling, words that made no sense, explosions of sounds that welled up within her and burst forth with no rhyme or reason. Jack tried to grab her again and she pushed him away. Missouri had the phone to her ear. Gary started into the kitchen, paused, unsure, while Darcy and Jamie stood frozen behind him in shock at her outburst.

What was she doing? Screamed and echoed through Chabal's mind. But she couldn't stop. And then she saw Jack's face, terrified, sad, worried—and suddenly she was seeing him at four years old with the same face. He was her baby. Her first boy. She sank to the floor, sobs starting to ripple up through her body in huge wracking convulsions.

Her children gathered around her, kneeling and sitting on the floor, their faces a rotating cyclorama of emotions. An image of Vera Miles screaming in the shower in *Psycho* popped into Chabal's mind and she started laughing gasps of air that careened from her mouth like an exploding balloon.

Then Langdon was there. He kneeled and picked her up and carried her into the bedroom and held her tight. And for the first time in a long while, she felt safe. Maybe she could get through this. Maybe it was going to be okay.

Chapter 17

Langdon woke the next morning with his body fully encasing Chabal in a big spoon position. She was so tiny curled into him, her body melding into his like Silly Putty. Yet, he felt an awkwardness as the contact, the connection, sleep, lack of sex—all led to him being aroused when that was the last thing his wife needed at this emotional morass point of her life.

Chabal sighed and wiggled her butt, grinding into him. An action that did not help his current situation. He didn't want to roll away from the contact—whether due to the protective nature of it, just the touch and connection with his wife, or his sexual arousal—it was tough to tell. Most likely a combination of all three as Chabal shoved herself even tighter into his body if that was possible.

Langdon vainly tried to dampen the raging desire that flamed through his body and pushed rational thought from his head. Chabal rotated her hips, her bottom rubbing him, and then she reached her hand back and into his boxers.

"Are you sure?" he asked.

In reply, she released him and pulled her sleeping shorts and panties down and wiggled them from her feet. That seemed to be a plenty clear enough answer.

~ ~ ~ ~ ~

Langdon was still in a fog of satisfaction when he breezed into the bookstore later that morning. After his morning nookie with his wife, he'd gotten up and cooked a breakfast of bacon, eggs, and his famous potato surprise, a throwback to when all the kids had been younger. It was just past eleven as he came through the open door and was greeted by Raven, who'd opened this morning. She asked if she could cut out early after Starling came in at noon.

"Not a problem," he replied. "Chabal is going to be in soon to help out."

Raven, to her credit, kept most of the surprise from surfacing on her face. "Great. I hope she gets here before I leave. It's been ages."

And it had been a long time since Chabal had been to the Coffee Dog, much less worked here. A few weeks after the incident with the wendigo, she'd returned to work, but it'd proven to be too much. Over the next couple of months, she'd attempted to come in, but gradually had just phased it out until it was not at all. That had been eight months ago. For the last four months, she'd barely left the house. Except to buy wine.

Langdon had suggested she let him drive her in to the shop, but she'd insisted that she wanted to do it on her own and would be along shortly. What was the saying, he wondered? Don't hold your breath, but he was, and hoping for the best.

His phone buzzed in his pocket. It was from Washington, D.C. The White House. Cooper Walker. "Hello. This is Langdon."

"What part of over do you not understand?"

Langdon waved at Raven as he walked back toward his office. "Excuse me?"

"Agents Delgado and Thomas told you that the background check on Judge Cornelius Remington was complete. You have submitted your final report. A check is in the mail. You are done."

"I understand that."

"Why the fuck are you still poking around, then?"

Langdon sat down and put his feet up on his desk. "I didn't feel like the task was complete, to be perfectly honest with you. There seems to be several loose threads that still need to be run down."

"I just got reamed out by my boss. I don't like it when that happens. You will cease and desist from muddying the waters of Judge Remington's hometown."

"And by your boss, Cooper, do you mean the Chief of Staff herself, or do you mean the President?" Langdon had always found humor and sarcasm a good way to evade when under attack and not wanting to respond to something.

"You are no longer being paid for your efforts."

"I understand that."

Cooper made a sound between a cough and a splutter. "Why, then?"

"I told you. There appears to be a lot of smoke."

"Smoke?"

"Yeah, you know, where there's smoke, there's usually—"

"Fire. I got it." Cooper sighed. "Okay. I'll bite. What smoke?"

"First of all, did your agents, Delgado and Thomas, speak with Chris Taylor, aka, Shannon Undergrove?"

"Shannon Undergrove?"

"I put it in my report that I found Taylor. That he'd transitioned from a male to a female. That she moved to Ogunquit. Did you read it or was that for FBI eyes only?"

"I read it. So what?"

"I'm going to assume from that answer that nobody has spoken with Shannon. Well, I did, and do you know what Remington's nickname in college was with his closest friends?"

"Neely."

"All his friends call him that. Even I call him that. But his inner circle, the boys of Mayhem, they called him Corn Porn."

A sound like grating teeth came over the line. "Judge Remington has told us he occasionally watched porn in college. Like most young hormonal men of that age."

Langdon chuckled. "Every day. Five guys in a room with one

color television attached to a VCR. I know, much like the pranks they played, just 'boys being boys' stuff."

"Look, Langdon, it seems excessive if what this Shannon Undergrove is saying is correct. Judge Remington shared that it was only on a rare occasion that he'd watched pornography in college."

"His word against hers."

"Not something a Senate Committee will mire themselves in, if you know what I mean."

"And you also know that Corn Porn dated Tara James. That is why she was on my list of people to find."

"Yes."

"And did the FBI speak with her?"

There was a pause, a hesitation suggesting that Cooper didn't know how much he wanted to share. "Briefly. But when I tried to follow up, the phone number was no longer valid. Her address is just a P.O. box in Marathon."

"Would it be safe to say that many of the people without a phone and no physical address are people who don't want to be found for one reason or another." When there was no answer, Langdon continued, "Shannon also told me that after Corn Porn and—"

"Please stop calling him that."

Langdon chuckled. "Okay. Shannon said that Judge Remington got real strange the spring of his junior year. He wasn't his normal gregarious self, but withdrawn, as if he'd been through a wringer."

"That was most likely because he'd just broken up with his girlfriend."

Langdon nodded. "Tara James."

"Yes."

"It turns out that Tara James just happened to intern with a man named Jonathan Starling up in Madison, the town here in Maine, not Wisconsin, the summer between her junior and senior year. And she told him a story about passing out in her boyfriend's bed and waking up to having sex with somebody else before passing out again."

"Okay, you have my attention."

"The suggestion was that Judge Remington orchestrated this… sexual interaction."

"Again, nothing concrete. Innuendo. Nothing more. Anything else?"

"The strange death of Michael Levy."

"It was indeed a freak accident."

Langdon chuckled. "Sitting on the toilet taking a dump listening to music on your headphones, sticking the wire in your mouth creating a conduit of electricity via water through your body, causing a jolt through your body that tweaks your weak heart to go into cardiac arrest. What's freakish about that?"

"Your point, Mr. Langdon?"

"Don't you think it quite possible that Levy was killed, and his murder was made to look like an accident?"

"I believe that it would be an even more bizarre way to murder somebody than if it was an accidental death, is what I think."

"Maybe not the whole headphone and shitter thing but jolted with a shock that leads to a heart attack."

"It's possible. But where's the proof?"

"But possible."

"To what purpose?"

Langdon pondered this for a few seconds before answering. "Levy was a close consort with the judge in college. Where there are hints of malfeasance taking place. Right before Remington is nominated for the Supreme Court, Levy suddenly dies. Coincidence? I think not." The phone line was dead silent, long enough for Langdon to worry he'd lost the connection. "What do you think?"

"I can't decide whether I'm more shocked at your use of the word malfeasance or your quote of *The Incredibles* on the coincidence thing."

Langdon smiled to himself. He had Cooper Walker believing. The assistant to the chief of staff of the White House, a young man who'd probably been no more than eight years old back in 2004 when *The Incredibles* came out. He'd probably watched it ten times.

"That it?" Cooper asked.

"Just the fact that Corn Porn, sorry, Judge Remington, came to visit me on a fishing expedition. He seemed concerned at what this background check might reveal and wasn't happy that I wasn't more forthcoming with information regarding the status of his investigation."

"Look, Langdon, I'm not giving credence to your accusations but there does seem to be some smoke on the water."

Langdon noticed that Cooper had dropped the Mr. "I wouldn't have pegged you for a Deep Purple fan, Coop. Isn't *Smoke on the Water* a song before your time?"

"My parents were part of the back to the land movement in the '70s. That's the music I grew up listening to. Sure beat what was popular when I was a kid."

You're still a kid, Langdon wanted to say. But then wondered if Cooper's parents knew Starling, who'd been quite involved in the back to the land movement and was about the right age. "Back to the land? You mean here in Maine?"

"Yes."

"They still live here?"

"What is it you want to do, Langdon?"

"Did they go to Bowdoin? Did you go to Bowdoin?"

Cooper laughed, perhaps the first unguarded sound Langdon had heard from him. "I got out of Maine as fast as I could. Went to Stanford. Got my law degree from UNC. The other day was my first time back in years."

"Why?"

"My personal life is not the topic of this conversation. What is it that you would like to do?"

"I'd like to follow some threads. See where the smoke on the water is coming from."

Cooper sighed. "I've already talked to my boss, not the big boss, but my boss. She said that if you were adamant, that we, the White House, would like to know what you find. On the down low, of course."

"Off the books, you mean?"

"More, shall we say, informally. You will report directly to me. If asked, you are doing this on your own. There will be no ties to the White House, at least on paper."

"Does that mean I don't get paid?"

"Within the hour you will have a $5,000 retainer in your bank account. Let me know when you need more."

Langdon wondered if this was some special hidden slush account. Figured it didn't really matter. "Let me at least hear you say it."

"Say what?"

"That you, that the White House, would like me to continue. I don't want to misconstrue any of this. I'm not used to this secret agent thing, you know."

Cooper laughed. "Okay, then. The White House would like you to continue your investigation into the background and life of Judge Cornelius Remington."

Chapter 18

Langdon decided it was time to check in with Susie and see if he could find out more about Alice, the woman who'd been pressured into prostituting herself to Remington for five-hundred bucks. He'd meant to follow up with Susie the previous day but had gotten that phone call that Chabal was freaking out.

The first stop was at Hog Heaven, but he was told that it was her day off. Langdon had done his due diligence and had looked further into the life of Susan Quinn. She lived at Blueberry Estates, the trailer park out by the high school, was twice divorced, currently single, and had two grown children. Some of it, Langdon knew a bit of. She'd been born and raised in Brunswick, dropped out of school when she was seventeen, and had been arrested twice on drug charges.

Raven had helped out by stalking the woman through social media, and from this Langdon knew that she'd recently broken up with a fellow by the name of Ralph and had two cats. She drove an old Corolla, dyed her hair blonde, and was a fan of watching reality television like *The Bachelor* and *Naked and Afraid*. She liked to hang out at McSorley's, the biker bar on Pleasant Street, and attended the Catholic church down the street from her drinking haunt.

When she wasn't at her home, therefore, Langdon's next stop was McSorley's. The third time was the charm. Her red Corolla was in the parking lot, and she was belly up to the rough-hewn bar that was in a U-shape around a cracked mirror and shelves of cheap liquor. The taps were commercial in quality—Bud, Miller, Coors, and Michelob, with not a single craft beer in sight.

"Hey, Susie." Langdon slid into a stool next to her, his shorts immediately sticking to the surface, making him wince, and he wasn't much of a wincer. "Funny running into you here."

Susie snorted. "Whaddaya want, Langdon?"

"Thought I'd get a…" Langdon was not much of a fan of the commercial beers in sight. But it was hard to find a bad brown liquor. "Knob Creek, on ice."

The bartender had approached, nodded, and grabbed a glass with a chip in the rim, plunked several cubes into it, and poured a generous amount of whiskey into it, before sliding the cocktail in front of Langdon. "Five bucks."

That was damn cheap, Langdon thought, and a fine reason that people would brave the sticky seats for a beverage. "And whatever the lady's having."

The bartender and Susie looked at each other and snickered at the same time. He slid a tequila shot in front of her and poured a pre-made margarita into a glass.

"Now I know you want something." Susie knocked the shot back. "Been quite some time since a man bought me a drink before midnight."

Langdon looked at the clock tacked to the wall just past the cracked mirror. He judged that it was probably about correct or was just coincidentally broken to the right time. "Half past midnight, noon, all the same thing."

"Ha. You was always a wisecracker, Langdon, even back in high school."

Langdon's senior year, Susie was a sophomore. She was quite the athlete and had been incredibly pretty. He'd noticed her, but they'd never had anything but a cursory conversation. "High school was a long time ago, Susie."

Susie raised her margarita. "It's been a fucking ride."

Langdon clinked her glass with his and they drank. "Quite a surprise, you showing up with Bart at my house the other night."

"He ain't all that bad for a cop." Susie scoffed. "Hey, how is your wife. Don't figure you had much of a chance to answer me the other day. That was quite some fireside ghost story she told."

Again, Langdon winced. "Sorry you had to be there for that. She's been going through a rough patch but seems to be on the mend."

"Sorry? That was the fucking bomb. I get fucking chills every time I think about that sick fuck, what'd she call him? The wendigo. Man, that sounds like it was pretty whacked."

"It was all that and then some."

Susie shook her head, took a drink. "Suppose you're here about Remington. Or to pass me a note from your cop buddy telling me to meet him at the Oak Tree during recess."

Langdon chuckled. "He is quite smitten with you, much like a schoolboy and his first crush, but I am, indeed, here about the former."

"Told you I'm not sharing deets on my friend."

"Wouldn't be hard for me to find her, you know." Langdon nodded at the bartender who was chatting with a man and a woman across the way. "I imagine I could ask him if he knows an Alice who comes in here, slip him an Andrew Jackson, and he'd hook me up."

Susie started to speak, stopped, glared, and took a sip. "She'll deny it ever happening. Won't do you no good."

Langdon nodded. "I figured as much. That's why I'm talking to you. Maybe you can convince her."

Susie scoffed. "You want to play your cops and robbers games—you go right ahead. You'll end up smelling like roses. But it's people like me and Alice who always lose those games, get chewed up, spit out. Fuck that. It ain't no game for us."

Langdon swirled the liquor in his glass. "I understand."

"Do you? Do you really?"

"My childhood wasn't all sunshine and roses. My dad ran out on us when I was eight years old. I worked on a lobster boat from then until I graduated before school every day. Ten years. To help my mom out, so that my younger brothers would have something to eat."

"Mm. The twins. Couldn't tell them apart, but they were both fine. Lord and Nick. Whatever happened to them?"

"Fifty years old and still wandering the earth like nomads. But, my point is, I'm not some fellow who was born with a silver spoon in my mouth. And that's why it irks me to let people like Remington stomp all over poorer people. Women like your friend Alice, thinking his money, prestige, and power allows him to use, demean, and humiliate her."

Susie sighed. "I'll see if I can set up a get-together for the three of us. Not my call to make."

"Thanks, I appreciate that." Langdon stood, having barely touched his drink. "You got my number. Call me."

"You know, one thing sticks out about what she told me. Sex and subservience. Sure, that's what a lot of guys want. But she was kind of freaked out by the look on his face when he'd call her Tara. You like that, Tara? Roll over, Tara. Touch yourself, Tara. Over and over again. Tara this, Tara that."

~ ~ ~ ~ ~

Marsha Verhoeven lived out past Cook's Corner on the Princes Point Road overlooking Harpswell Cove. Langdon could only imagine that the sunsets were magnificent. The house was not massive, but had a variety of contours, peaks, and edges. He pulled in the dirt driveway, parked, got out, and went up to the front door and banged the knocker twice. No answer.

Strange, he thought, as he'd called her after his conversation with Susie, thinking that the woman had not quite shared everything she knew. That had been just twenty minutes ago, and she'd said she was home. He walked around the side of the shingled home to a fence, lifted the latch of the gate, and went into the backyard.

A small, but not too small, swimming pool glittered in the sunlight. The back of the house was an array of windows that reflected the light of the descending sun. Just on the other side of the fenced in pool was a rocky coastline, thirty feet wide, that led to the ocean. This expanse of blue glistened with tiny whitecaps like stars in the heavens.

Blinded by the brightness, it took Langdon's eyes a moment to adjust, the blurry figure of Marsha Verhoeven coming into focus reclining in a poolside chair. She had on a wide-brimmed hat from which her voluminous hair sprung in haphazard directions. Her sunglasses were circular, tinted green, and larger than her bathing suit top of the same color. Her lipstick was an orangish-red to match her hair, and she held a coupe glass, originally modeled on the breast of Helen of Troy, in her right hand. Only, it was the larger margarita variety, the modern version of the champagne glass, enlarged to meet a heightened appetite. Helen of Troy after a boob job.

"Welcome to my humble abode, my dear Langdon."

Langdon felt like a troll who'd stumbled into the land of fairies. "Hello. I knocked at the front but—"

"Here you are. Would you like a cocktail?"

He couldn't but help compare the two women of this afternoon. Both approximately the same age, both drinking margaritas, both fascinating—but, oh, worlds apart. Susie and Marsha. An example of the educational and financial polarization of Brunswick.

"Earth to Langdon. Would you like a cocktail?" Marsha's voice flirted with teasing.

"Uh, yeah, sure."

"Blender on the bar is strawberry margarita. Fresh strawberries in the bowl to garnish. Patrón if you want a bit more kick. Or there are more choices underneath." Her eyes flickered down her body, his following as if magnets.

"Uh, sure. Margarita would be great." He stepped to the Tiki Bar and poured the red-frozen liquid into an enlarged coupe goblet.

"I was about to go for a swim when you called. I'm sure we could rustle you up a bathing suit if you want. Double X-L?"

"I'm fine, thank you." Langdon sat down in a chair at a round glass table facing Marsha. "If you don't mind, I have a couple of questions I wanted to ask you, but if this is a bad time, I can come back."

Marsha laughed, a girlish giggle. "Do I make you uncomfortable, my dear Langdon?"

"Not at all."

She didn't look like she remotely believed that. "My swim can wait. What is it that you wish to know?"

"Did Remington and Tara James date back in college?"

"I'm thinking you're asking me that because you already know the answer."

"Humor me."

"Yes. They were an item from the middle of their sophomore year until sometime in their junior year. On and off, I think it was."

Perhaps it was the largely naked and beautiful woman he was talking to, but the comment of on and off sounded sexual to Langdon. He refrained from shaking his head to clear the confusion. "And do you know why they broke up?"

"He was an asshole?"

Langdon chuckled. Took a drink. He liked her frank manner. "Did something happen that winter of their junior year?"

"Like what?" Her voice dropped an octave.

"You tell me."

Marsha looked out over Harpswell Cove. "No, not that I know of. Other than he was a real prick."

Langdon nodded, not sold in the slightest. "Tell me about Michael Levy."

"Him and Chuckie were the best of them. The mayhem assholes, that is. The two of them were just weak, afraid to upset Neely." Marsha shrugged, pushed a loose strand of hair from her face. "He'd talk at length about anything. A real chatterbox. Mikey was a nervous dude, you know, all kind of jittery and hiding his real self behind his words. I got the feeling he didn't much care for the pranks and stuff that Neely forced upon them."

Langdon leaned forward, elbows on his knees, eyes locked on her face. "Did the two of them ever have a falling out?"

Marsha took a sip, licked her lips slowly to clean the salt, and set her glass down. She sat up and scooted forward to the end of the recliner, her knees almost touching his. "I did come upon them shouting at each other once. Thought it was going to come to fisticuffs if you know what I mean."

"When was this?" Langdon was well aware of her nearness, her sexuality, and his bloodstream raced with testosterone like electric cars on a track. He kept his eyes pinned on her green-tinted sunglasses, the gleam of her white teeth, the curl of her lips.

Marsha put her hand on his knee. "It was right before finals, senior year, so it must've been end of April, early May? Something like that."

Langdon swallowed. Sat back. "What were they fighting about?"

Marsha sighed. Stood up. "I need to cool off. You sure you don't want to jump in? Wear your boxers. I won't tell anybody." She removed her hat and sunglasses and laid them on the side table next to her margarita.

"I'm fine." He watched as she sashayed to the pool. He thought she'd probably wade delicately in up to her waist, but was wrong, as she walked to the far side of the pool and dove in.

She was definitely a fascinating woman, he mused, and had most certainly been flirting with him. Langdon wondered how this encounter would've gone if his one year of celibacy hadn't just been broken this morning with the wife he adored. Lust and love were a strange dichotomy, and were best when packaged in one container, but that was not always the case.

He stood up to leave, while the getting was good. Marsha was now wading out of the shallow end toward him, water streaming in rivulets from her body, her red hair clinging to her cheeks in wet curls and Langdon had to forcibly restrain his eyes from roving down her mostly naked body in appreciation.

"I'll be off, now, and out of your hair." He could hear the huskiness in his voice.

"Grab me that towel behind you before you go, would you?"

Langdon turned and grabbed the towel and stepped to meet Marsha as she emerged from the pool. "Here."

"Thanks."

He turned to go.

"Langdon?"

He stopped. Turned back. She was just about a foot from him. "Yes?"

"They were fighting about Tara. I just now remembered. Neely and Mikey were having a row regarding Tara."

~ ~ ~ ~ ~

Princes Point Road was a winding affair and Langdon's thoughts were preoccupied with Marsha Verhoeven. True, he was shaken by her boldly flirtatious manner and voluptuous body, but his thoughts had turned to the why of her attempted seduction, if that is what it was. Thus, as he came around the corner prior to the short bridge over the narrows of Buttermilk Cove, he almost clipped a man waving him down from the side of the street.

He pulled the Jeep to a shuddering stop on the far side of the road and got out, caught between anger and helpfulness. "What's going on?"

"Look, man, my buddy got his hand ripped up in a winch and my truck won't start, can you give us a ride to Mid Coast?"

Langdon looked at the truck. It was parked in the pull-off parking for the boat landing. A man was hunched in the passenger seat. Behind the truck, in the water, was a small outboard motorboat moored to a tree with a hastily-done look to it. "Sure."

"Help me get him over to your Jeep, would you?" The man was about Langdon's age, even if a bit more weathered looking. He was broad of body, but not overweight, built more like a block than a person.

Langdon let a car pass and then crossed over the road to the truck. Blockman was already at the side door helping his buddy get out. There was a red-stained towel wrapped around the passenger's hand and arm up to his elbow. Langdon grasped the man's good arm. As they stepped back from the truck, the man's legs gave out and he slid to the ground.

Langdon lost his grasp as the man tumbled down. He immediately leaned over and that was when something crashed into the back of his head. Thunk. He fell on top of the injured man who shoved him off. Everything spun around like a carousel turning too fast, rushing faster and faster, a roaring in his ears like being at the racetrack.

He fought off the darkness that started creeping upon him. Tried to ask a question—he didn't even know what—but no sound came out. Langdon rolled to his side, pushed himself up to one knee, tried to stand. Had he been struck by a car?

He took a gasping breath, the oxygen steadying the spinning carousel of his brain, pushing the darkness to the corners, and looked at the injured man who was now standing. Over his shoulder, Blockman was stepping toward him, something in his hand raised over his head. The hand swung down, with what appeared to be a tire iron, and Langdon had a fleeting realization that he'd been set up and then everything went black.

Chapter 19

Cornelius Remington checked into the posh New York City hotel at just after 4:00 p.m. on Thursday. He'd driven himself down to the city from Brunswick, eschewing public transportation or limousine service. There were things to be done that required anonymity. Officially, he was meeting with the chief of staff, not that assistant Cooper Walker, but the head honcho, the top dog, Saylor Ball. Joining them would be the head of the FBI and the lead counsel for the White House.

He was early, purposely so, having planned a massage and body work. The Four Seasons Downtown offered some of the best spa services in the city and he meant to make use of them. The past weeks had been very stressful. It started when the president, yes, the President of the United States, had called him. *Neely,* the man had said, *I'm considering you for a seat on the SCOTUS.*

It took Cornelius several moments to wrap his head around the fact that SCOTUS was the Supreme Court of the United States. The highest court in the land. A position that would cement the legacy of Cornelius Remington into the history books.

We have a chance to balance the scales of justice, the President said. *And I think that you are the proper man for the job. Left of center, but not so far that Congress will throw a hissy fit.*

And the life of Cornelius was forever changed. Sure, he'd had background checks before, as an appellate judge, but the scrutiny was nowhere near the same as what had been only the start of a deep dig into his personal life and history.

There was a knock at his hotel door. He opened it to a pretty brunette with a cart carrying the tools of her massage trade. She was dressed in a blue tunic that looked much like nurse scrubs and Cornelius could feel himself stir. He had always liked a pretty nurse, real or in costume.

At another time, prior to being considered for the position on the SCOTUS, Cornelius might've tried to seduce this pretty young thing. She must've been in her early twenties, had smoldering dark eyes, and her scrubs couldn't hide the swell of her breasts or the shapeliness of her ass. For the time being that was all on hold, though, and truth be told, he already had plans in that department for later, and he'd reached the age where a repeat performance the same evening as afternoon sex was problematic.

No, this was foreplay for the main event, nothing more. Once he was seated on the Bench, the spotlight would be off him, and he could continue his philandering without the high degree of clandestine care that had been put into this evening's affair.

The masseuse said her name was Julie, had a friendly smile, and got busy setting up the table and lotions for his spa experience. She turned her back demurely as he removed his robe and climbed naked underneath the sheet. Sure, he wasn't as physically fit as he'd been back in the day, having put on fifty pounds since his twenties, but his intellect and wealth more than made up for that, he figured.

Cornelius wondered if he'd have to let Julie down. Tell her that this was just a massage. Nothing more. He felt his loins stir again and turned his thoughts from the beautiful Julie and her hands on his back, his neck, his scalp. With him, he knew, there was certainly a point of no return, and if this beautiful young thing aroused him too far, well, then, all bets were off, and his evening would be ruined.

So, he turned his thoughts to his wife, a woman he'd occasionally still make love to, but it was not much more than the motions, for any lust between the two of them had vacated the bedroom long ago. It wasn't that Toots was ugly. Sure, she was a bit broader across the bottom to match her face, but it was more the fact that she'd lost interest in sex within a few years of getting married. After their kids had been born, the passion had been put away in an ice box and the key thrown away. Luckily, she seemed happy enough to look the other way at his infidelities. Come to think of it, he couldn't remember the last time he and Toots had had sex.

Oh, well. There were plenty of fish in the sea. Much more attractive fish. Not so old. Not so inhibited. Like Julie, the stunning vixen currently rubbing all over him. Tally, his name for his pecker, rippled again, stirring to life as if a dragon awakening. Cornelius quickly turned his mind away from thoughts of Julie's perky tits, forgoing his frigid wife this time, and on to that damn nuisance, Langdon. He knew of the man, of course, having lived in the same town as the clod for the past thirty-some years.

Saylor had told him the local investigation was done, but the damn private dick kept poking his nose into things, and now had her assistant, Cooper Walker, interested in looking further into Cornelius' background. Maybe it was time to turn up the heat on Langdon, see how the man handled pressure. Of course, Neely had investigated the man, and Langdon had dealt with some seriously high-profile cases over the years. Maybe he could be bought off? Or made to disappear?

When Julie finished caressing his body, Cornelius gave her a large tip, thinking if not now, maybe at a future time he could return the favor to the young and nubile vamp. He showered, shaved, and had put the robe back on when there was a knock at the door.

He opened the door with a wide smile. "Hello, my lovely. Come on in."

Saylor Ball smiled wickedly in return and entered the room.

~ ~ ~ ~ ~

After Langdon left, Marsha went inside her house and showered. Her thoughts were on the six-foot four-inch red-haired man who'd just visited. He was certainly sexy, in a low-key sort of way. It seemed nothing perturbed the man. She'd tried to seduce him, just to see his reaction, and might've even followed through on it if he had. Damn. He was sexy. But he was also just a tool.

She thought of his blue eyes, his lanky figure, the calmness to his words and actions. The water trailed down her body and cascaded into the drain below. Much like she needed to let the provocative affections she was experiencing to drain from her person and trickle down and away. She had waited a long time for this. Too long.

Back in her college days, Marsha had been much heavier, more insecure, and a target for mayhem. Just a girl from a small town in Pennsylvania. She'd spent her undergraduate years in and out of therapist appointments. She'd been weak, unable to cope with the testosterone and hormones of two-thousand young people loosed from parental control and unleashed into campus life in Brunswick.

Boys had mocked her. Girls had avoided her. Marsha had been invisible to teachers. She'd been given a single dormitory room her freshman year. Saddled with a roommate who hated her sophomore year. And then back to living alone for her final two years.

There had been one boy who'd been nice to her. And one girl. Two people in four years. Luckily, those days were behind Marsha. She'd buckled down to her studies, done her time, gone on to graduate school, gotten a good job, and risen through the ranks to becoming a powerful businesswoman. She'd lost her flab. Matured into a curvaceous and beautiful woman desired by others. Marsha had day by day left her insecurities behind and become a confident and dynamic woman.

She stepped from the shower, grasping a towel to pat herself dry. Looked at herself in the mirror. Naked. Hair askew on her head. And smiled.

~ ~ ~ ~ ~

He was weightless. Suspended in space. Rocking gently back and forth.

It would've been peaceful if not for the excruciating pain ripping through the interior of his skull.

Jagged fragments of thoughts and memories smashed and crashed in his head. Shards of elusive cognizance swirled in spinning pieces of an impossible puzzle.

There'd been a man. His face was missing. He needed help. His buddy had injured himself. A beautiful woman in a bathing suit. Water dripping. Tiny droplets coursing down her neck. A dog. A woman named Chabal. A hand caught in a winch. The water ran in rivulets over the rounded breast and took flight toward the ground below.

His name was Langdon. His wife was Chabal. His dog was dog.

Looking up. A man swinging something in a downward motion. A tire iron. Salt on lips. A tongue cleaning the granules from the ripeness. A judge. A man dead on the toilet. A man now a woman. The crash of metal into skull. Blackness.

Langdon gasped, spit out seawater. Shook his head. A freight train of misery barreled through his existence.

He was in the water. The ocean. Bobbing in the waves. It was dark. Not a star to be seen. He tried to tread water, but he was suspended backward. Attached. Reclined. Unable to incline. Cold.

The men on the side of the road had ambushed him. He'd been coming from the house of Marsha Verhoeven. On the Princes Point Road.

His head felt like it was cracking in half. A melon smashed on the road. Movement was pain. It was easier to bob in the waves and not move. Give in.

Chabal.

Giving in was not an option. Langdon twisted this way and that way. He was attached to a mooring. In the middle of the ocean. No. There'd be no mooring in the middle of the ocean. He must be close to shore. Attached to a boat mooring. He tried to twist his arms to find what held him secured but could not reach.

Langdon ripped his shirt open and was released from his captivity, plunging down into the freezing water. The pain in his head subsided, just an iota, allowing him to realize how chilled he was, his teeth chattering, his fingers numbing. That was a good sign. There was still feeling. Which way to go?

Langdon tread water, looking this way and that. It'd be a shame to strike out in the direction of Iceland. He heard a sound to his right. A rumble. The sound of a vehicle. It must be a road. Land. He started doggy paddling in that direction. His limbs sodden and weighed down like anvils to his body.

It wasn't really the doggy paddle, but more akin to the breaststroke, Langdon realized, as his head submerging every time he kicked forward, the icy water clearing the cobwebs, if not the pain. Why had he been attacked?

Paddle. Kick. Submerge. Spit seawater. Repeat.

He didn't know how far it was, or how long it took, but eventually he smashed his face into a rock. His knees were touching bottom. Langdon pushed himself to his feet. Floundering like a teenager drunk on whiskey, he staggered toward land. It was a rocky shore and he tripped and fell repeatedly before making it to the brush and scrub trees that scratched at his face, clawed at his legs, and poked into his ribs.

Lights illuminated the foliage around him. The sound of a vehicle on a road reached his frozen ears. Langdon stumbled into a ditch as a Ford F-150 went rumbling past. He scrabbled his way up the incline, hand over hand, dragging his legs behind.

More lights. Langdon came to his knees. Pushed himself to a standing position. Waved his arm. He felt like a deer frozen, literally frozen, in the headlights.

The car came to a shuddering stop. A door opened. A man's voice demanded to know what the hell was going on.

Langdon sank to his knees and fell forward on his face without bracing his fall. Gentle darkness embraced him.

Chapter 20

The *Columbo* soundtrack broke the silence at the Langdon household just before midnight. This was the ringtone Chabal had assigned to Bart. She was sitting at the dining room table with her daughter, Darcy. Missouri and Jamie, along with dog, had taken their car and gone searching potential haunts of Langdon, while Gary had gone with Jack to do the same thing.

She'd first called the cop when her husband was an hour late getting home for dinner and wasn't answering his phone or text messages. Bart had been placating. Chabal had held her temper.

At nine she had called him back. At this point, worry had now tinged his voice. Bart had promised to put an unofficial BOLO on Langdon with the Brunswick PD. It was far too early for an official 'be on the lookout' for a missing person, but somehow, Bart had gained friends and respect recently in the department, and the word had gone out.

At a bit before ten, Bart had called to inform Chabal that the last person to have seen Langdon was Susie Quinn, just after noontime, at McSorley's. Chabal faintly remembered that this was the woman Bart had brought to the barbecue the other night, and had been present, most likely, for her meltdown. It was all a bit fuzzy.

Then nothing. Until now. Chabal picked up on the first notes of the theme song. "Tell me you found him, Bart."

"He's at Mid Coast Hospital. I'm on my way now."

"Is he okay?"

"A passing motorist found him unconscious on the Mountain Road out to Harpswell. Hauled him into his truck and drove him to the hospital. Officer Scott recognized him when he showed up there and immediately called me. That's all I know."

"We're on our way." Chabal stood, keys in hand. "He's at Mid Coast. Text the others from the car."

"I can drive," Darcy said.

"I will drive." The flatness of Chabal's voice brooked no argument.

For six hours now, Chabal had been pondering all the wonderful gifts that she was blessed with. Four great caring and loving kids. A wonderful house. She lived in a fantastic community. A friend set that would, and had, risked their lives for her. And a husband that she loved more than anything in the entire world.

These gifts bestowed upon her were being ignored, discarded, discredited—by the fear that resided within her mind. Instead of turning to those who were important in her life, she'd shut the whole passel of them out, especially her husband, and instead, turned to alcohol to ease the edges of her dispirit.

As of late, unburdening her body and soul at the barbecue, the arrival of her children to surround her with love, and the act of lovemaking this morning had cracked the door of the living world. But it was the worry and concern for Langdon that opened the egress wide and swallowed the fear that resided within her by the larger terror of losing her husband.

What had Langdon got himself into now, she wondered? At the same time, she felt a measure of disgust with herself, because she didn't even know. For too long now, she had wallowed in her own morass, the entanglement of her spiritual and emotional world, and ignored everything around her. Gifts endowed upon her, privileges given, and she'd turned her back.

No more. With these thoughts zigzagging through her mind, Chabal pulled into the long twisting driveway of Mid Coast Hospital. And the path aligned and became straight.

~ ~ ~ ~ ~

A seagull was cawing. *Keow. Keow. Keow.*

Another seagull laughed at the first. *Ha-ha-ha.*

A whirlpool swirled in ever-widening circles, threatening to pull Langdon into the vortex. The sky was black. Dark. The fin of a shark circled deadly in the maelstrom.

"Langdon."

The North Star rose into the sky and shimmered, growing in brightness, and then it was the rising sun.

"It's okay. I'm here."

Langdon glanced back at the tourbillon which had shrunken to a small eddy. He looked up. Opened his eyes. Everything was fuzzy. There were lights. Too bright. His head rang.

Focus, he thought, but it was a battle.

"It's okay. It's me. Chabal."

Was he home, in bed, Langdon wondered? What had happened? Was he hungover? Why was his mouth so dry?

Slowly, the image of Chabal's face came into focus. Her cheeks, puffed out slightly, bulged like a squirrel with a nut in each cheek, a trait that he found absolutely adorable. She was smiling at him. It'd been a long time since he'd seen her smile. Truly smile.

Langdon tried for his best Groucho Marx. It came out as a barely audible rasp. "'Will you marry me? Do you have any money? Answer the second question first.'"

Chabal snickered. "No, all you get is me, babe. Take it or leave it."

"Do you at least have some water?"

She was saved from an answer by a nurse who breezed into the room. "Mr. Langdon, welcome back. Let me get the doctor."

"Can you get water as well, please," Chabal said.

"What happened? Am I in a hospital?" Langdon asked.

"Yes. Mid Coast." Chabal put her hand on his brow. "As far as what happened? I was hoping you'd tell me."

"I saw Susie at McSorley's. Barely touched my drink. Everything keeps circling back to Tara James."

"Is that the last thing you remember?"

Langdon was quiet for a long moment. The nurse came back with a cup of water and a straw and Chabal helped him take a few small sips.

"Then I went out to pay a visit to Marsha Verhoeven. At her house. By the pool. She was in her bathing suit. I think she tried to seduce me." Langdon stopped, his fuddled brain thinking he probably should've kept that part to himself. "And again, Tara James. Cornelius Remington and Michael Levy had a fight about Tara."

After a minute, Chabal cleared her throat. "And then?"

"I left, I think." He furrowed his brow. "I remember getting in the Jeep."

A woman with a clipboard came into the room. "I'm Dr. Strader. Can you tell me who you are?"

The doctor went through a series of questions about what the date was, what he remembered, and whatnot. She also told him that they'd be doing some tests, but from the crack in his skull, she was guessing that he had a fairly severe concussion at best. They'd put seventeen stitches into the top of his head. Langdon tentatively raised a shaky hand and touched the zipper that held his noggin together. Winced.

After the doctor left, Bart came into the room and Chabal left for a moment.

"Doc says you don't remember who did this to you?" Bart said.

"No. Last thing I remember is leaving Marsha Verhoeven's place out on Princes Point Road. Nice house."

"Marsha? That broad who Jimmy brought to the barbecue? That hippie lawyer is always getting himself involved with questionable chicks."

"If you saw her in the bathing suit like I did, you'd know why. She's one sultry woman."

Bart looked down his nose. "What exactly were you doing with her in a bathing suit?"

"Stopped by to pay a visit, ask some questions, and she was out by her pool."

"What time was this?"

"Later afternoon. Maybe four o'clock."

"Motorist found you at midnight. What we gotta do, is figure out what happened during those eight hours."

"Doctor said there's a good chance things will keep coming back to me."

The nurse came into the room. "Okay, enough for now. Mr. Langdon needs to sleep."

Chapter 21

Missouri was driving the Jeep with Langdon in the passenger side and dog in the back. The top was off and the breeze felt glorious. It would've been better without the raging headache, Langdon thought, but it was important to look on the bright side of things. He was out of the hospital, even if it was against the strong recommendations of the doctor. And he was getting some one-on-one time with his daughter.

There was no sense in dwelling on the negatives. Such as, somebody who he couldn't remember had waylaid him, hooked him to a boat mooring in the Atlantic Ocean, and left him to die. Or did they? Leave him to die, that is. Why not just kill him? Langdon mulled this puzzle over, his brain still a bit muddled, but improving as the pristine air cleansed his being.

If the intent had not been to kill him, then what? Whoever did this certainly didn't seem concerned that he very possibly could have died. But attaching him to a cinder block and not a mooring would've done the job of killing him and hiding the body much more effectively. It was possible that it was an enemy from long ago, some psychopath, or an overly aggressive robber, but Langdon didn't think so.

This attack had to do with his investigation into the background of Cornelius Remington. Thus, the prime suspect had to be no other than the judge. That is why their second stop of the day was at his house. It was Saturday morning, making it at least possible that the man would be home.

The first stop of the day had been to replace his phone at the Verizon store. The techs did their magic and his missing texts and voicemails popped up on the new iPhone 14. The young lady at the store had suggested he could wait a couple of months and get the newest of the new, not seeming to understand that he needed a phone immediately.

There were many a text and voicemail from Chabal and the kids, and it tore him up to think about how much he'd worried them. Not that he'd intended on getting seized.

There was a text from Marsha Verhoeven. **Maybe you can come back over to my place this weekend so we can talk more about the case. I feel like we have unfinished business.**

Another text from Starling. **You coming into the store this morning?**

That had been yesterday, right before Bart called him to let him know that Langdon was in the hospital. He'd shut down the bookshop and he and Raven had come over to the hospital for a few hours before going back and reopening. Langdon could only imagine what sign they'd hung on the door. **Back soon. Langdon got his noggin addled. Again.**

There was a text from a phone number not in his contacts. **Alice said that she would meet with you and at least hear you out. Next Friday at 4. McSorley's.**

Susie. Langdon added her to his contact list. Alice was the woman who'd been paid by Remington for sex. If he could get her testimony, that might be enough to cripple the nomination. Probably not, as his people would undermine and destroy the credibility of Alice. Langdon worried about even bringing this poor woman forward to be torn apart by the machine. He'd meet with her, build his case, and then would decide. That is, if she was even willing.

There was a voicemail from Bart. "Where are you, big man? People are worried."

Langdon looked at the date. Thursday. Two days ago, when he'd been missing. No need to reply to that one. He deleted it and hit play on the next message.

"Langdon. This is Cooper Walker. I'm sorry to inform you that your investigation is officially over. It has been squashed by my boss. Please bill us for any hours you have logged in up until now. I... well, things don't always play out as we want them. I'm sorry."

Hm, Langdon thought. Hired, fired, rehired, refired. The White House was as hot and cold as a teenage girl. This caused him to smile, his thoughts drifting back to those volatile years in the life of his daughter. There'd been some rocky times for sure. At one point, he'd sighed, shook his head, and wished her well, telling her he'd see her again on the other side when she returned as a real person. Luckily, the journey had been much less perilous than many, and the good times had far outweighed the bad.

The third voicemail was even more jarring. The voice was modified in some way, the metallic hollow speech articulated in a robotic monotone. "Looks like you survived. I figured you would. You won me a dollar by not drowning. Next time we won't be so nice. How good of a swimmer is your wife? Or your daughter. Stop what you are doing."

Langdon looked sideways at Missouri, her tangled blondish-red hair blowing crazy in the openness of the Jeep. She'd insisted on driving him around today if he was going to refuse to go home and recuperate. Both her and Chabal had known that winning an argument with him to mend his wounds and loosen the grip of his teeth on the bone was not going to happen. It had been settled when Missouri said she wanted to spend some time with him before she returned home, which might be happening as early as tomorrow.

Now, some faceless voice had just threatened her. Could he let her go back to Brooklyn? He didn't know how far these people were willing to go. But the threat lingered in his ear. Steely. Foreboding. Threatening.

"What?" Missouri asked. "I can feel you staring at me."

Did he share the threat with her? Of course. He'd always believed in honesty and openness in their relationship of father and daughter. Missouri had never been a girl he'd kept things from. Sometimes, when asked a difficult question, he'd reply asking her if she *really* wanted to know the answer. Usually that emphasis on really had been enough to get the young Missouri Langdon to say no, that was okay, understanding that she didn't really want to know how women got babies in their belly or some such thing like that.

"Some fellow was wondering how good a swimmer you are."

Missouri turned to look at him which made him very nervous as her driving skills were suspect when her eyes were *on* the road. "Say what?"

Langdon put the speaker on, turned up the volume, and played the voicemail.

"Fuck him," Missouri said. Her eyes were flashing.

Langdon pointed weakly at the road. "Watch out for that car, hon."

She twitched the wheel and missed an oncoming Prius by less than a foot. "How are we going to find this prick?"

"Thought you might be going back to Brooklyn tomorrow. Doesn't give *us* much time."

"That was before my swimming skills were called into suspicion."

"Stop sign."

The Jeep came to a shuddering stop at the end of the Middle Bay Road.

"Are you suggesting that you don't want me to drop the case?" Langdon asked with a grin, full well knowing the answer. "Go right here."

Missouri turned right. "No, you are not dropping the case. Not until we find the rock that this filth is hiding under and drag him out and kick his ass."

"Just to be clear. Is it truly the fact that your swimming skills were called into suspicion that has you this angry or is something else?"

Missouri glared at him. Then they both broke into laughter. They also narrowly missed a mailbox, almost ending up in the ditch.

Judge Cornelius Remington lived off Route 123 on a small dirt road that serviced five or six houses. His house touched upon one of the many inlets of ocean licking the coast of Brunswick. In this case, it was Middle Bay. Solar panels adorned the roof and there was a large greenhouse in the side yard. The two cars in the driveway suggested that at least somebody was home.

The door opened before Langdon was able to knock. Langdon knew from pictures that it was Mrs. Remington. Angela. She was of medium height with black hair that was so dark it must've been dyed. Her skin was smooth with just a touch of crow's feet wrinkles in the corners of her eyes, any other signs of aging carefully concealed under a layer of makeup. She wore a multi-colored blouse and a plain blue skirt.

"Can I help you?" Her voice was honeyed. Her tone carefully constructed.

"Mrs. Remington? My name is Langdon, and this is my daughter, Missouri. I was hoping to speak with your husband."

"You own that bookshop downtown."

"Yes."

"Do you have the new Barbara Ross book? *Scared Off*?"

Langdon shook his head. "No. I'm sorry. That comes out on Kindle later this month."

"Shame. I don't do that Kindle thing. Not the same thing as a book, you know? But I do love all of Barbara Ross' books."

"I agree. She is fantastic and books are meant to be held."

"Cornelius is not here right now. He's out on the boat. But he should be back any moment. Would you like tea or coffee while you wait?"

Before Langdon knew what was happening, Mrs. Remington had shown them into a sitting room. He had to rearrange throw pillows to fit onto the too-small couch while Missouri sat in an armchair and their hostess, who insisted they call her Angela, had bustled off to get them food and beverage.

Langdon had to shift down the couch to see Missouri around the flowers on the cushioned table. The entire room seemed to consist of ruffles and chintz. Even the lights had large ornate lampshades and produced no more than a glow.

The one practical aspect of the room was the wooden bookcase that was at the end of the room. Upon closer inspection, Langdon realized that it was filled with a set of encyclopedias, a throwback to an era before the internet and smart phones, and a scattering of self-help books. *Meditation for Mothers, Fly Tying for the Beginner, Fixing your Electrical Problems Without Paying a Lot*, and other things like that. No mysteries. No fiction, for that matter.

Angela bustled back into the room with tea for Missouri, coffee for Langdon, a basket of scones, and a trolley of jams and jellies.

Once he'd taken the obligatory bit of scone, rather dry for his taste, Langdon cleared his throat. "What do you think, Angela, about your husband becoming a Supreme Court justice?"

"Oh, my understanding is that he is being considered for this position. It's quite an honor just to be thought of for the Bench of the high court. Yes. Quite an honor, indeed. Cornelius has always been very ambitious. Always wanted more than he has."

Langdon noted the tinge of bitterness that seemed to cloak this last statement. "That's the American way, I suppose. Never satisfied with what we have. Always envying the grass on the other side of the fence."

Angela turned and looked narrowly down her nose from her round-silver spectacles. "Coveting one's neighbor is different than climbing the ladder of success."

Langdon blushed. He'd tried to be delicate and subtle when

referencing the *grass on the other side*, but she'd caught his drift. He looked to Missouri for aid in subtlety.

Missouri returned his stare with a look that clearly told him to keep his mouth shut. "That's not what my father meant, Angela. As a matter of fact, I believe that if anybody is envied, I'd think it would be you and your husband. A beautiful house. A fine marriage. An illustrious career."

Angela looked only slightly mollified. "You mean that Cornelius has had an illustrious career, I believe."

Missouri shook her head. "I know that a person does not follow the stellar path that your husband has traversed without the incredibly strong support and backbone of their spouse. I'm sure that you are responsible in a million ways for his success."

"It's not always easy. You have no idea the things I must do."

"I'm sure."

Angela looked pensively out the window toward the bay. "One must always smile, be gracious, appreciative, and be able to look the other way." She gasped and put her hand over her mouth.

"It is a man's world."

Langdon knew that Missouri must've gritted her teeth to utter that line.

"Yes, it is dear. Certainly for my generation. On the face of things, anyhow. Maybe not so much for you."

Missouri moved from her armchair and sat on the sofa next to Angela. "Why are men like that? My boyfriend seems to think that I don't notice him looking at other girls. Constantly."

Langdon smirked. Then wondered if his daughter's female fiancé really did look at other girls constantly. Then gently chided himself. He knew better. Jamie was a fine woman who loved his daughter. Missouri had always been a good actress and was merely playing her role.

Angela patted Missouri on the knee. "Oh, don't you worry about all that. Boys will be boys. I'm sure he cares for you in his own way.

Men and women are just different, is all."

"How do I know if he does more than just look? What if he's cheating on me?"

"What does it matter, really, dear? If he loves you, what does it matter if he goes around with other girls?" Angela had a faraway look in her eyes. She was no longer referring to Missouri and her fabricated boy problems. "If you land yourself a catch like I did with Cornelius, there's always going to be jealous whores out there, but as long as he comes home at the end of the day, what does it really matter?"

Langdon felt his mouth gaped open and quickly closed it. Angela had spit out jealous whores in a monotone, as if reciting a grocery list, and seemed unaware that they were even still in the room with her.

"We all have our secrets," Missouri said.

"Yes we do. As long as it's just sex. Not love."

Langdon thought it sounded much like a 1950s marriage. This awkward moment was interrupted by the sound of a door opening. "Toots, I'm home. Whose Jeep is that outside?"

Remington came to the doorway and froze when he saw Langdon. The man looked like he'd been out yachting, and Langdon's mind filled with an image of the judge from *Caddyshack* when he went boating and got swamped by Rodney Dangerfield. The man had on a captain's hat, white with a blue brim that matched his khakis, his shirt as white as the driven snow.

"What are you doing here?" he asked.

"Just wanted to ask you a few questions, Judge." Langdon stood. "This is my daughter, Missouri Langdon."

"How long has this man been here, Toots?"

"What, oh, I don't know, just a few minutes. We just sat down for tea. Do you want some?"

"This man has been attempting to fabricate stories about me, Toots."

Chapter 22

Mayhem smiled wickedly. They had never planned on being androgynous. Never even contemplated it, as a matter of fact. They had been brought up to believe that men were men and women were women and everything else was wrong. They had lived a good life based on that principle. But always, in the very back of who they were, the unseen attic, the seldom used closet, the deepest recesses of their being—there'd been an unsettled anxiety shifting and tweaking about.

They were neither male nor female. They were both female and male. Society wanted to pigeonhole you into one category when the reality wasn't that at all. It had taken crisis to open the eyes of Mayhem to their own reality. They were not man nor woman, human nor beast, but rather, they were Mayhem.

It felt good to unleash this primal self upon the world. Increasingly, it became difficult to rein in the need to gallop, to run, to sprint, and to entertain the world on their own terms and not those thrust upon them by some societal expectation. They were meant to blossom. To grow. To flourish.

The mistake had come by consigning out the killing to others. When playing croquet, it was best to have the mallet in your own hands. Others could not always be trusted to strike the wickets when necessary. They shouldn't have allowed the two bozos the important task of killing Langdon.

Mayhem would not make that mistake again. Of course, it was

like that game of chess, it would be fun to pit the bozos against Langdon. If given the choice of murder or exposure, which would they choose. This time they'd gone halfway. Next time? If they could be trained to kill, what a great asset the bozos would be.

They realized the taser was out and in their hand. Before they knew what they were doing, Mayhem pointed it at their own midsection and depressed the trigger. The jolt was unbelievably painful. The first feeling was that of the prongs stabbing into them like a short knife and then every muscle clenched fiercely. The pain surged through them. Mayhem rode it like a bronco buster in a rodeo.

When the pain subsided, Mayhem smiled weakly. And then did it again.

Chapter 23

Langdon got off the plane in the Miami International Airport and followed the line of people toward baggage claim and ground transportation. Not that he had checked a bag. He had, after all, come to Florida, and needed little more than a couple pairs of shorts and two Jimmy Buffett shirts to go with the one he wore. This was a quick trip, as things were percolating back in Maine.

There seemed to be little choice after Judge Remington threw him and Missouri out of his house. All possible leads of wrongdoing had dried up, all except one, that is. Tara James. The Tara who had shut her phone down and only had a PO Box. The same Tara who'd disappeared from Maine around the time that the position of Supreme Court justice had been first bandied around.

It was unlikely that he'd recuperate his travel expenses, as he'd been fired by the White House for a second time, not to mention any sort of payment for services rendered. He was on his own. Doing this because he couldn't let it go. He felt like a basset hound on the scent—that breed of dog used to hunt rabbits—due to two important factors. Their incredible keen sense of scent and the fact that they were extremely slow, and thus, easy to keep up with. Oh, and yes, a stubborn nature that once on the trail, would never stop.

Once Langdon had been given a scent, teased by a case, intrigued by a wrongdoing—he couldn't let it go, even if he was no longer being paid for the hunt. At the same time, he felt like he was plodding along, taking two steps forward, and one step back, or even two or three back. And the missing piece that kept popping up was the elusive Tara James who had a PO Box in Marathon, Florida.

When he emerged from the airport to the rental car shuttle bus waiting area, the oppressive heat almost knocked him over. It sucked the oxygen from his lungs and set him to sweating almost immediately. Summer in Florida. He was hoping that it wasn't too hot to put the top down on the rental. It seemed that in Florida, a Mustang convertible rental was no more expensive than any other car that would fit his size.

The Mustang turned out to be lime green, similar in color to key lime pie, and not very unobtrusive for doing private investigative work. Oh, well, Langdon figured, sometimes it was easier to hide right in plain sight. He decided to take the slightly longer route, according to the GPS anyway, and head right over to the 997 instead of taking the smaller roads that would more than likely have him stopping at lights and for traffic.

The air was plenty cool at 80 MPH. It was the middle of the day, and everybody was either at work, at the beach, or safely encased in air conditioning somewhere. In less than an hour he was onto the Keys and buzzing his way through Key Largo. Realizing his empty stomach, he followed a sign to Snapper's Tiki Bar on the water. There was something about being in the Keys that demanded him to order a mango margarita to start, followed by two mahi fish tacos, blackened, and completed with a second drink before getting back in the car.

With a slight buzz, his stomach sated, and rolling along in a key lime Mustang convertible with the top down—Langdon truly felt on top of the world. Even if the top of his head still resembled a zipper. He wished that Chabal had come along with him, but he was leery of putting her right back in the field doing investigative work.

As it was, he'd convinced her to stay with Bart while he was gone. And to help out at the bookshop. Jack had gone home to Portland. Missouri and Jamie had returned to New York but agreed to stay with Jamie's parents in Queens for a few days until things got sorted out. Darcy was back to South Carolina. Gary to Boston. The family had spread back to their own homes and lives as quickly as a funny dog video gone viral.

Whereas Snapper's had been a nice waterfront spot, the drive out through the Keys was quite ugly, Langdon thought. A series of strip malls and billboards promising everything from fishing excursions to useless knick-knacks. Junk to bring home from vacation to those people you only sort of like. Plenty of food options, but Langdon wondered who might come to the Florida Keys and eat in an ugly building resembling a gas station on the side of a busy road?

The post office in Marathon was a concrete affair in a strip mall. He went in to find a heavy-set middle-aged woman with tight gray curls working behind the window. Langdon dawdled looking at cards with cute sayings while several people conducted their business. When he was alone with the postmaster, if that was indeed her title, he went up to the counter.

"Hello, Ma'am."

"Can I help you?" Her voice was screechy, like a window that hadn't been opened in a while welcoming spring.

"I sure hope so. I'm looking for a woman."

"Ain't we all."

This slightly flummoxed his prepared speech. "I, uh, the one I'm interested in has a PO Box here."

"It gotta a number?" The woman looked as if she were about to have an epileptic fit and then burst out in a grating cackle. "Maybe you should call it."

Langdon smiled thinly, realized the game he was playing, and chuckled. "Now that's might funny Miss…" He looked at her name tag. "Miss Earline. You got you some sense of humor."

"Laughter is an instant vacation, that's what my momma always said."

"A day without laughter is a day wasted."

"Got that right. How about you, feller. You got any jokes?"

"What do you get if you put an alligator in a blender?" He'd read this on a sign at lunch.

After a moment, Earline shook her head. "What?"

"Gatorade."

Earline smirked, scoffed, and then guffawed loudly. "S'pose you would at that."

"Nice running into somebody who likes to laugh." Langdon laid a picture on the counter. "This is the woman I'm looking for. Her name is Tara James. She's Box 1480. I was hoping you might have a home address for her."

Earline picked up the photo and turned it this way and that way. "She is some sweet pie, that one. Yeah, she comes in here. Can't share an address with you, as that is a Federal offense, and I don't much think I'd like prison. Or maybe I would." She looked at Langdon and raised one bushy eyebrow.

"Is there anything you can tell me that might point me in the right direction?"

"I seen her 'round other places."

Langdon looked at her wide gray eyes. He pulled out his money clip and peeled a fifty off. Set it on the counter. "I'd sure appreciate it."

"What do you want with her?"

Langdon had a story all ready to go on this tangent but suddenly felt that honesty was the best policy with Earline.

"Just to talk. Ask her some questions about something that happened quite some time ago."

"You ain't finding her for no wife-beating asshole, are you?"

Langdon shook his head. "No, Ma'am."

"And she ain't wanted by the law?"

"Not that I know of."

"You swear you got no ill intent aimed toward that woman?"

"I swear."

Earline took the fifty-dollar bill, folded it lengthwise, and stuck it down the front of her shirt. "Sometimes after work I stop into a place out the road a piece on Big Pine Key. 'Bout twenty miles west of here. Joint called the No Name Pub.

Langdon had been to the Keys once before and remembered the endless Seven Mile Bridge right outside of Marathon. Off to the side was the old bridge, now a walking and cycling path, and boats and jet skis passed underneath. The traffic was moving along well, it was a beautiful day, and he had a lead on Tara James.

He struggled to appreciate these slices of empyrean that surrounded him, though, as his mind was back in Maine. Chabal was on the mend, but he wasn't sure he should've left her at this critical juncture in her mental recovery from last year's ordeal. Although, he thought with an audible chuckle, after a couple of days staying with Bart, Langdon was going to be looking mighty damn good when he got home.

At least she was safe, for Bart could be trusted with his life or wife, of that he was certain. A few days with Bart should be fine as Langdon attempted to get to the bottom of the whole Remington fiasco and uncover who was behind the threats to him and his family. And Tara James seemed to be the wild card in the deck.

In Big Pine Key, Langdon banged a right, and drove off into nothing. Even with the GPS, he missed the No Name Pub on the first pass, instead crossing a bridge onto what was actually No Name Key, which made sense for the location of the pub. But no, it was back across the bridge, tucked into the palm trees and foliage, located on Big Pine Key. There were seven or eight cars and twice that many motorcycles in the gravel parking lot. The sign over the door was apropos, *No Name Pub; You Found it.*

Langdon wondered what the smaller structures, seemingly deserted, across the parking lot were, or once were, but shrugged and went inside. The interior was dark. It took him a moment to adjust. He took a stool at the bar, marveling at the dollar bills. Every possible interior surface of the pub had dollar bills taped, stuck, and posted multiple layers thick, most with messages and names in marker.

The bartender was a young lad with tousled hair who said he was fifth generation Big Pine Key. Langdon knew that this area had been inhabited by pirates, outlaws, salvagers, people on the run, and those not wanting to be found since the beginning of time. A perfect place for Tara James to get lost if that is what she desired. He knew better than to flash the picture and ask about her in a place that fiercely protected anonymity. At best, he was sure to be rebuffed, and at worst, beat to a pulp and deposited outside.

He was on his second beer and contemplating a brown liquor, a choice he knew was a bad one, when Tara James came in the door and sat down next to him. She ordered a tequila on ice and was on a first name basis with the bartender.

Her hair was blonde, her bangs cut across at eyebrow height, the sides and back just below her ears. When she took her sunglasses off, she had extremely blue eyes. Her cheeks were narrow, her lips full, and her chin oval.

"Hot one out there," Langdon said without looking at her.

"You must not be from around these parts," she said.

"Nope. Down from up north."

"Oh, yeah? Where at?"

"Maine."

"How 'bout that. I'm from Maine originally. Where in Maine you live."

"Brunswick."

Tara turned and stared directly at him. "What'd you say your name was, mister?"

He turned to meet her gaze. "Langdon."

She threw her tequila in his face and headed for the door at a run. Langdon wiped his eyes and climbed from his stool to follow, thinking that that could've gone better, but the gent next to him, as wide as he was tall and wearing a leather vest with the skull of a joker on the back, slid into him and knocked him to the floor. When he went to stand, he was bumped by another man, and by the time he got to his feet and made it to the door, all he saw was the back of Tara James as she roared away on a Harley Davidson.

But she was going toward the bridge to No Name Key. And Langdon had, by mistake, just ascertained that there was only one way onto that particular island, and one way off. He went back inside, paid his tab, smiled genially at the man who'd knocked him down, and went to his rented convertible.

Chapter 24

Langdon crossed over the bridge to No Name Key. Three men and one woman had fishing lines dropped over the side, coolers next to them, either for cold brewskies or for caught fish, he was not quite sure.

When he'd missed the pub on the first pass, Langdon had driven across this key all the way to the end. It was less than two miles from bridge to the far end. There appeared to be just two small clusters of houses, too small to even be called neighborhoods, maybe a couple dozen in all on the entire island.

The first grouping was based around three short streets to his left. He cruised up and down them looking for signs of the Harley Davidson that Tara had been riding. It was on the second road, between two canals, that he saw the shiny red fender of the bike poking out from a shed. There was a chain link fence enclosing the property, not tall, just four feet, but this also held three dogs that looked to have Rottweiler in them.

Dogs were not something that Langdon had ever had any problems with. Something about his laid-back manner put even the most aggressive of canines at ease. He parked on the road, now wishing he had a more nondescript rental. The lime green Mustang might fit in out on the main road, but back here, in No Name Key, it was a target asking for a load of buckshot.

There was a gate with a padlock. Langdon paused, called Tara by name, told her he just wanted to talk. There was no answer unless you counted the panting of Cerberus, standing at attention, six eyes inquisitive, six ears cocked. Langdon shrugged, put one foot over the fence, and then the other. He immediately bent over to rub the dogs who were not nearly as fierce as they looked. At least not with him.

Once due diligence had been accomplished to pay Cerberus back for not chewing him to bits, Langdon walked to the house, but before he could start up the steps, heard a sound from the back that made him quickly move around the side of the house. Tara was on the short dock in the canal about to step into an outboard motorboat.

"I need to talk to you, Tara. Nothing more than that."

She stopped, turned, and glared at him. "I just want to be left alone."

"I understand. But we can't always just ignore our problems. Sometimes we must face them."

The cocking of a rifle garnered Langdon's attention. A man had emerged from the house with a shotgun nestled loosely in his arms. He had on coveralls with no shirt underneath, a scratchy beard, and appeared to be extremely bowlegged. "My cousin said she didn't want to talk with you, numbnuts, so why don't you slink your ass out of here."

Langdon assuaged the threat. Turned his back on the man to look again at Tara. "Did you know Michael Levy was killed?"

"Killed? I knew Mikey died, but I was told it was an accident."

"I believe it was a cover-up."

"What's this all about?"

There was the roar of a truck coming down the road and brakes sliding it to a stop out front. More company. Langdon sensed movement behind him and turned as the butt of a shotgun swung at his head. He caught it with one hand, somewhat surprising himself, and punched the man in the face.

Cousin Scratchy held grimly onto the weapon as Langdon tried to wrench it free. He sensed movement and turned to see a blur coming fast and then a body jettisoned into his like it'd been released from a cannon.

"Whoo-hoo, you sure hit him," Cousin Scratchy said as Langdon tried to reassemble his wits. "That was some Friday night under the lights shit, right there, Rusty. Them Noles don't know what they was doing letting you go."

Langdon panicked for a second when he realized he was unable to move, but then realized that Rusty had him in some sort of wrestling hold. He was willing to bet it was called the pretzel.

Two men closer to his age than that of Scratchy and Rusty stood over him looking down. They wore baseball caps, had narrow faces, scraggly facial hair, and eyebrows that looked to be trying to escape their faces.

"What's going on here, Tara?"

"This fellow came into the pub looking for me, Cousin Ronnie. He's a private investigator from Maine."

Cousin Ronnie was a good thirty years older than Cousin Scratchy, Langdon thought. Maybe everybody down here just figured they were some kind of cousin. The man could be distinguished from the other gent by a jagged scar running across his cheek.

"Let him up, Rusty. Jughead, you keep that shotgun on him and fill him full of shot if he does anything funny," Cousin Ronnie said.

Langdon chuckled. Scratchy's name was Jughead. He wondered if it was a nickname or bestowed upon him at birth.

"Hold on."

Cousin Ronnie stepped forward and put a pillowcase over Langdon's head. Rusty spun him facedown and he could feel zip ties being put on and then tightened around his wrists. Then Langdon was roughly pulled to his feet.

"I just want to have a conversation with Tara. Nothing else. Just a few words." The pillowcase was stifling in the heat of the day.

"Jughead, give me that shotgun and you and Rusty run up to the shed and get the Boobie Bouncers. We're gonna take this feller out to the gator hole."

All the men except Langdon cackled in laughter.

"Don't hurt him, Ronnie," Tara said. "There's been enough of that."

"I promise on Grandpa's grave I won't hurt him."

"Can't say the same for ole Bloody Bill Anderson. He's probably got a right fierce hunger about now."

Langdon figured this voice for the fourth man. Cousin Ronnie and the Fourth Man laughed loudly, and then one started wheezing and coughing. "Tara, I don't know what you're running from, but I can help."

The sound of ATVs sprang to life out front at the same time as the outboard motor on the dock. Langdon was helpless, zip tied, head covered in a pillowcase, the woman he was pursuing now leaving him behind with her hillbilly clan.

They attached his zip tied hands to the rear bar, slopping him onto the bed of the ATV, and off they went. The dogs followed, barking excitedly. They went out through the gate onto the paved road, a few moments of smoothness, before they were back onto a rutted trail, and he was bouncing this way and that way. At one point, Langdon was bounced off the bed onto the ground, his hands still attached to the rear bar, and he dragged along behind for a bit before he could clamber back on.

After what seemed an eternity, but was probably no more than five minutes, they came to a shuddering stop. Langdon sensed, rather than felt, a knife sawing him free from the ATV which the boys had called the Boobie Bouncer. He went to step down and his legs gave out and he collapsed on the ground.

The pillowcase was pulled from his head, and he took several gulping breaths of air, never so excited for the moisture-filled and scalding air of southern Florida to be pulled into his lungs. After a bit, he picked his head up, aware that the four men stood around him in a semi-circle. They were smiling, chortling, grinning—filled with unbridled excitement.

"We gonna let you go," Cousin Ronnie said.

"All you got to do is swim across the gator hole to the other side and you is free to go," Rusty said.

"With this here chicken tied to your back," Jughead said.

The four men guffawed loudly.

Langdon turned his eyes to the water hole. It was just about perfectly round and a couple hundred feet across. After a bit, he could see two eyeballs floating out in the middle. And then the outline of what must've been a twelve-foot gator.

"That there is Bloody Bill Anderson," Jughead said.

Langdon was the only one who didn't laugh.

Chapter 25

"That's enough."

The voice came from up on the trail where the four wheelers were parked. Langdon was ankle deep in the water of the gator hole with a live chicken duct taped to his back. It was squawking and thrashing around and scratching up his skin something fierce, but he barely noticed, intent as he was on the beady eyes of the alligator floating in the middle of the water like some prehistoric monster from a sci-fi flick.

Cousin Ronnie had said the gator was more scared of Langdon than he was of it.

Rusty had been betting the gator took the chicken off his back without so much as touching Langdon.

The Fourth Man had just shaken his head sadly.

Jughead had been giggling like a little schoolgirl in anticipation of her first kiss.

Langdon, his hands now untied, stripped to the waist so as to attach the chicken, had been contemplating rushing Jughead who held the shotgun, a fear that paled in comparison to swimming past Bloody Bill Anderson. You didn't get a nickname like that without a few kills.

At the sound of the voice, Langdon looked back over his shoulder. Like a vision of a goddess, Tara James was walking down the small foot trail to where the four men ringed Langdon, prodding him forward into the pond. The sun was low on the horizon, filtering through the scrub brush, casting dancing shadows in her path, which she strode through like Athena cutting a path through her enemies.

Tara stopped five feet behind Cousin Ronnie. "You all know Bloody Bill is going to eat some fellow one of these days by mistake and you're all gonna end up in jail."

"We just havin' some fun," Jughead said. "He ain't even pissed himself yet."

Tara brushed past and grabbed the chicken and yanked it free from the duct tape restraints.

"Thanks for that." Langdon turned and faced her. "Been meaning to wax my back hair for some time now. You can't see it all that well, on account of it being red, but it's there sure enough, well, up until a few seconds ago it was there, anyway."

"Nobody told me you was so tall."

"Wait until I put my Hey Dudes back on. They give me another tenth of an inch."

"Was Mikey really murdered?"

Langdon stepped from the gator hole. "I believe he was but have no proof."

Tara stepped back. "What'd you want to talk about?"

Langdon looked at the ring of faces. The four men were now stoic, waiting to see if they could resume their fun, or if it was indeed, ruined. Tara was smiling but her blue eyes remained cold.

"Did you know that Cornelius Remington is being nominated to be a Supreme Court justice?"

Tara's face blanched. Then she laughed but there was no humor in the noise. "Of course he fucking is. That's why you called me with all those questions about him."

"I was hired, fired, rehired, and refired to do part of a background check on him."

"Sounds like somebody is pretty fickle."

"The White House."

"Politicians." The tone suggested that Tara didn't think much of politicians. "Sounds like your current status is fired. So what are you doing here?"

Langdon shrugged. "Consider it my civic duty. Sort of like jury duty. Or voting."

"You're trying to find dirt on Neely so he doesn't get appointed judge for life."

Langdon nodded. "Something like that. There seems to be a gray cloud in his past that is shrouding various monsters, sort of like that Stephen King story, *The Fog*."

"It was called *The Mist*. But I get the gist."

"You suppose I can get my shirt back? Even filtered sunset sunshine burns gingers like me."

Tara laughed, a genuine guffaw that reached her eyes and contained humor. "It's a twenty-minute walk back to the house. I'll give you that long to ask me what you want."

"We ain't gonna make him swim?" Jughead asked. A tinge of whine had crept into his voice. He didn't much like having his fun curtailed. "Bloody Bill weren't gonna come near him, no how, not even with that chicken on his back."

Langdon made a mental note to come back down to the No Name Key at some point in the future and shove a chicken up Jughead's ass and bring him down to the gator hole for a little skinny dipping with a squawking rear end.

"How 'bout we tie a line around the chicken's foot and see how close to shore we can lure ole Bloody Bill," Rusty said. "First one to run away loses."

"I'll watch the two of you," Cousin Ronny said.

"You wuss," Jughead said. "Ya scared of a little pet gator?"

Langdon pulled his shirt on, wiped his feet dry on the grass, and slid his shoes on. He and Tara walked up past the ATVs and Tara led the way to the left down the trail they'd come as the four men argued, fought, laughed, and insulted each other behind them.

Tara asked him to fill her in on what he knew so far. Langdon started at the beginning with his hiring by the White House staff and counsel, and then the FBI. How his search led to Marsha Verhoeven, who told him that Chris "Chuckie" Taylor was now Shannon Undergrove, and how both told stories of the mean pranks played by Remington and the Maine Men of Mayhem. How Remington cheated on his wife with women he paid for sex. The only sound Tara made as he recounted the details of his investigation was when he mentioned that Jonathan Starling now worked with him and had recounted the story shared with him by Tara.

"Jonny? Works in your bookstore?"

It took Langdon a moment to realize that Jonny was Starling. "Sure enough."

"How 'bout that."

"Every direction I turn, your name comes up. Tara James. That made me wonder about the death of Michael Levy. Ruled an accidental death but in light of all the surrounding information? An elaborate murder to silence the man, made to look like an accident. Electrocuted on the shitter. Why? Well, I'm wondering if he was the man who sexually assaulted you when you were drunk and maybe, just maybe, Remington was concerned that him being complicit in that assault would ruin his bid to become one of the nine most powerful people in all the land."

After Langdon finished speaking, they walked in silence for a few minutes before Tara broke the quietude. "Doesn't surprise me that Chuckie transitioned to a female. I think even Neely questioned his masculinity."

"What makes you say that?"

"Well, for one, because it wasn't Mikey who screwed drunken me. It was Chuckie. Goaded to do so by Neely. I think Neely was testing him, you know, see if he had what it took to have sex with a woman. And I don't consider it assault. I'm from the generation that believes I got drunk and got it on with some drunken boy and I'm at fault as much as him. I guess that's not always the case, but in this situation it certainly was. Chuckie came to my room that fall, after I interned with your friend Starling, crying one night, and apologizing. Said that Neely told him that I liked him, that I wanted to have sex with him, and that Neely was giving his permission for it to happen. Chuckie said he tried to say no, but that Neely accused him of being gay, being queer, and wasn't I pretty enough for him, things like that, until he finally gave in and crawled into bed with me."

Whoa, Langdon thought, that was a lot to unpack right there. "It was Chuck Taylor, now Shannon Undergrove, who… who you realized you had sex with when you were blotto drunk back in your junior year of college?"

Tara nodded. Shrugged. "Not my finest moment. But Chuckie was always sweet. I don't regret it. He was a helluva lot nicer than Neely. I don't know why I even dated that prick."

Chapter 26

Chabal sat in the Subaru Outback parked in the cell phone lot at the Portland International Jetport. Dog sat in the shotgun seat, as ready to offer protection as any guard on the stagecoach line of times past. Langdon's return ticket had been for Saturday, but he'd called last night to say he'd found what he wanted and would be back the following afternoon, on Thursday, a full two days ahead of what he'd allotted to find Tara James.

That was great as far as Chabal was concerned. Nothing against Bart, but he lived in a bachelor pad and had a prickly way of doing things that brooked no change in the pattern, and Chabal was certainly a burr under the saddle of his life. If Langdon hadn't called with the good news, she most likely would've been leaving Bart's today anyway. To where, she wasn't sure, but anywhere would be better, if not safer.

And what danger was she in, really? Last year she'd faced down a Satan worshipping cannibal and come out on top, or at least with all her appendages. That was better than the wendigo had fared. An investigation into some hoity-toity Bowdoin alum being nominated for a position on the highest bench in the land paled in comparison to the wendigo. Even if some bastards had bopped her husband over the head and latched him onto a boat mooring in the ocean.

Chabal reached her right hand across her chest, slipping it in through the neck of her blouse, and grasped the butt of the M & P Shield in a shoulder holster. She wasn't going to be caught unaware, unprepared, again. If some asshole wanted to come at her she was going to shoot first and ask questions second, if at all.

A sparkle of anger had begun to simmer in her core when she'd visited Langdon in the hospital, beaten and injured, but alive. He was okay. And at that point, a flicker of ire had been lit, fanned by a growing fury, blossoming into a full-blown rage. Somebody had tried to take Langdon away from her permanently. While she hid in her house terrified by memories of a beast locked away, no longer a menace, long since extinguished as a tangible threat anywhere except in the crevices of her tortured recollections.

But this threat was real. A living, breathing, enemy who walked amongst civilization and threatened the existence of what Chabal held most dear in the entire world. And then Langdon had shuttled her off to stay with Bart while he went to the Florida Keys. Like she was a fancy piece of China to be hidden away and protected, a delicate flower vulnerable to the breeze, the sun, the cold—not of hardy Maine material but a southern belle to be protected and cherished.

"Fuck that," Chabal said aloud.

That was not who she was. She'd grown up in Maine, the youngest of a passel of older siblings, all brothers. Her mother's hopes of one demure young lady of good manners had been dashed when Chabal was eleven-years old. Her brother Jacon, two years her senior and the closest of her four older brothers in age, had made a disparaging remark about the tangled mess that was her hair. Not once, twice, or even three times, but the fourth jibe had been the final straw.

They were having a Sunday evening dinner. Mom, Dad, Chabal, and her four older brothers. When Jacon compared her hair to a robin's nest, Chabal had calmly stood up on her chair, stepped onto the table, and charged the surprised sibling. She hit him with a flying tackle, but failed to realize she still held her fork in hand, and inadvertently stuck this into his cheek in the process. As Jacon screamed and writhed on the floor, Chabal had gone back to eating her dinner, forced to use a spoon.

She had not been a victim since then, back when she was eleven, and learned on that day that trouble had to be confronted head on or it would merely grow. Like that wendigo creature. If somebody had nipped him, literally, in the bud, all the awfulness would've never happened. Chabal reached under her blouse again and fondled the butt of the pistol. She had been acting like a victim, but in reality, it was her who'd taken care of the wendigo, and she wasn't going to lie around being some wallflower anymore.

There'd been a light rain falling but it seemed to have eased, and Chabal stepped out of the car just as Langdon came striding out through the airport doors, looked both ways, and crossed to the cell phone lot. Chabal met him with a hug and kiss that lingered, a kiss that was normally the public display of emotion reserved for younger lovers.

"Successful trip?" she asked once they were back in the car and dog had had his head suitably rubbed and been banished to the back seat where he happily hung his head out the window and watched all the activity outside.

"Interesting might be a better choice of words."

His tone implied that *interesting* was an understatement. "Do share."

"Well, I almost went swimming with a gator named Bloody Bill Anderson, for one." Langdon went on to tell Chabal about the post office, the No Name Pub, pursuing Tara onto No Name Key, where he ran into Jughead, Cousin Ronnie, and the others, who took him to the favorite water hole of an alligator with a name that suggested a penchant for butchery. "But I ended up having an enlightening conversation with Tara James."

"After she suggested that the rednecks let you go."

"Yep. We walked back from the gator hole to the house and my rental car. I told you about Starling's story where Tara interned with him, slept with him, and shared a story of sexual assault with him back in the late eighties, didn't I?"

"You sure did. Not the man's finest moment. Or summer. As far as I'm concerned."

Langdon nodded. "Tara has forgiven the person who assaulted her in college. She believes that she was just as complicit, and the man in question was badgered into his part by Remington, and that the two of them had always had a curiosity for the other. An emotion that Tara acted upon under the influence of alcohol and that this fellow acted upon under the coercion of the judge."

"Was it Michael Levy like you thought?"

"Nope. It was Chuck Taylor."

Chabal processed this for a few moments. "Chuck Taylor who is now Shannon Undergrove."

"The one and the same."

"Wow. Tara have anything else to say?"

"She was real interested in my theory that Michael Levy was murdered rather than died in a freak accident."

"She have any input on who or why somebody might've killed him and attacked you?"

Langdon shook his head. "Not really. She does think that the judge is capable of doing something like that if he thought it necessary. I believe her words were that he is 'one cold hearted bastard.'"

Chabal went through the fast lane at the toll on the Falmouth connector and moved to the right to get onto Interstate 295. "Big stretch from cold hearted bastard to murderer."

"It seems that it's time to have a pow wow with the judge."

"Didn't that White House fellow, Cooper, tell you to steer clear of the judge?"

Langdon chuckled. "But then they fired me. As in not paying me. So, I suppose I can do what I want. I figure once we get back, I'm going to hunt him up for a little confab."

"Not immediately when we get back."

Langdon looked at Chabal. "Is there something else going on?"

"Well, for one, the kids are all gone, and the house is empty."

"Empty houses are good."

Chabal turned her head and looked him in the eye. "Me thinks you have other things to do first."

~ ~ ~ ~ ~

Neely Remington was in the process of lining up his ducks. Duffy and Boyle had never strayed from the path. Michael Levy had been a weak link but now that problem was no longer. Tara James had taken her big mouth and moved to the Florida Keys. Chuckie Taylor had up and disappeared. This was a good thing, but then it'd been brought to his attention that Langdon had found Chuckie, who was now Shannon, that the former Maine Man of Mayhem was now a woman, and she lived right down the street in Ogunquit.

This was the reason why he found himself behind the wheel of his BMW M4 convertible cruising down I-95. The car was a metallic blue and shimmered in the sunshine. He had on Ray Bans, and while his thinning hair no longer blew in the wind of the open top, he still felt like a million dollars. Soon, he would be appointed a Supreme Court justice for life, and then the real windfall would begin.

Just as an appellate judge, Neely received favors, disguised as tokens of friendship, to gain his support. The bigger the ask, the bigger the offering. Soon, he'd be basking in luxurious resort vacation sites, riding private jets and helicopters, and getting VIP seating to sporting events and concerts. All just considerations between friends. And Neely would merely have to vote as he would have anyway.

And the women, he thought, who would to flock him and his new prestige. No more cheap hookers. No more sad middle-aged women on business trips in hotel bars. Neely would be reveling in beauty, ripe skin and nubile bodies—women who knew how to please a man of his stature. It had been years since he'd even contemplated making love to his own wife. Toots was a fine woman, an important ornament for his ambitions, but she didn't know the first thing about pleasing a man in the bedroom. Which was fine, because wives weren't created for naked sport, but were rather set upon this good earth to be the assistant to their husband in their career path.

Saylor had confided in him that the background check had been completed and that he was ready to be nominated, presented to the Senate, and confirmed as justice, all in rapid order as no skeletons had been found in his closet. In her role as chief of staff, Saylor had polled possible opponents to his nomination and found little for concern. He was the choice of the democratic president, which was good with that party, but his borderline republican stances appealed to that party, making him the perfect candidate.

It certainly didn't hurt that he was screwing the chief of staff who had the ear, no, both ears, of the president. The poor sap probably didn't even know that Remington had not been his choice but had been planted there by the *sotto voce* of Saylor Ball.

His path to becoming one of the nine most powerful people in the universe was now clear of obstructions and he merely had to coast toward the finish line and receive his prize. Into his victory lap, though, kept appearing the image of a tall, red-haired, middle-aged, bookstore owner slash detective who kept popping up and stirring shit around and threatening the very dream that Neely was so close, oh so close, to realizing.

The house was in a small neighborhood just a couple blocks from the beach. It was a small Cape Cod with a white picket fence around the minuscule yard. Neely half expected to see some small dog with a specialized hairdo. He wasn't quite sure what he was expecting. Maybe garish neon lights, rainbow flags, or some other sign that a member of the queer community lived in this nondescript house.

Neely unlatched the gate and went up the three steps to the covered front porch. There were two rocking chairs on one side and a table on the other covered with flowerpots.

He knocked.

The door opened. A woman stood there with hair poofed in a swirl, a sundress casually encasing her body. She wore no jewelry nor shoes.

Neely smiled broadly. "Hello, Chuckie. Did you do something with your hair?"

Chapter 27

The waves were lapping over the top of Langdon. He couldn't move. He was attached to something. It was an alligator who opened his jaw impossibly wide and exposed teeth that flashed like sabers in the Coliseum. His head was pounding.

Langdon woke in a cold sweat. He quickly looked next to him where Chabal slept. He knew she was naked under the covers and smiled.

Somebody was banging on the front door. Dog started barking.

Langdon slipped on a pair of shorts and a shirt and eased out of the first-floor bedroom. Bart and Susie were on the front porch. He opened the door. "What time is it?" Dog brushed past him and jumped up on Bart.

"Time to get up and make the doughnuts." Bart pushed past with Susie in tow.

Chabal was in the kitchen with her M & P Shield in hand. She nodded to Bart and went back in the bedroom to put the pistol away.

Bart looked at Langdon. Raised his eyebrow. "Did I interrupt role playing morning?"

"What brings you by my humble abode at such an early hour?"

"Got any coffee?"

As if on cue, the coffee began to percolate. Langdon had set it for six, so that must be the time. Bart had always been an early bird and didn't adjust his schedule for others.

Chabal came back out having returned the pistol to the safe and adding a long-sleeve shirt to her morning wardrobe. "Morning Bart. Morning Susie. To what do we owe the pleasure?"

"I thought you'd be staying with me a few days, at least." Bart grabbed a cup and poured the first of the strong brew into it. "Missed you, this morning, is all, and thought I'd come over and see what was for breakfast."

"I think we have some apples." Langdon poured himself a tad of gourmet creamer and a cup of coffee and then sat down at the table. Susie and Chabal joined him. Bart remained standing. "Maybe leftover Thai food?"

"Just joshing with you." Bart poured a bit more coffee into his mug. "We're gonna stop at Mae's in Bath for breakfast on our way DownEast."

"DownEast?"

"Gonna go up to Lubec for the weekend." Bart put his hand on Susie's shoulder.

"That'll be nice," Chabal said.

"You stop by just to tell us you were going to be away?" Langdon chided away at the surly cop who presently looked like a preteen in a candy shop.

Bart cleared his throat. "Thought I'd update you on the Levy… murder."

"Murder?"

"Well, not officially, but I been asking around and there seems to be some sketchy stuff going on. I'm gonna give it some thought over the weekend and decide whether I want to stick my neck out and ask the chief about reopening the investigation."

"You mean the State Police? If it's a homicide."

Bart nodded. "But it's gotta come from the chief. They ain't going to do anything on my say so. Unless we use your Jackson Brooks angle. Did you talk with him yet?"

"Ach, no. Kinda got distracted." Jackson Brooks was the friend who worked for the State Police. He was no longer in the Major

Crimes Unit that investigated murders, but his tech job seemed to overlap with the unit responsible for all the murders in the state, and he kept himself current on what was going on. Langdon had called in favors with him several times before. It almost always had behooved the man as well, but sometimes the skirting of protocol also got him into trouble with his bosses. "What'd you find out?" Langdon asked.

"There was some light bruising on the back of Levy's arms and ankles. Not much, mind you, but something caused that while he was still alive."

"Like he was dragged?"

"More like carried. One had his ankles, the other had his arms."

Langdon nodded. "That it?"

"The ME told me in private that the chances of Levy electrocuting himself with ear buds plugged into a cell phone were pretty darn steep but the word came down the chain to wrap things up and so he did."

"Down the chain, huh?"

"From the chief medical examiner."

Langdon smirked. "Ole Floppy Bum himself." This was the nickname the two of them had bestowed on the corpulent CME.

"Yep. Told the investigator to tie things up. When he put up mild resistance, got his ass chewed out, and capitulated."

"Who is the medicolegal death investigator?"

"Dallas Barbeau."

"Don't really know him."

"New feller. Just started last year."

Langdon sighed. Took a sip of coffee. "Any chance you can get the three of us together for a confab?"

"I'll see what I can do." Bart nodded, touched Susie on the arm. "Hey, baby, I'm starving. You ready to get on the road?"

"Yeah, sure." Susie stood up, looked at Langdon. "Alice changed her mind about meeting up with you at McSorley's today at four.

Said she can't risk everything."

Langdon had forgotten about the meeting in all the hubbub. "You need to convince her, Susie, how important this is."

Susie sighed. "She's got a little Yorkie. Takes him out on the bike path for a walk every morning. Right about seven o'clock. One mile out. One mile back. That's where you can find her."

Dog was not very wise in the ways of the leash. The poor guy had never had to face one very much, only in the rarest of circumstances. But Langdon didn't want the big galoot scaring Alice's little dog by just being his normal clumsy, enthusiastic, and oafish self. So, he, Chabal, and dog on a leash, found themselves meandering along the bike path at a few minutes before seven.

They'd only gone a couple hundred feet, not even having passed under the tunnel, and Langdon's arm had been whipsawed back and forth numerous times. As far as painful went, it was right up there with getting clunked with a tire iron and latched to a buoy or taking a hit from a former college linebacker and taken for a swim with a man-eating alligator.

On the other side of the tunnel underneath the bypass, they began their dilly dally. Dog was happy to sniff for a few moments but then looked up inquisitively, wondering why they weren't careening down the bike path at full speed. Luckily, the woman matching the picture Susie had shown them came along at that moment. Alice Rehnquist. A Yorkshire terrier with Ewok ears pranced along in front of her.

Dog did his part and strained at his leash. Alice, as most little dog owners are, was rightfully nervous that her Yorkie might get eaten or trounced by the bigger dog.

"Okay if he says hi?" Langdon took a few steps closer, making the question a moot point.

"You're the private investigator." Alice's eyes got big as she looked at him. She had lost her worry about her dog and replaced it with a larger fear. "The one Susie told me about."

One of the things that had occurred since the case of the wendigo had been splashed across every media outlet in the entire world was Langdon had lost any shred of anonymity he had left. Even though he'd been involved in some high-profile cases prior to that, he'd mostly kept his name and face out of the spotlight. Ever since he'd been shot in the head, anyway.

"I was hoping we might have a few words, Alice."

"That bitch. She told you where to find me."

"I thought you agreed to see me?"

Alice guffawed. "I look stupid to you?"

Langdon shrugged. "I have your address. Not hard to find. Isn't this better than me coming to your house?"

"What do you want from me?"

"To talk about Cornelius Remington."

"Judge Cornelius Remington."

Langdon nodded. "Let's walk and talk."

Alice looked like she was considering turning around and going back home. Then, with a resigned look to her face, started walking. "I have nothing to say to you."

"Remington was nominated yesterday by the President of the United States to serve on the Bench of the Supreme Court."

Alice smirked. "The POTUS and the SCOTUS."

Langdon chuckled. "I don't believe the man has the moral integrity to serve in that capacity. I fear that he's done some extremely bad things but can't prove anything and therefore I will be ignored by anybody with the power to do anything about it."

"What does any of that have to do with me?"

"Susie told me that you were paid to have sex with Remington."

They walked in silence for a bit before Alice broke the blaring hush. "Nobody cares about a man paying a woman to have sex that is not his wife. Not anymore. Not one bit."

"Certain people have to be held to higher standards than the run of the mill."

"Oh, most people would be pissed. If the guy who bags my groceries got caught cheating on his wife with a prostitute, he'd be in a world of trouble. Probably get fired on the spot. It's exactly the certain people you are referring to that nobody cares about. Not their wives. Not the voting public. Not anybody."

"I guess you're right about the last president." Langdon sighed. "Nobody cared about that, or at least, not the courts nor half the country. But the SCOTUS is different. They are determining the laws of the land based upon the principles of integrity and honesty."

Alice snorted. "Yeah. Somebody tell that to the last drunken whore dog that got appointed. Better yet, tell it to the women he groped and the one who got her face slapped with his dick. At least I was paid for my abuse."

Chabal put her hand on Alice's elbow and squeezed gently. "It can't be easy."

Alice stopped walking and stared at her. A tear trickled from the corner of her eye and ran down her cheek. She was quite a striking woman. Her face angular and defined. Long blonde hair. Plump lips and sultry eyes.

When she spoke, her voice was cracked, but firm. Unapologetic. "I'm a single mother raising three kids under the age of ten. No help from their fathers. I work two jobs but still can't pay the bills. I'd be homeless, we'd be homeless, if I didn't supplement my piss poor jobs with additional income. Real money. And all I gotta do is be compliant. Appreciative. Less than an hour. Remington paid me five hundred bucks. That's twice what I normally get. That goes a long way, you know, in putting cereal on the table. Keeping the lights on. Heating in the winter. Boots. Winter jackets. You know?"

Chabal nodded. Stepped forward and hugged Alice. "A tale as old as time," she whispered in her ear. "We do what we must. With what we have. But it's people like this fucker Remington who stack the deck against us. Take our ability to choose from our hands and let rich white men decide what happens to us and our bodies."

Alice laughed coarsely. "If it's not him, it'll just be another one like him. It won't make a lick of difference."

Chabal stepped back. Shook her head. "No. The president is a good man. If we expose Remington for what he is, the nomination will be revoked, and then extended to a person with moral integrity, not some cheating bastard who puts a dollar number on women."

"I can't. I just can't."

"Why not?"

"I can't stand up on national television and tell the world that I'm a sex worker. A hooker. A whore."

"The world will forget about you before the week is out. And they will unremember him as well. He will just be an asterisk in the history books. Make him forgotten."

"The world might forget. But my kids won't. My neighbors won't. My kids' teachers won't. My father…" Alice choked up and began sobbing.

Chapter 28

"Where's that leave us?" Chabal asked Langdon as they watched Alice Rehnquist walk on down the street with her Yorkie. "Can't really make somebody testify that they were hired to perform sexual services if they don't want to."

"Sure, you can," Langdon said. "I just don't know if it's the right thing to do."

"Yeah, I suppose. The Senate Committee could call her as a character witness and get her to testify on her oath of honor, and if she lied, face possible perjury."

"Yeah, but at what cost? We'd be tearing that poor woman's life apart."

"But if we don't, and Remington becomes a Supreme?"

"Ha. Not sure he'd fit into a Black girl group."

"He's no Diana Ross."

Langdon opened the back gate and gave dog a little boost into the Jeep. The fellow was slowing down just a tad with his jumping ability, especially after see-sawing Langdon all over the bike path. "Is Remington really that bad?"

"What? He's a pig." Chabal climbed into the Jeep and slammed the door.

Langdon got in the driver's side. "What have we turned up, really? The guy liked to watch porn in college, play pranks on other students, and cheats on his wife."

"Porn and pranks are one thing, but adultery shouldn't be

tolerated."

"What if Toots doesn't care?"

"Toots?"

Langdon chuckled. "That's Remington's wife's nickname. Given name, Angela, adopted name, Toots."

"What do you mean if she doesn't care?"

Langdon started the Jeep and pulled out of the parking lot. "A marriage of convenience. Plenty of those to go around. Lot of loveless marriages out there. Either you're too poor to get a divorce or you're too rich and powerful to split."

"If Toots divorced Remington, she'd no longer be the judge's wife."

"Half the money. None of the prestige. Have to figure out life as a single woman."

Chabal snickered. "That's the only reason I stay with you. Money, prestige, and fear of being single."

"So, you'd be okay with me sleeping with other women?"

Chabal smacked him on the arm. "We are neither too poor nor too rich for divorce, bucko, just you remember that. But if you sleep with another woman, that would be the least of our worries, believe you me."

Langdon rubbed his arm. "I'm documenting this abuse, just for the record."

"Suck it up, buttercup."

"She might even be happy that he's getting his jollies in somebody else's yard. Heck, plenty of women out there not interested in sex. Especially as they get older."

"So, what are you saying? We just drop the whole thing. Porn, pranks, and playing the field are not character flaws enough to prevent Remington from becoming a Supreme."

"Not if the White House, the FBI, and the Senate don't seem to care."

"Somebody cares." Chabal sighed. "There's gotta be an entity, a person, somebody worthy and with clout, who will slam on the brakes of this shit show if we get some proof of the man's infidelities and generally poor moral character."

Langdon pulled into the parking lot behind the bookshop. "Cooper Walker, the assistant chief of staff, seemed to care. But he shut me down. I'm thinking it was on orders."

"A fellow who doesn't have the clout we need."

"But an ally."

Chabal opened the door, got out, and let dog flash by her on his way to investigate what had been going on in the parking lot in his absence. "Might be interesting to know who ordered Cooper to leave it alone."

"Hm. Yes. Did the order come from the president himself?"

"Or the chief of staff. What's her name?"

"Ball. Saylor Ball."

~ ~ ~ ~ ~

Starling was at the counter in a very empty bookshop when Langdon, Chabal, and dog walked in, or rather, dog ran in, and received the proper treat for his effusive greeting.

"Back from Florida early," Starling said.

Langdon grinned. "Found your girlfriend."

Starling winced.

Langdon felt bad. "She was staying down on a little tiny islet called No Name Key living with some redneck cousins of varying ages." Then, because he couldn't help himself. "You ever get to meet the family?"

"We didn't quite get to that stage." Starling's voice was dry. "I'm not sure I was up to her standards. Might've embarrassed her in front of her family."

"Not these cousins, you wouldn't have, well, maybe they'd think you a bit too stodgy and prissy. There was Ronnie, Rusty, and Jughead. Not sure the fourth guy even had a name."

"Like the key," Starling said.

"The key?"

"No Name Key. No name cousin." Starling cleared his throat. "If you're done busting my balls, how was Tara?"

Langdon raised an eyebrow. "She's a good-looking woman. Was asking after you."

"Really?"

Langdon chuckled. "No. We didn't get around to talking about you as we had more pressing things to discuss. Once she had saved me from an alligator with the moniker Bloody Bill Anderson, that is."

"Of the Anderson Gator dynasty?" Starling laughed hoarsely.

"That'd make for a good television series," Chabal interjected. "Gator Dynasty."

"Think you might be stepping on the toes of the duck people," Langdon said.

"Okay, okay, enough." Starling held up his hands in surrender. "Just tell me what you found out from Tara."

"Tara James?"

The voice came from the open doorway.

Langdon turned to find Shannon Undergrove standing there, poised as if a wax figure, one hand on her forehead, her mouth making a perfect circle, feet stopped in the middle of taking a step.

"Hello, Shannon. Shannon, my wife Chabal, and this is Starling." Dog ran over to her wagging his tail. "Oh, and yeah, this is dog."

Shannon came unfrozen, reached down, and scratched dog on the head. "Hi." She looked up. "Were you talking about Tara James?"

Langdon nodded. "Yes."

"Is she around? I haven't seen her for ages."

"What brings you to Brunswick?"

"I remembered something that might be helpful."

"You want to come back to my office?" Langdon waved her to the back of the bookshop. "Right this way."

Shannon preceded him into the office and proceeded to walk around the dingy office with no window, dim light, and scuffed furniture, looking at everything, before settling into one of the chairs across the desk from Langdon.

"You know, I grew up in Jackman," she said. "Not too many people from Jackman go to college, let alone Bowdoin."

Langdon nodded and said nothing. Keeping his mouth shut had never got him into trouble yet, unless you counted the questions from Chabal like 'do you like my new haircut? Do I look like I've gained weight? Should I make brownies?' These were things that a careful and correct answer had to be immediately given.

"That's why I didn't leave Brunswick, I suppose. I should've gotten out of town. But I didn't want to go back to Jackman and Brunswick was the only other thing I knew. You know, I'd never even left the state until spring break, sophomore year, when a group of us went to Fort Lauderdale."

"No offense, but I don't imagine there are many Black people in Jackman."

Shannon chortled. "Nope. It wasn't easy."

"All the good reason to not go back after college."

"Not much for me in Jackman."

"And you got married, I understand. Reason to stay around."

Shannon nodded. "Karen. Met her at the Maine State Music Theater. She was alone. I was alone. We sat next to each other. Two lonely souls."

When nothing more seemed forthcoming, Shannon lost in reflection, Langdon prompted, "When was that?"

"It's not really all that important." Shannon shook her head, banishing the past, returning to the present. "I remembered something about Tara that might be helpful."

Interesting, Langdon thought, for Tara had shared information pertaining to Shannon. "Yeah? What's that?"

"Well, you said that you think Mikey was murdered?"

"The thought has crossed my mind." Langdon thought about the recent update from Bart about the light bruising on Michael Levy's wrists and ankles. "But that is only a theory right now."

"About five years back, I ran into Tara James in a bar. Goldilocks. It was late. I was drunk. I think she was drunk as well." Shannon sighed. Leaned back. Her skirt flared open, and Langdon looked away.

After a bit, he leaned forward and looked her in the eyes. "Go on."

"It was before I began transitioning. I was confused and in a messed-up place. My divorce had just been finalized. I knew what I felt but I was fighting against it with every fiber of my being. Anyway, we decided to go back to my place for a nightcap. I was living in an apartment downtown, you see, and so we stumbled back to my place. We were flirting, I suppose, having moved on from catching up on the past, covering all the mandatory family and job crap, studiously ignoring the time we knew each other in college."

Langdon steepled his fingers and waited for her to continue.

Shannon sighed loudly. "We were sitting on the couch of my shithole apartment and then we were kissing fiercely."

Langdon waited but Shannon seemed to have gone to a faraway place in her head. "And?"

"I couldn't do it. I pulled back and started crying. Confessed to her that I was a woman and not a man, my body just didn't know it yet, but my mind did. I came clean. Told her everything. It was then, in that drunken moment, on the cusp of having sex with another woman, a blast from the past, that I finally grasped what I was going to do, and that nothing was going to stop me. And here I am, a changed person, happier than I've ever been, with more confidence." She guffawed loudly. "If my friends from Jackman could see me today."

"Is it safe to say that Tara James was one of the first ones to know your secret?"

Shannon nodded. "The very first."

"And?"

Shannon sighed. "After my confession, might've as well been in one of them closets in the Catholic Church where you renounce your sins, we both cried a little, laughed a little, and then poured another drink. That's when Tara shared with me that she couldn't get past being raped by Mikey. Told me there was only one way to get over what he'd done to her, and that was to end him."

"End him?"

"Her words, not mine. I think I asked what she meant by that, but I don't think she expounded, and if she did, I can't remember. But yeah, she'd been tortured by what happened ever since, and she was going to end him. And that would end her nightmares. Or something like that."

Interesting, Langdon thought, wondering if he should keep his cards to himself or play them to see what reaction they produced. He chose the latter. "I spoke with Tara a couple days ago. She told me that it wasn't even Michael Levy who… abused her. She said it was you. And that she didn't hold a grudge, realized that you'd both been drinking, and she was just as culpable as you. Not sure that I agree with her, but that's what she told me."

"What? She said I… wait, you're fucking kidding me, right?"

~ ~ ~ ~ ~

The day only got more interesting for Langdon from that point forward. No more than twenty minutes after Shannon left, steaming mad about what Tara had claimed, Chabal texted to say that Marsha Verhoeven was out front in the bookshop wanting to see him.

Langdon was just sitting at his desk, feet up on top, hands clasped behind his head, trying to unsort the whole mess. Somebody was lying. Maybe everybody was lying. He texted back.

Busy out front?

Not so much but Star went to get some lunch so I'm out here by myself.

Send her on back.

A few seconds later, the door opened, and Marsha came in. As always, she was dressed very fashionably in a jumpsuit of varying shades of orange, matching her hair, lipstick, and clutch.

Langdon gestured for her to have a seat across from him, but she ignored him, coming around the desk and pulling his baseball cap off. "Oh, my," she said. "Jimmy said you got accosted by a couple of gents down to the end of my road after you left the other night, but this? Shitake mushrooms! That looks terrible."

Langdon took his cap back and put it on, covering up the zipper on top of his head. "It looks worse that it is."

"Did they rob you?" Marsha put her hand on his shoulder. "You poor boy."

"Please have a seat."

Marsha patted his cheek gently and cooed, but then followed directions and went back around the desk and sat down. "Why would anybody do that?"

"Do you believe that Cornelius Remington would hire somebody to kill me? That he is capable of such an act?"

Marsha covered her mouth with her hand, but not so close as to smudge the lipstick. "You don't think?"

Langdon took a deep breath. "I have no idea. That's why I'm asking you." He was starting to tire of the melodramatics of Marsha Verhoeven. It was as if she were starring in her own self-produced soap opera.

"After Jimmy told me, I looked it up online and found that two men attacked you and that you only escaped by jumping in the water and swimming away. Is that what happened?"

Bart had been instrumental in downplaying the story for the media. If the true nature of Langdon being knocked out and attached to a mooring in the bay had come out, it would've been a feeding frenzy that very well might've included national syndicates.

"That's about the gist of it," he said. "But they weren't there to rob me. They either wanted to kill me or send me a message. I've made quite a few enemies over the years, and it could be any of them, but it could also involve my current case investigating Judge Cornelius Remington."

"Could Neely actually try to harm somebody?" Marsha said softly, as if to herself, a faraway look in her eye. Then louder, "He's a world class prick but I can't see him hiring somebody to assault you. He doesn't have the mettle for something like that."

Langdon nodded. "What brings you visiting today?"

"To see how you are. I wanted to come earlier, but the fellow at the counter said you'd gone to Florida?"

"Following a lead," he said noncommittally.

"Heard Tara James moved to Florida. Somewhere on the Keys."

"As you can see, I'm fine. Just a scratch."

"Chabal looks to be doing better than last time I saw her."

Langdon looked for hidden meaning in the woman's eyes. The last time, and only time, that Marsha had seen his wife was a couple of weeks back at a barbecue when Chabal was, well, not at her best. There seemed to be no guile, just concern. But Langdon was starting to realize that Marsha could play many roles.

"She is doing much better. Thank you."

"Have you managed to track down Freddie Duffy or Johnny Boyle?"

The fourth and fifth men of mayhem, Langdon thought. Neither man had been home nor answering their phones. "No."

"Do you know about Freddie's cottage out to Harpswell? They might be staying out there. It's in his cousin's name, so you might not know about it. But I think he spends a big chunk of the summer there."

Langdon said nothing. He felt a little silly. He did not know of this cabin. How did she know about it? Didn't she say she hadn't seen them in years? This woman, Marsha Verhoeven, seemed to have the ability to make him feel uncomfortable. Unworthy. Somehow wanting.

"No worries," she said. "I'll text you the address. I just wanted to stop in and check on you. I can see myself out."

She stood and moved toward the door and Langdon followed. He thought it right to walk her out, but was feeling flustered, put out by her lightning changes of hot and cold. "Thanks for coming by," he said, opening the door for her.

She leaned into him ever so slightly. "Too bad your wife is working."

"What?"

"Oh, I thought I could've stopped by and checked in on her as well. Tell her we must have a cup of coffee sometime."

There was a woman at the counter with Chabal. As they started down an aisle of bookshelves, she turned. "There he is," she said. "I knew he was here."

It was Mrs. Remington. Angela. Toots to her husband, and perhaps friends.

"Mr. Langdon, I have come to let you know that I did not appr—" She stopped in the middle of the sentence as she caught sight of Marsha, her eyes going large behind her horn-rimmed glasses, large and hard, a gasp emitting from her mouth that sounded to be wrenched from deep in her belly. "It's you. Tramp. Tart. Trollop. What lies are you telling about my husband?"

Marsha looked from her to Langdon. "Do I know you?" she asked.

Toots spluttered in rage, spittle flecking her wide cheeks. "I know you. Flaunting yourself and throwing yourself at married men."

"I think you have me mistaken." Marsha walked hurriedly toward the door, but Toots stepped in front of her blocking the way. "Get out of my way you Puritan prude."

"Jezebel."

"Priss."

Toots' face went red. "Slut."

Marsha shoved her. Toots' arm flailed up and she grabbed a handful of the rich-red hair and yanked hard and they both went tumbling to the floor. Marsha raked her nails across Toots' cheek. Toots bit Marsha's arm. Marsha rolled her over and sat astride of her and punched Toots in the face.

Langdon stepped over, grabbed Marsha, and pulled her off the other woman.

Toots rolled over heavily, clambered to her feet, and glared at Marsha. "You're going to pay for that you… you… you *bitch!*" And then she turned and walked out the door.

After a minute, thinking it was safe, Langdon released Marsha. She kicked a bookshelf, cursed at Langdon, and stormed out the door.

Chapter 29

Langdon and Chabal were still standing in the bookshop with mouths agape when Starling came back through the door.

"Looks like you pissed off another customer," he said. "Was that Jimmy's lady friend? Marsha something or other?"

"Holy shit," Chabal said.

"What happened?" Starling asked.

Langdon told him, best he could, of the events that had just transpired.

"Sounds like the judge's wife, Toots, is it? Sounds like she believes that this lady friend of Jimmy's, Marsha, had an affair with her husband, is what it sounds like to me." Starling unwrapped a Reuben from Sugar Magnolia's and took a bite. "Chabal said the two of you were going out for lunch, so I didn't get you anything."

"Yes. Yes it does." Langdon reached over and snatched a chip. "And more recently than back in college, would be my guess. That was some pretty fresh anger right there."

"She seems so nice," Chabal said. "But I guess a person can be nice and be involved with a married man. No one is all good and no one is all evil."

Langdon glanced at her, wondering what this reflection meant. "She, uh, is actually quite flirtatious."

"What's that mean?" Chabal asked.

"Every time I see her, there is an underlying invitation to come experience more, whether it is just harmless coquetry or actual seduction, I don't know."

"Come experience fucking more?"

Langdon kept the grin from his face. His wife, the foul-mouthed one, was coming back. Cursing coupled with a glint of fierceness to her eye were both good signs. "An invitation that I have returned unopened."

Starling snorted, choked. "She's a pretty woman."

Chabal glared at him, then snickered. "But with some serious issues, it would seem."

Langdon's phone buzzed. He looked at it. Put it back down.

"Who was that?" Chabal asked.

Langdon looked sheepish. "Marsha. She sent me an address to a cottage out to Harpswell." He paused a beat but then hurriedly continued. "Where I might find the fourth and fifth men of mayhem. Boyle and Duffy."

~ ~ ~ ~ ~

Jimmy 4 by Four was reading a case file at his desk when Marsha came barging into his office, slamming the door open, and propelling across his office toward him. Her hair was uncharacteristically astray upon her head, tossed and wild, sprouting in all different directions of tangle. Her face was red, and one cheekbone was slightly discolored.

"That goddamn battle-axe. I should've ripped her eyes out of her skull. Coming at me with her saggy tits and fat ass! No wonder the man cheats on her. She has no—"

"Whoa, whoa, what's going on?" Jimmy asked.

"I was just assaulted by Angela Remington, and I want to press charges."

"Assaulted? Angela Remington?"

"The wife of the judge, yeah, that's the one. That harridan just bit me. She bit me!"

"Harridan?"

Marsha took a choking breath. "Yeah, you know, a cold and vicious shrew who nags her husband all the time. A harridan."

"Let's slow down a bit. Where did this woman attack you?"

"The Coffee Dog Bookstore."

Jimmy nodded comfortingly. "Were you there visiting Langdon?"

Marsha sighed. Sat heavily down in a chair. "Yes. I was checking up on him, you know, because I haven't seen him since his unfortunate incident. Just to see how he was doing. And then when I was leaving, I ran into Angela buggering Remington and she started insulting me, so I shoved her, and she grabbed my hair and—"

Jimmy held up a hand. "Slow. Slow the roll. I'm sorry. I just need to know what happened."

"That's what I'm goddamn telling you!"

"Why did she insult you?"

"I don't know. She was calling me names."

"What names?"

"Jezebel. Slut. Things like that."

"Why?"

"I don't goddamn know why. For no reason. Because she is a sad, sad, sad woman. Jealous that I look like this, and she looks like that. I don't know. She is a mean-spirited shrew who has attached herself to Neely like a leach and is trying to ride him all the way to the finish line, except, without riding him in that way, if you know what I mean. She's a self-serving, cold-hearted, manipulative bitch, is what she is."

"And you want to press assault charges against her?"

Marsha breathed deeply. Stood. Walked around the desk and straddled Jimmy. "No. No. But I do want you inside of me right now."

~ ~ ~ ~ ~

Harpswell was shaped like a trident, three prongs of land poking their way into the Atlantic Ocean. Fred Duffy's cousin's cottage was near the end of the closest prong to downtown Brunswick and the Coffee Dog Bookstore. Fifteen miles south. Chabal stayed back to help Starling in the shop and dog stayed as well, knowing he had a better chance of eating his dinner on time if he didn't go off on an adventure as that particular mealtime began to near.

The cottage was almost all the way to the end, off Basin Point Road, just about a half-mile shy of the tip where the Dolphin Marina & Restaurant was located. It was not a large place, but its location right on the water suggested that it was far from cheap. It was possible that it had been handed down through the generations from fishing family to fishing family, but Langdon doubted that. It reeked of a summer residence.

The driveway entered between a rock wall, carefully constructed, the work of a master craftsman and not a fellow piecing together rocks ripped from his own land. The grass was perfectly manicured, green grass mown to look like AstroTurf, well-landscaped shrubberies, flower beds, and stone lawn ornaments.

The house itself was not large, but a substantial wraparound porch doubled the size. Langdon parked behind a Ford F-150. A second vehicle, perhaps a Jeep Cherokee, was backed into the turnaround. Langdon went up the three granite steps to the front door and gave it two sharp raps. There was no answer. He repeated the sequence. When nothing stirred, he looked in the window. No lights on. But there seemed to be a casual lived-in look, the pillows on the couch crumpled, a coffee cup on a side table, and other signs of some presence.

He walked around the side of the porch and looked in another window. The side view of the living room. Then a small window that peeked into the bathroom. The veranda continued on around the side of the house. The view was spectacular at the back, sweeping views of water egresses into Maine, Maquoit Bay, Broad Sound, as well as dotted by islands, the largest being Chebeague and Cousins.

And beyond them was the mainland, Yarmouth.

Set up to take in this view were two rocking chairs with a small square table between them. Sitting in them were two men smoking cigars. Langdon had looked at photographs, of course, of Duffy and Boyle. These two men didn't look much like their pictures, he thought, but it was them all the same. Just slightly older, a harder look to their faces, perhaps a lifetime of smoking and drinking, but maybe more.

More importantly, seeing them caused a shift in Langdon's brain. Like a rocket docking to the space station, two large fragments of his memory clicked into place. An image of a man waving him down, leading him to a truck where another man huddled on the front seat, a tire iron rising high, impossibly high in the air, and then descending upon the back of his head. These were the two men who ambushed him, cracked his skull, and left him floating in the ocean attached to a mooring.

"Hi, fellows," he said.

Boyle was inclined in his direction and merely shifted his eyes to see Langdon. "Oh, shit."

Duffy had to turn his head, but he was the first to react. He came out of the rocking chair and down the steps to the rocky shoreline below. Boyle went to follow, but was slower, and Langdon hit him with a tackle that would've made his old football coach proud. The impact sent the two of them sprawling down the stairs. Langdon's head smashed into the ground, and it was as if a rap flash mob exploded in his noggin.

Boyle struggled to his feet, but as he went to run, Langdon grabbed his foot and flipped it, sending the man crashing back to the ground. Langdon crawled the few feet to him and straddled him, his hands on the man's chest. There was a roaring in his head that was a mixture of crunching his still-delicate head, and anger at the man who'd been the reason for the concussion and zipper in his egg.

"Why?" he yelled in the man's face.

A boot slammed into his ribs and Langdon toppled sideways. Duffy grabbed Boyle's hand and pulled him to his feet. Langdon lunged at them, but his hands came up empty. He got to his feet, gasping in pain from battered ribs, and stumbled after them down the rocky coastline. He tripped, almost fell, righted himself, and continued on. Through the fog of pain his blinding rage guided him in pursuit—gave breath to his muscles and strength to his legs.

The two men turned to the left and cut up the side of a neighbor's yard. Langdon vaguely noted the immense size of the dwelling as he followed them around the side, down the drive, and across the dirt/gravel spur road off Basin Point Road.

He scuffed his foot on a rock and went ass over tea kettle, landing flat on his face. When he looked up, the two men had disappeared into the thin strip of foliage between the two roads. But they were heading further out the peninsula, and Langdon, who was a big fan of the Dolphin Restaurant, knew that the end of land was not far and that they were running themselves into a dead end.

At the same time, he was in no shape to catch them, and if he did, lacked the fitness to do anything constructive by running them down other than getting his ass kicked. Just about a hundred feet back was his Jeep, and in his Jeep, his Glock. That seemed to be the wiser choice than pursuing two men in his weakened state on foot and unarmed.

The Glock was in the lockbox between the two front seats. The ammo clip was in the glove compartment taped to the back. He unlocked the box, took the pistol, pulled the ammo free, and slid it into place. He placed the weapon on the passenger seat, put the Jeep in reverse, and went back to the main road, the only road between here and the Dolphin, and began trolling his way along.

The trees on either side thinned out. The two men could have gone to ground and hid before leaving their protection. But Langdon didn't think so. There were houses and yards, places to hide, and he might be missing them. But he didn't think so. They had a plan, and he was starting to catch on to what it might be. There'd been no dock, no boat, at the cottage. The marina. Langdon punched the accelerator.

The road narrowed even further and then emerged onto the point. Erica's on the left, the Dolphin Restaurant straight ahead, a parking lot between them. Langdon slammed the brakes, and the Jeep came to a shuddering stop at the top of the gangway to the docks. He grabbed the Glock, jumped out, and came to a halt before going down. A metal skiff was about a hundred yards out, pulled up to a boat, and two men were stepping from one to the other.

Duffy and Boyle.

In the movies, Langdon would've commandeered a passing speedboat, chased them down, and after some heroic high-speed fisticuffs, he would've knocked them unconscious and dragged them off to the police. In reality, that opportunity didn't exist. There were no idling banana boats to be jumped into. There were two people sitting on the back deck of a fishing boat at a mooring. With these thoughts churning in his head, *Mainely Mayhem*, the boat with Duffy and Boyle aboard, chugged into life, and then began moving away.

The Coast Guard, Langdon thought with a glimmer of hope, might be an option. He pulled his cell phone from his pocket. Went to look up the number. No service.

Chapter 30

Judge Remington was returning to his office in the Fort Andross building after lunch at Sugar Magnolia's. He decided to forgo the elevator and take the stairs. It was in the stairwell that he ran into Marsha Verhoeven.

Her face was flushed. Her hair was astray. Clothes disheveled. Her eyes were that of a feral cat. And he wasn't sure whether he'd ever been this turned on by the sight of a woman in his entire life.

It was on the landing between floors, he going up, she down, that they came face to face. "Marsha," he said.

"Neely." Marsha rolled the name off her tongue with surprise and anger tinged with tenderness.

To Remington, it was like she was caressing him gently prior to lovemaking. Their tryst had been hot and furious. He'd pined to be with her when he wasn't and couldn't get enough of her when he was.

"What brings you here? Were you looking for me?"

Marsha smiled, a wicked grin. "I was visiting a friend. You probably know him as he's a lawyer. Jimmy 4 by Four."

Remington could feel his lips curl in disdain. He did know the man. He'd had several run-ins with him in the courtroom, been challenged by him, and would define their relationship as adversarial. "A friend?"

Marsha tossed her hair to the side. Gave him the wicked grin. "A *very* good friend."

"My understanding is that the man never matured past that of juvenile, possibly a preteen."

"I saw your wife earlier."

Remington noticed that her cheekbone was slightly discolored. "Toots?"

Marsha snickered. "Do you have more than one wife?"

"What happened?"

"She called me a jezebel, amongst other things. And then she bit me."

"What? Bit you?" Remington's eyebrows rose in perfectly manicured arches.

Marsha stepped closer to him so that they were only inches apart. "Now I have been bit by both Mr. and Mrs. Remington. My love triangle. Neely and Toots." She shook her head. "Fuck."

Remington felt her nearness. Her skin. Her mouth. Her breasts. Almost touching. He burned with desire. "Tell me what happened."

"I ran into her in the Coffee Dog Bookstore."

He felt the shock rippled from his ears all the way to his toes. "You aren't talking with him, are you?"

"I thought you wanted to know about me and your wife writhing on the floor together. About her biting me."

He had so many questions. *What was Toots doing at Langdon's bookstore? What happened between Marsha and Toots? What was Marsha doing visiting with Jimmy 4 by Four?* As was so often the case with him, lust won the day. "Maybe we can go to our special place and talk more?"

Marsha leaned in and her lips brushed his, her tongue flickering gently into his mouth. "Oh, but you ended that, didn't you. We can't continue, you said. You seem to be sending mixed messages." She reached down and grasped his erection through the trousers, smiled, released, and walked on down the stairs.

Remington barely made it to his office, fumbling with the lock, pushing the door shut behind him, before sinking into his chair. He pulled a bottle of Blanton's Single Barrel from a drawer, along with a glass, and poured a healthy two fingers. Slugged it down.

As his arousal receded, and desire was pushed from his body, he began to be able to think logically again. First, Toots and Marsha had words that led to a physical altercation. He wondered if it was possible to not go home tonight. Maybe he could go to the lake cottage for the night? Because he most certainly did not want to face the ire that was his wife when angry.

He took his phone from his pocket and there were three voice messages and nine texts from his wife. He looked at the texts first.

Call me.

Saw your whore today.

We need to talk. Get home now.

CALL. ME.

And five more of the same. Remington sighed, put the phone down on the desk. He would let her calm down some before speaking with her. The lake cottage was probably not a good idea. He needed to engage in some domestic damage control, or his entire career could be derailed. He cringed as he realized this would probably even include cuddling his wife. And then she might, as she on very rare occasions did, want something more.

He poured another shot of liquor into the glass. Swirled it. Took just a nip. The phone rang a few bars of the *Law & Order* theme song. Not his wife. She had her own special ringtone. Remington looked at the phone. No name. He was going to ignore it, but wondered if it might be Marsha, changing her mind, agreeing to meet in their hotel room.

"Hello. Judge Remington." He smiled, thinking how Marsha liked it when he acted all official and judicial, a man in charge.

"Hello, Neely."

"Who is this?"

There was a pause. "Tara."

"Tara?" He hadn't spoken to her in years.

"How are you?"

"I'm… I'm just fine. What do you want?"

"I need to ask you something."

Remington held the phone away and looked warily at the screen. Put it back to his ear. "What?"

"Did you…"

"Did I what?"

"Did you have anything to do with Mikey's death?"

"Mike Levy?"

"Yes."

"Levy died in a freak accident."

"There was a man who came to see me. Told me that he thinks Mikey was murdered."

Remington gritted his teeth. *Langdon. Poking around. Stirring things up.* "First of all, he was not murdered. Second of all, why would I be involved in anything like that?"

"This man was pretty convincing."

"Goff Langdon?"

Again, a pause. "That's the guy."

"He's some shady private investigator just trying to shake me down. I'll handle him."

"Mikey said if anybody asked, he was going to tell them what you did."

"What? What'd I do?"

"You forced me to have an abortion."

Remington laughed hoarsely. The day just kept getting worse. "I did what?"

"You know what you did."

"Tara, I was just trying to help. You were pregnant and didn't even know who the father was. It would've ruined your life. I was just giving you wise counsel."

"You turned that Remington charm and laser intensity onto me and forced me to agree that it was for the best. But I'm not sure I really thought that."

Remington breathed in through his nose. Out through his mouth. Tried to calm himself. "You could've just said no and done whatever the hell you wanted."

"No. No I couldn't. Nobody ever told you no."

"That's hogwash."

"I didn't want to disappoint you. Not again. You were so adamant. I felt I had no choice. But let's not bog down in this. It was a long time ago. Water under the bridge. What I want to know is, did you kill Mikey?"

"Where are you, Tara?"

"A long way away. Tell me. Did you kill Mikey?"

"No. I did not kill Michael Levy. I don't know what kind of monster you imagine me to be. I'm a judge. A respected member of the community. A family man."

The other end of the line was silent for a bit. And then Tara hung up.

When Remington got home just after six, he found his wife in the kitchen making dinner. Shrimp scampi was cooking in a pan on the stove top, and she was cutting up vegetables for a salad. Her hair was carefully constructed on her head as if she'd just come from the hairdresser. The makeup was heavily painted onto her face, probably to disguise the thin scratch on her cheek, still barely visible, and the swelling under her left eye.

"Hello, dear," she said.

"Hello, honey."

He went up to their room, removed his suit jacket and tie, before coming back down to the study where he poured himself a gin and tonic.

"Will you open a bottle of white?" Toots called to him.

There was a wine cooler next to the bar and he pulled a bottle of Pinot Grigio out and corkscrewed it open. He poured a glass for Toots, put the wine back in a marble chiller, and carried it all to the dining room. The table was set and as he came in one door, Toots came in another with two plates of shrimp scampi. The salad was already on the table.

Once they were seated, Toots looked at him for the first time. "How was your day, dear?"

Remington thought about that. Marsha, Tara, and Toots. The perfect trifecta. Of regret, that is. The perfect trifecta of regret. "It was fair to middling, honey. How about your day?"

"About the same, I suppose. About the same."

Remington took a sip of gin and tonic to hide his relief. It looked like they were not going to address the elephant in the room. He had been temporarily pardoned from paying the piper for past indiscretions. He knew that the bill would be coming due before long, and his gut quailed at what the total would be.

Chapter 31

Langdon had skipped the gym this morning to have breakfast with Chabal. The television was on, and they were eating while watching the news, when the screen flashed over to a special announcement from the president.

"With the unfortunate death of Justice Benjamin Johnson, and my Constitutional responsibility to replace that justice, I have found a candidate with the strongest possible record, character, credentials, and detail to the rule of law. He is somebody who I have known since his days at Georgetown Law. It is my pleasure to nominate Judge Cornelius Remington to the Supreme Court of the United States of America. Judge Remington has been confirmed by the United States Senate three times in his career. He has had broad bi-partisan support each time and promises to bring an independent voice to the Bench who will appeal to all Americans."

The screen cut to a senator from North Carolina.

"Judge Remington is an outstanding choice. He will bring the right and left sides of Congress together and will undoubtedly win unanimous support. His record speaks for itself."

Back to the president.

"The experience that Judge Remington will bring to the Bench is immense. He has been both a prosecutor and in private practice as a defense attorney, as well as a Federal Judge. He has a mastery of the law, the ability to hone in on key issues and provide clear answers on complicated legal issues, as well as a commitment to impartial justice. Judge Remington has touched every rung of the ladder of law on his climb to this momentous day."

Cut to Judge Remington.

"The law is something that has always been of the utmost importance to me. Without that, we would have no justice, and without that, anarchy would exist. It is important to me that equality for all is achieved throughout the Constitution as we continue to interpret that document in an ever-changing modern world."

Back to the president.

"I can't wait for you to get to know Judge Remington as well as I do. America will be a better place due to his life-long commitment to bringing honesty, fairness, and integrity to the people of our great country. God Bless."

The screen cut back to the four members of the national news sitting in a semi-circle at a table.

"I think that Judge Remington is the perfect candidate to fill the void by the unfortunate death of Justice Johnson."

"He crosses the aisle with ease and pulls together Congress and the people of America."

"I mean, just look at the man's record. He is a brilliant mind with an untarnished record of fairness and honesty."

The lone woman on the panel cleared her throat and shuffled a few papers. "We do need to ask ourselves if America is best served by placing another middle-aged, middle-class, white man on the highest court in the land where he will serve for life."

Langdon clicked the television off. Stood up. "Interesting."

Chabal grabbed her plate and glass and stood as well. "Next step is to be evaluated by the American Bar Association's Standing Committee on the Federal Judiciary."

"Which he will pass with flying colors. His legal knowledge and history are not what is at question here."

"How long will that take?"

"I'm betting the president has already greased the wheels and it will take only a few days. And then on to the Senate Judiciary Committee."

"And they'll probably just give him a hearty welcome and send him to the full Senate for a vote."

"He might be confirmed within a week." Langdon shook his head. "Son of a gun."

"What can we do?"

"I don't think there is anything we can do about it."

"Nothing?"

"What do we have? He played pranks back in college. Some wild theory that he may've been involved with the death of Michael Levy, which, by the way, has no proof of connection whatsoever. He cheats on his wife. Who cares? Doesn't everybody?"

Chabal punched him in the arm. "Not everybody, bucko."

Langdon chuckled. "Well, not everybody. But fidelity certainly doesn't seem to be a trait necessary to be elected or confirmed to offices of power these days. Plus, all we have is innuendos. We have no proof."

"How about your friend *Marsha*?"

Langdon wasn't sure he liked how she said the name. Her tone belied the words of friend and suggested a much more intimate connection. "First of all, I would not classify her as *my friend*."

Chabal snickered. "One, it would seem obvious after being tackled to the ground by a lady named Toots that she has had a sexual relationship with the judge. And she seems to want to stop his nomination… confirmation as much as anybody. Why don't you persuade her to come forth and give testimony."

"I'm thinking that if she was willing to do that, she would've already offered."

"Don't really know until you ask the question, now, do you?"

They both had put their dishes away and were now in the bathroom brushing their teeth as they spoke.

Langdon spit and rinsed his toothbrush. Took a mouthful of

water. Spit again. Drank. "I can try."

Chabal followed suit. Turned and faced him. "Maybe use your manly persuasive powers on the poor woman. She won't stand a chance."

Langdon didn't really like how she laughed after this last statement.

On the way to the bookshop, the phone buzzed. It was just a number with no name but that wasn't all that unusual. He was going slow enough to be able to hear even though the top was off the Jeep, so he hit speaker and answered. "Langdon."

"This is Cooper Walker."

Hmm. Interesting, Langdon thought. Very interesting indeed. "That was quite the ringing endorsement that the president gave to Judge Remington this morning on national television."

"Where are you?"

"In my Jeep on the way to the bookshop."

"Can we meet?"

"In D.C.?"

"I'm in Brunswick. But I don't want to be seen. Especially not conversing with you. Is there somewhere we can talk on the down low?"

Langdon felt a bit like he'd just entered a spy novel. On the down low. Like Jason Bourne in Ludlum's thriller, was he, Langdon, being brought in only to be dispatched? "Talk?"

"I want to do what I can to make sure that this nomination is not a monumental mistake with long-lasting and disastrous consequences for the country."

That was quite a mouthful, Langdon thought. Just like something somebody would say to lure him into a clandestine meeting to silence him. "How about my house?"

"It might be watched."

This chilled Langdon to the bone. Here he was thinking that this was just a case of adultery, but in reality, it was far more complex and deadly than that. With frightening clarity, he suddenly realized that confirming or denying a justice to the Supreme Court was worth killing over. "How about the swinging bridge on the Androscoggin. On the Route 1 access across from Cushing Street?" That's where, Langdon figured, spies would meet. On a bridge on a river.

"Ten minutes."

"I'll be there."

Langdon hung up. At the stoplight he texted Chabal that he'd be in a bit later if she could get the bookshop opened up, that'd be great. He didn't really think Cooper was setting him up to be knocked off. That seemed a bit extreme. Plus, he liked the kid.

But it was possible that one man had been killed already in the process of making Judge Remington one of the nine most powerful people in the country. His vote would possibly determine any number of legal and social issues.

Judge Remington could be completely amoral in his ambition or there were other more powerful factors at work, machinations by shrouded figures to create the court that they wanted to achieve their own specific goals. Of course, it could all be just a figment of Langdon's imagination, and Judge Remington was no more than a philandering dog, a distinction that no longer mattered in the court of public opinion. If it ever had. History seemed to suggest that it was fine for men to step outside of their marital vows. Men would be men, or something like that. Ever since JFK took his affairs public, that is.

But Langdon knew that this was more than just a man stepping outside the bounds of matrimony. He could feel the stink of this whole thing in the marrow of his bones.

There was a tiny lot for parking on the Brunswick side of the swinging bridge. There were no cars in it on this Monday morning, a good opportunity for a surreptitious meeting with the assistant chief of staff at the White House about a nominee for the SCOTUS.

Langdon got out, convinced dog to wait a second, and then helped the fellow down. He'd recently come up a bit lame from jumping out of the Jeep, his head not realizing the aging of his body. Ain't that the truth for us all, Langdon thought.

They walked to the center of the swinging bridge, not that it really swung, but was a suspended walking bridge connecting Brunswick to Topsham. Down the river was the Fort Andross building where Jimmy's office was, and just beyond, the Sea Dog Brewery, an American pub and eatery with a fantastic view.

He didn't have long to wait as the suited lithe figure of Cooper Walker emerged from a rental car, looked left and right, before journeying to the center of the river to join Langdon and dog.

"Hello, Cooper."

"Langdon." A brief nod of the head. He leaned over and scratched dog's head.

"What brings you back to Brunswick?"

"Officially? My boss, Chief of Staff Ball sent me here to smooth things over. Make sure that you weren't making a nuisance of yourself."

"And unofficially?"

"One of the things that I'm supposed to control is the narrative of the death of Michael Levy. One of Judge Remington's old pals."

"One of the Maine Men of Mayhem." Langdon spit over the railing and watched the saliva splat into the river below. "Two of whom recently tried to kill me."

"What?" Cooper looked over at him with shock etching his features.

Langdon told him of his recent ordeal culminating in him finding and chasing Duffy and Boyle.

"Can you connect it to Remington?" Cooper asked.

Langdon shook his head. "Maybe if the cops can catch them. Not if they keep their mouths shut."

"Lot of circumstantial evidence."

"Lot of smoke on the water."

Cooper chuckled. "Leaves me with questions."

"Like what?"

Cooper leaned forward over the railing and looked down at the Androscoggin. Normally, this time of year, the water would be low and lazy. The spring rains had continued through June and July this year and the river swirled angrily.

"Do you think Levy was murdered?" he asked after a bit.

Langdon sighed. "I have it on good authority that there was bruising on his wrists and ankles like he'd been carried from somewhere and placed next to his toilet. Probably shit himself when he died and they just had to yank his pants down to make it look like he was doing his business, got zapped, and it was too much for his fragile heart."

Cooper nodded. "I saw the report. So, let's say he was murdered. Who do you think is good for it?"

"Couldn't say. Jealous lover. Robber. Road rage. Could've been anybody."

"Could've been Judge Cornelius Remington."

Langdon shrugged. "They knew each other. Seems a coincidence his buddy was murdered right before he's nominated for SCOTUS and is about to face intense background searches. But as far as evidence? Nothing."

"First of all, this was not an intense background check. Between having recently had one done and Chief Ball telling me the POTUS wanted this done in a hurry with no hiccups, it was more like a friendly meander down memory lane."

"Chief Ball?"

"That's what she likes to be called by her underlings." It was Cooper's turn to shrug. "You know, Chief of Staff Ball. Chief Ball."

"Seen her on the news. She seems to think highly of herself." Langdon watched Cooper's face for his reaction, and got just a flicker, a mixture of disdain and dislike.

"Next to the President, Chief Ball is the most powerful person in the country."

Hm, Langdon thought, wondering how correct that truly was. He'd always assumed that the Speaker of the House, the Senate Floor Leader, or even the Whip, held the most sway, but Cooper might be right. "Interesting."

"Do you have anything that might prevent the Senate Judiciary Committee from confirming Remington for the SCOTUS?"

"I got a woman who Remington paid to have sex with, and things got a little strange and naughty, as you might imagine, but she refuses to come forward in an official capacity. Seems to think that she'd be vilified, and he'd be placed on a martyr pedestal for having to deal with her lies."

"We could force her to testify."

"She's a poor mother with kids who took money for sex to put food on the table. He's Judge Remington. Who's anybody going to believe?"

"Gosh dang it, Langdon, I'm trying here."

"I think that there's another woman who Remington may've committed adultery with. Let me speak with her."

"And keep digging into the death of that Levy guy. See if anything connects back. We have three, maybe four days, and then it's too late."

Chapter 32

As Langdon watched Cooper drive off, he texted Chabal. You okay at the shop for a bit?

Sure. What's up?

Gotta go see Marsha and try to convince her to testify.

Hmm. Keep it in your pants, sailor.

Will do, Captain.

What sent you her way?

Cooper in town. Seems to be wanting to find way to hold up nomination.

Be careful.

I'll use protection.

The reply was a series of curses and emojis. Langdon had no idea what they meant. One definitely looked like a turd pile, though.

Next, Langdon called Marsha. She answered in a sleepy, yet sultry voice, with a 'good morning my handsome detective'. She agreed to speak with him at her house in half an hour, once she was *decent* and presentable.

As Langdon turned onto the Princes Point Road, he realized that he was a bit ahead of schedule, and he pulled into the boat landing, the site where he'd been bushwhacked by the two men, who he now knew were Fred Duffy and John Boyle. Two of the five Maine Men of Mayhem.

He visualized the memory, Duffy in the road, waving him down. Boyle in the passenger seat with a towel wrapped around his fake injury. The tire iron rising and descending. They must've then carried him to the fishing boat. One of them pulled his Jeep off the road where it was later found.

All, still in the light of day. It'd been a chance they'd taken. To not be seen. Sure, dusk was approaching, but was certainly not here yet. Did one of them take him in the boat while the other drove the truck to a rendezvous point?

If they moored the boat at the Dolphin Marina, is that where they'd met? Had one of them taken him by boat, hooked him to a buoy, and then met the other at the marina, and the two men had driven back to the cottage just down the street? There were so many questions, Langdon thought, and yet another new one popped into his head.

Langdon had seen their faces. The two men had not tried to hide who they were. That seemed to suggest that the plan was to kill him. A cement block attached to the leg would've done that trick just fine, but instead, he'd been attached, albeit unconscious, to a mooring in the bay, and left to live or die on his own devices. Had one of the two men gone rogue, broken the plan, and given him an opportunity to live?

His next thought had been roiling around in his brain since it'd recovered from being addled. The two men knew where he was because they were following him. Or somebody had told them where he'd be.

The latter would point the finger directly at Marsha Verhoeven. It would've been easy for her to let them know that he was coming and then notify them that he was leaving and on his way. But that didn't make any sense. Or did it?

Langdon's phone buzzed. It was Bart. "You made it back from your romantic weekend away?"

Bart said nothing for a few moments. "Hey, bud, I think I might be in love."

A fleeting thought that all first girlfriends ended up being the love of a boy's life flashed through Langdon's mind. Just, in this case, the boy was a sixty-something year-old man. "Susie, is, uh, quite a nice lady. Good for you. I'm glad you're happy."

Bart began to share what they'd done up to Bar Harbor, or down to Bar Harbor, however one wanted to look at it, but when he started to devolve into the romantic first evening they'd shared, Langdon interrupted. "Did you get my messages?"

"Yeah. There's an arrest warrant out for your two friends, Duffy and Boyle. They best hope I'm not the one to find them."

Langdon looked out at Buttermilk Cove, his eyes fluttering to the strait that went to Winnegance Bay where he'd been moored just a bit more than a week ago. *Had* one of them shown mercy and given him a chance to live?

"There's more." Langdon went on to fill Bart in on his meeting with Alice Rehnquist and how she refused to go public with her story. And how Shannon came to the bookshop claiming that Levy had been the one to have sex, or, rape, Tara, and that Tara wanted vengeance. Bart kept quiet throughout, whistling just once when Langdon shared the physical fight between Angela 'Toots' Remington and Marsha Verhoeven at the Coffee Dog Bookstore. "And this morning I met with Cooper Walker who wants me to keep looking for dirt on Remington, but this is being done without the knowledge of his boss, the chief of staff, Saylor Ball."

Bart chuckled. "You been busier than a one-legged man in an ass kicking contest."

"It's been a time of it." Langdon climbed back into the Jeep.

"Wait, didn't you tell me that Tara said that it was Chuckie, now Shannon, who had the drunken horizontal refreshment with her?"

"Yep. So, one of them is lying."

"Or too drunk to know."

"Suppose that could be true."

"What's the plan now?"

"I'm going to talk with Marsha. Find out what truly went down between her and Remington, which seems to be some sort of affair, and see if she'll testify before the Senate Judiciary Committee to that effect."

"She still bopping Jimmy?"

Langdon grimaced, as he often did when speaking with the politically incorrect Bart. "Think so. Look, I gotta go. I'm almost to her house."

"I'll get Susie to talk to Alice, see about getting her testimony, and I'll hunt down those two pricks who mashed your melon."

At least Marsha did not seem to be trying to seduce Langdon this time, he thought as he sat down across from her with a cup of coffee in a mug that said *Be the Voice, Not the Echo*. He kind of liked that. Marsha sat across from him in a bathrobe, not some silky sexy thing, but an old and bedraggled jobbie that was probably pretty darn comfortable. Her hair was askew upon her head, jutting in various directions, and her eyes looked swollen and baggy.

"I'm so sorry about what happened in your bookstore on Friday," she said. "So terribly embarrassing."

"It seemed that Mrs. Remington was quite irate with you." Langdon held back a smirk with some trouble. Irate was *quite* the understatement.

"Is that who that was? I had no idea."

"You just thought some random lady verbally and then physically accosted you?"

Marsha shrugged. "I thought she'd mistook me for somebody else."

Langdon set his coffee down and steepled his fingers under his chin. "That's not quite the truth, is it?"

"What?'

"I believe the names you levied at her were Puritan, prude, and priss. Interesting choice of insults for a woman you don't even know. I probably would've gone with something along the line of crazy, loco, or delusional to a stranger who buttonholed me in that manner."

Marsha laughed dryly. Took a sip from her own mug. "Okay. So I know who Toots is. Maybe I met her at a reunion or something."

"Or maybe you slept with her husband."

Marsha's eyes widened in momentary shock, a gut reaction that bespoke her lie, and then she seemed to realize the jig was up and her mouth compressed into a hard line. "Maybe I did."

Langdon took a sip. Waited.

Marsha stared at him.

Langdon leaned back and crossed his legs.

Marsha sighed. "It was a few years back, okay. We ran into each other down in Boston. I was at a conference. He was staying in the hotel. One night, I went in, sat down at the bar, and there he was, next to me. We hadn't seen each other in years. We talked. Had a few too many drinks. I ended up in his room. We had sex. Happy?"

"Just the one time?"

"Maybe a few times more than that."

"How many is a few?"

"Why do you want to know?"

"You told me that you hadn't spoken with Cornelius Remington since college."

"I lied."

"Why?"

Marsha's eyes seemed to have reversed vision, no longer looking out at Langdon, but inside at herself. After a few long moments, she cleared her throat. "I didn't want you to think that I'm just some spurned woman trying to get even with some bastard for dumping her."

"Are you?"

"What?"

"Are you a spurned woman trying to get even with Cornelius

Remington for breaking off your affair?"

"No. Not at all."

"How long did your affair last?"

"About a year. Every Friday night. His wife thought he was working at his office in Boston. In reality, he was with me."

"Where?"

"All over. We'd stay in cheap motels, fancy hotels, in Portland, DownEast. Rarely the same place twice. I think he thought it less likely somebody would recognize him, and me not his wife, if we kept moving. Me? I liked the adventure."

"When was this?"

"Look, everything I told you about the prick is real. I just omitted our affair, for obvious reasons."

"Obvious reasons?"

"Well, I wanted you to believe me, sure, but I also don't want to testify that I had a longstanding affair with Neely. I don't want to stand in front of a bunch of white men Senators and share the lurid details of my less-than-ideal life. Hello America, my name is Marsha Verhoeven, and I fucked a married man who I despise. Every week for a year."

Langdon watched as a tear rolled down her cheek but that was the only hint of her distress as she glared at him. "Why did you?"

Marsha shook her head slowly back and forth. "I don't know. He is incredibly charismatic. And a great lover. But a despicable human being. What's wrong with me? I've theorized that it's some twisted version of Stockholm syndrome. The judge holds power over me as he was my tormentor during college. It's like I'm one of fucking Charles Manson's groupies."

Langdon nodded. A year ago, he would've thought it hogwash. But he'd seen the hold that a man could have over a woman. In the case of Chabal, it was fear, and not lust, but the two emotions perhaps weren't all that far apart. "You told me that he never bothered you in college. That you witnessed him bullying others, but never you."

Marsha stood and crossed the living room and sat on the sofa next to Langdon. She took his hand and looked him in the eye. "The heavyset girl whose door that he propped the smelly fish water in a barrel against? That was me. I was the dork with no friends. Not a one. And any chance I had of breaking open my shell was crushed by Neely Remington. Until I graduated and left Bowdoin. Went off on my own. I told myself I wasn't going to be a victim anymore. And I wasn't. I was woman. I was powerful. I was me. And then about a year and a half ago, I ran into Neely at that hotel bar and… and it fell apart. He didn't even know who I was. We'd been fucking for several months before I told him I'd known him back in college. He still didn't remember me. But I remembered him. He possessed me." The tears were now flowing freely down her cheeks. She made no move to wipe them. Just stared Langdon in the eye.

"You could stop him." Langdon squeezed her hand gently. "You could prevent him from becoming a Supreme Court justice."

"No. No I couldn't. People would never believe me and if they did, who would care?"

"There must be receipts. People who saw you together. Witnesses."

Marsha smiled but it wasn't a bit happy. "Nobody witnessed us having sex. They will just say it is the delusions of a fat girl from Pennsylvania striking out at the popular college boy years later. People would care so little they wouldn't have to try very hard to lie to themselves and believe the bastard. Because they want to believe him. Brilliant and charismatic sociopath that he is."

Chapter 33

Mayhem was at Regal Nails in the Tontine Mall getting a manicure. They needed this as it had been too long. Fingernails were the first thing that others saw when they looked at Mayhem. Or so they presumed. Obsessed? Ha, Mayhem thought, knowing that this bordered on a fetish, this weekly trip to Regal Nails. Once, when their appointment had been postponed for two days due to a sick technician, they had gone completely bonkers and smashed a set of very expensive China.

A manicure provided many things, and one was the ability to think. The young lady attending to their cuticles at the moment knew that Mayhem didn't want idle chitchat, but absolute silence. There was gossip blather in the background from others, but it was like the flow of a brook down a mountainside to Mayhem, relaxing and soothing.

And there was so much to consider. The one blaring warning was that darn Langdon. Their mind was constantly filled with an image of the tall ginger with the sleepy eyes. At random times, his figure sprang into their mind, pulsing in warning, a horn blaring threateningly, almost like in some sci-fi movie when the spaceship has entered an asteroid field. WARNING. DANGER. WARNING. DANGER.

Langdon had to be dealt with or all their plans would be for naught. Nothing. Zilch. The only question was whether they would take care of the problem or if it would be farmed out to those two bozos? Duffy and Boyle. Two of the original five. The Maine Men of Mayhem who had existed in a long-ago universe, gone dormant, now brought back to life. A notion of the past that threatened the now and promised to destroy the future.

Of course, Duffy and Boyle would have to be dealt with at some point. Loose ends. There was no room for loose ends. Threads that threatened to unravel the best laid plans. But everything in its own due course. First Langdon. Then… Mayhem paused in their thinking. No, the next obstacle that needed removing was not Duffy and Boyle. They were insignificant fleas on the dog.

Saylor Ball. Chief Ball. The bitch knew too much. Had too much power.

Mayhem smiled. Looked at their nails. They looked good. Powerful.

Chapter 34

Late Monday morning in the bookshop was a slow time, giving Langdon and Chabal a chance to catch up on the events of the day so far. "And that about sums it up," he concluded. "Cooper is risking his career to help but I got nothing. Alice won't testify. Marsha won't testify. Duffy and Boyle are MIA. All I, all we, have is loose ends blowing in the wind."

Chabal leaned on the counter. "Maybe it's time to get to the real crux of the matter."

"What's that?"

"You've said it yourself. Marsha and Alice have said it. Adultery, even if proven, might not be enough to derail this fast-track nomination of the judge."

"But?"

"But murder certainly is."

"Levy."

"It must be connected. Too much of a coincidence not to be. And you don't—"

"Believe in coincidences." Langdon let his gaze wander out over the store. The answer probably lay within one of the thousands of mystery and thriller titles on the shelves out there. "What'd that fellow Booker claim? There are only seven basic plots, just written in different ways."

"Overcoming the monster. Protecting our innocence. That's where we're at."

Langdon nodded. "It seems that the monster began his reign in college and has continued right up until the cusp of now. And along the way, that monster killed Levy. Why?"

"Levy was going to spill the beans about Remington. Come clean. Tell everything."

"The judge couldn't have that. All his dirty little secrets spread into every crevice of society."

"So he killed Levy. Or had him killed."

"The judge would know about Levy's heart condition, as they were friends for almost forty years."

"He kills him and makes it look to be a freak accident. Or, he has Duffy and Boyle kill him, more likely. The two loyal minions."

"The death of Levy spooks Tara James, who flees to Florida to hide out." Langdon walked around the counter to the customer side and leaned in facing Chabal. "The problem is, I've been trying to dig up whatever Remington is hiding, but in reality, the doorway into the past is to find proof that he was involved in the murder of Levy. In the now."

"A recent murder certainly trumps a decades old sexual indiscretion."

"We connect Remington to the murder, him being a life-long philanderer and bully doesn't even matter."

Chabal snickered. "I think proving the judge to be a murderer should be enough to get his Supreme card revoked."

"Ha. Yes, that's true. Hard to pass judgment from behind bars."

Langdon's phone buzzed. Text from Cooper. *The American Bar Association has passed Remington on with the highest mark of 'Well Qualified'.*

Langdon looked at the time and pecked out his reply. *Isn't that extremely fast? I thought it would take a week, not four hours.*

Chief Ball started them in on their peer review back when we began our investigation. She says the word from the POTUS is to make this happen sooner than later.

Langdon looked up at Chabal who was staring at him and waiting. "The Bar Association seems to be behind him. As long as he stays ahead of them, he's not going to be behind bars. He will be the bar. Once he becomes a justice, there won't be any chance to touch him. He'll be far too powerful."

Chabal groaned.

Langdon wasn't sure if this was due to the ABA recommending Remington or the corny word play he'd used regarding jail bars and legal bars.

~ ~ ~ ~ ~

Fred Duffy and John Boyle sat on two stumps in the woods of Bowdoin. The town, not the college. They were only twelve miles from Brunswick, just across the Lisbon Falls border, but it felt like Siberia. They'd gone off trail. There were no bodies of water for fishing. It was not hunting season. Meaning, there was only the slightest of chances that anybody would stumble upon them. Across from them, side by side, were two one-man tents, green. What they ate was cold and from a can, not wanting to risk a fire.

"This sucks," Duffy said.

Boyle grinned painfully. "We knew it was all going to catch up to us eventually."

"Thirty-four-years. That's a long time."

"We should just turn ourselves in. We didn't do anything wrong."

Duffy spit. "Covering up a murder?"

"What choice did we have?"

"There are always choices. We just keep making the wrong ones."

"Neely's got clout. He'll make it go away."

"He better if he doesn't want his whole life to fall apart."

Boyle stood and threw a rock irately into the trunk of a pine tree. Even doused up with repellent, the mosquitos devoured them, and the black flies that hadn't gotten the memo they were supposed to have passed by now, swarmed around their heads in an angry tsunami of annoyance.

"How'd we get to this point?" he asked.

"One step at a time."

"You think he even knows?"

Duffy shrugged. "Hard telling."

~ ~ ~ ~ ~

Langdon walked into Blyth & Burrows on Exchange Street in Portland just before five p.m. It was a cocktail bar with a speakeasy vibe. He asked to be seated in the back room and upon passing through the opened-up bookcase and going down the stairs, he found Shannon Undergrove had beaten him here.

He'd no sooner sat down then the waiter came to get their drink order. Shannon got the 'Tom Yum Punch', and Langdon, who'd been here once before, didn't hesitate to order the 'Mutiny on the Bounty', which was an Irish whiskey with charred coconut, house falernum, pineapple absinthe, and tiki bitters. The tagline was that it drank like a Sazerac and tasted like a mutiny. The description was spot on, and he'd been looking forward to once again having another of these specialty drinks that came in its own small bottle with a glass to pour into.

"Hello, again, Shannon."

"Hello to you, Langdon."

She wore a green dress that didn't come close to reaching her knees and had a sparkly, but subtle, pattern on the front. Her natural hair was cut short, giving her a much more wholesome look than the first time he'd met her when she was wearing the platinum wig.

"Thanks for calling."

"I take it you're still investigating the case, or you wouldn't be here."

"That I am."

"I saw on the news that Corn Porn was formally nominated, approved by the ABA, and is being reviewed by that Senate committee thingy."

Langdon grinned. Corn Porn, he thought. What a nickname for a Supreme Court justice. That last thought transformed his grin to a grimace. "Yep."

"Does that make your investigation… unofficial?"

The drinks were delivered, and they both waved off ordering any food. "Well, yes, officially unofficial." Langdon grinned. "The assistant to the chief of staff of the president, Cooper Walker, has asked that I keep digging. On the down low."

"I need to reiterate something." Shannon leaned forward over the desk. "I did not rape Tara James. I did not have sex with that woman. Not in college and not five years ago."

Langdon wasn't sure who to believe in this convoluted mess of a case. "Okay."

Shannon stared at him. "I don't know why she would have said that I did."

Langdon said nothing.

"Tara wasn't a bad sort. She was just so in love with Neely that it clouded her decisions, I suppose."

"What do you mean?" Langdon asked.

"I don't know how well you know Neely. I mock him now, call him Corn Porn and whatnot, but the truth is, the man has an inner charisma that lit the souls of the people he came in contact with on fire. Probably still does, but I haven't seen him in years. When you were in his presence, it was like you were hypnotized, agreeable to whatever he suggested."

"Like a cult leader?"

Shannon slowly nodded. "Exactly like a cult leader. His power was immense. I did things that embarrass me to this day. Mistreated people. Bullied people. But where I drew the line was having drunk sex with his girlfriend."

"Tara James?"

"Yes."

"And he tried to get you to… have sex with her?"

"Yes. When I refused, he called me a homosexual in a colorful array of terrible slurs. Didn't talk to me for weeks afterward. It was like a shadow had descended upon Brunswick. I was in a fog, in the dark, depressed, kicking myself for refusing—and then he invited me back into the bright glow of his being."

"Why did he welcome you back into his realm?"

"He needed his disciples. His minions. People to do his bidding."

"You told me that it was Michael Levy who took advantage of the drunken Tara?"

Shannon nodded. "I'm sure it was on the urging of Neely. It was during the time that I had been cast out, expelled from his world for refusing to do the same thing. And then he reached out and brought me back into the fold. It wasn't for several weeks, but at one point, Mikey told me what he'd done."

"So, you were welcomed back because Remington found somebody else to do his bidding."

"Yes."

"Why?"

Shannon's eyebrows arched high. "Why what?"

Langdon contemplated this. There was a great deal to unpack here. "Why did Remington want somebody to have sex with his girlfriend?"

"I don't know. The power of it? The perverseness of it? I truly can't tell you. But I do know something that might help you out."

"Yeah? What's that?"

"He took a video of it."

"Of what?"

"Of Mikey having sex with Tara. A drunken blacked-out college junior who didn't have any idea what was going on. In other words, raping her. And, what's more, of him convincing Mikey into raping her."

"How do you know?"

"That he took video? Because he videotaped everything. Made us watch pranks we'd played, crazy things we'd done, when we weren't watching porn, that is. He loved to chronicle the adventures of the Maine Men of Mayhem, as he called it."

Langdon wondered if he'd filmed sex with Alice. Or Marsha? Was he still filming things, or had that stopped back in college? "I'm sure that any old footage has long since disappeared."

"Maybe not."

Langdon waited.

Shannon breathed deeply. Stared at a spot over Langdon's shoulder. "The last time I spoke with Neely was probably about ten years after we graduated. He'd asked me to come by his office. Same one he has now, I believe, on the river there in that old mill building. He was a prosecutor down in Portland, then, a rising star in the legal world.

"He, uh, wanted to know why we didn't hang out, do things together. I told him that I'd broken his hold on me, and that his actions and behaviors were repulsive. It got quite heated. At one point I suggested that maybe I should share some stories of who he really was with his family, peers, the ABA, and the media. Let them decide if he was a bad person or not."

Langdon realized that as Shannon traveled back in time, so did her voice, now deeper and huskier, and he could almost picture a young Chuckie Taylor sitting there across the desk from him. "What was Remington's response?"

"The room went deathly chill. His eyes seemed to glow red at me. I thought he was going to leap across the room and strangle me there and them. After a few seconds, he restrained himself. Told me that would not be a good idea because he'd documented everything. Filmed it all on the camcorder his parents gave him for Christmas his freshman year."

"Recorded the assault of Tara James by Michael Levy, you mean. What'd that have to do with you?"

"Neely stood up, walked over, and locked his office door. He then went to the closet, opened it, and unlocked a small locker or safe. From this, he pulled a VHS tape. There must've been ten or twelve to choose from. He told me this one was all me. He turned on the television, put the tape on the VCR, and played several minutes of footage. He said there was almost two hours in all."

"Footage of what?"

"Me. Christopher 'Chuckie' Taylor engaging in a myriad of horrible pranks and mischief."

"Bad enough to blackmail you into keeping your mouth shut?"

Shannon nodded.

"And he has a different tape for all of you? Duffy, Boyle, and Levy as well?"

"I don't know. I only know there was a whole stack of tapes that day. The night that I was out drinking and ran into Tara? Part of the reason for me being so upset was that I'd just gotten a note in the mail. It simply said that my history had been converted from VHS to digital. It was a simple enough reminder for me to keep my mouth shut."

"Not the sort of thing you want to store on your computer or on the cloud, not if you're worried about the FBI doing a search or being hacked by some criminal you sentenced to jail."

"Not that he is in any of the videos." Shannon spoke bitterly. "He was the puppeteer and cameraman."

"Oh, I don't know. The Remingtons of the world like proof of the power they have over other people. I'm betting that he has film of himself. Dirty little perversions that he watches in secrecy and privacy. That's how he gets his jollies."

"I think you might be right."

"Why are you telling me this? If you're afraid of it coming out?"

Shannon stood up. "Sometimes you have to hold your breath and jump. I did things back in the day that will embarrass and humiliate me. But I've come to realize that my past is something that I have to face up to, especially now, when I'm aiding and abetting a sociopath into becoming a Supreme Court justice."

Chapter 35

Bart said there was absolutely zero chance of getting a warrant to search Judge Remington's office in Fort Andross.

Langdon had no idea whether the video footage kept by the judge would incriminate him in any way. Or if it would be admissible to the Senate Judiciary Committee if obtained illegally. He figured that he would cross that bridge when he came to it.

What was it Shannon had said? Langdon wondered, as he sat in his Jeep parked behind the Coffee Dog Bookstore. Sometimes you have to hold your breath and jump.

The case was going nowhere. As far as Langdon was concerned, there wasn't an innocent one in the entire passel of former Maine Men of Mayhem, girlfriends, and victims.

The judge had a sexual relationship with Tara James in college and shared her when drunk with his friend, Chuck Taylor, or maybe it'd been Michael Levy, or both?

Marsha Verhoeven had been bullied by the judge and his Maine Men of Mayhem in college, and then, more recently, had an affair with the man, one that Toots Remington knew about.

Fred Duffy and John Boyle had clunked Langdon in the head and left him on a mooring to die but had now vanished into thin air.

Michael Levy had most likely been murdered and it'd been covered up to look like an accidental death. But he'd kept quiet all these years, suggesting his own level of guilt and involvement in everything. Was he the lynchpin upon which the entire case rested?

Langdon sighed. Smiled. At least his wife had returned to him from the nightmare that had been the legacy of the wendigo.

Uncovering the buried secrets in the closet of one Judge Cornelius Remington promised to be dirty and smear everybody nearby. Who would it benefit? Langdon knew the answer to that; he'd just been waiting for the universe to pose it directly to him. The entire world would benefit.

He reached in his console, pushed the Glock to the side, and retrieved the kit of lock picks, before locking the compartment with the pistol back up. Langdon was not as adept at picking a lock as those in the movies, but generally speaking, if not too complicated, he could fumble his way through the process and gain entry.

With another sigh, he opened the door of the Jeep and got out. It was a short walk to his destination from the back of the bookshop. This time of night, the parking lot at Fort Andross would be largely empty, and the Jeep would stick out like a sore thumb.

Langdon's lips moved, mouthing the words, *I really have no choice.*

A sane man would just walk away from this whole mess, he thought, and go home to his wonderful wife. Have a nice dinner. Watch the next episode of *Bosch: Legacy* on Amazon, or Freevee, or whatever it was. Go to bed. Make love. Sleep.

But he was a dog with a bone, as the saying went. Once begun, he couldn't let it go until he was done. Not until his gums were bloody and his teeth were chipped. Unfortunately, this bone was still attached to whatever elusive beast he was chasing, and he would have to first catch it before finishing the job at hand.

The streetlamps were lit, the sun now down, as he ambled down the sidewalk of his hometown to break into a judge's office in an effort to find proof of his being a miscreant, or at the very least, not of the highest moral fiber required of a man about to be confirmed to the Bench for life. Perhaps, a man, who should be condemned to prison for life, though.

The bar at the Wretched Lobster was one of the few places still open on this Monday night, as evidenced by three smokers in his path. He knew two of them by sight, one by name, said hello, and continued on his journey of illegal intent. The night was thick, the humidity of the day refusing to relinquish its stranglehold, turning back the coolness of the night air as if a greenhouse over Brunswick.

This was his town, a place he'd lived in his whole life, except for a short stint away at college. He'd played sports here. Had been a business owner for going on thirty years. He knew the owners of the places he walked past. The gelato place, the deli, a furniture store, an optician, natural foods, Indian food, Italian food—places he frequented and people who were his friends. Good people. And now, his Brunswick, was on the verge of sending that asshole, Cornelius Remington, off to Washington, D.C. to represent them and besmirch its good name. That wasn't going to happen.

Luckily, the Thai restaurant in Fort Andross still had a scattering of diners finishing their meals, and the entrance to the building remained unlocked to accommodate them. There was also a pizza place on the river side of the building, but it was closed on Mondays. He put on his Red Sox cap and pulled it low over his eyes to protect from prying eyes and security cameras.

Langdon walked past the Thai restaurant entrance to the stairs as if he belonged. Nobody gave him a second look as far as he could tell. The judge had his office on the third floor, facing Maine Street, the opposite of the river where Jimmy 4 by Four's law office was.

Langdon paused as he passed the repurposed artist studio that he, his family, and friends had hidden out in some twenty-five years earlier. That had been the time and incident that resulted in him being shot in the head, which on the face value, was not all that great, but the long-term effects had been a boon to both his PI practice and mystery bookstore as the resulting media coverage had been fantastic advertising.

He walked around the upstairs area and found it empty. The silence was thicker than the humidity outside. Now or never, he figured, as he approached the judge's door. The tools were already in his hand. He slid the tension wrench into the plug, or the keyhole, to apply pressure, and then delicately followed with the pick.

Langdon would never be a lock pick artist. He was not a delicate fellow. But practice allowed him to locate the six pins in this particular locking mechanism, sliding them up one at a time and keeping the pressure on them with a wrench, a tiny tool smaller than a key, until the last pin slid up, and he was able to turn the tool and open the door. Five minutes. Not too bad.

Luckily, nobody came by, even if the hushed quietude of the third floor of the old mill building roared in his ears the entire time. He stepped into the office of Judge Remington with a sigh of relief, pulling the door closed with the slightest of muffled clicks. He turned and faced the room.

A light, left on overhead, illuminated the desk, easily the most imposing thing in the room. It was over six feet long, was made of some sturdy dark wood walnut in color, offset by gold inlays of ornate craftsmanship that twisted and twined along the edges, each corner being a golden eagle. Langdon half-expected to see Judge Remington sitting in the high-backed chair facing him with a gavel in one hand and a derringer in the other.

But Langdon had the room to himself.

He went to the closet first, the place that Shannon had told him that the original VHS tapes were hidden. Langdon briefly thought that it was odd that they'd been converted from the tiny camcorder tapes to VHS, but supposed that Remington in all his perversions, liked to watch, as much for the power he held sway over people as the intimate and ugly things on screen.

Shannon had not been very forthcoming as to what he might find, other than proof that it was Michael Levy having drunken sex with a blacked-out Tara James. Proof that it was Michael, and not Shannon, then Chuckie, who had engaged in this assault.

And possibly, Corn Porn, Neely, Cornelius Remington, Judge—convincing him to assault his own girlfriend.

There was no locker in the closet. A set of judge's robes. A suit. Several pairs of shoes. One looked to be running sneakers. There was a shelf that had boxes on top. Langdon pulled these down and went through them. Knick-knacks and pictures. Nothing illegal, illicit, nor immoral.

He went to the desk. Tried the drawers. Figured that it was the locked one on the bottom right that was most likely to contain secrets. It took him two minutes to pick the lock. Just as he pulled it open, Langdon's phone buzzed.

Text from Cooper Walker. Where are you?

Langdon looked at the phone, looked at the drawer, put the phone down, and pulled out a metal box from inside the drawer. It was locked.

His phone buzzed again. He ignored it.

It took several minutes to get the metal box open. His phone buzzed several more times. He didn't think he should be telling Cooper Walker where he was.

Finally, the lock tumbled clear, and Langdon opened the box.

There was a single picture with a Post-it note. The picture was Judge Remington with a huge smile, his hands held to the side and slightly above his head, making victory signs. Langdon was reminded of Nixon.

On the Post-it note was written: *Bazinga*.

A chill crept up Langdon's spine. He looked at the text messages. There were three more from Cooper.

I hope you're not in the office of Judge Remington.

There was a tip of somebody breaking and entering.

The FBI and police are on the way.

The door opened. Two people stepped into the office with guns drawn. The right-front-breast pocket of each said FBI. Behind them were a host of blue uniforms.

"Hello Royal. Hello Parker." Langdon leaned back in his chair. "What can I do for you?"

Chapter 36

Langdon knew the Brunswick police station well. He'd been in it many times, both the old one on Federal Street, as well as the newer facility on Pleasant Street. While he'd spent some time in a cell in the old building, he hadn't had that pleasure in the ten years since they'd moved across town.

He was slightly surprised when he wasn't read his Miranda rights, miffed to be refused a phone call, and confused that he wasn't thrown into a cell block with other short-timers who would either be out soon or, if a longer stay was expected, transported to Portland.

Instead, Langdon was put into a room that might've been an interrogation room, or possibly a room for those high on booze or drugs, he wasn't quite sure. And left alone. They'd taken his phone, so he didn't know how long he'd been there, but was guessing maybe four hours, when the door opened, and a woman walked in. She looked vaguely familiar.

"Do you know who I am?" she asked.

"Do you think I might use the men's room first and then we'll do introductions?" he replied.

She smiled. Opened the door. A uniform who Langdon didn't recognize led him to the bathroom, waited outside the door, and brought him back.

The piss had been long and satisfying. This had provided him the opportunity to sift through his mind who the woman was and develop some theories as to why she was here.

She was still standing alone in the room when he was deposited back inside, the door pulled shut behind him.

"I am Saylor Ball."

Langdon stepped forward and held out his hand. "Chief Ball. Langdon. Good to meet you."

She made no move to take his hand but merely glared at him.

"Don't worry, I washed my hands. Soap and all. If they're a tad bit moist yet, I might've rushed the drying process a bit."

"Have a seat, Mr. Langdon." She gestured to a metal chair separated from another one by a table that was also metal.

He pulled his hand back and sat down. "Thank you for coming to my office today," he said. "What is it that I can do for you?"

Her smile was thin and didn't reach past her flared nostrils. "You are a royal pain in the ass."

Langdon smirked. "That's funny, see, as the man who arrested, well, no, detained me, I suppose, as I was not read my rights, well his name is Royal. Royal Delgado."

"Yes, I know. Agent Delgado works for me."

"Well, that's not quite true, now, is it? Royal Delgado is an FBI agent, and the FBI reports to the Director of the National Intelligence. Hm." Langdon shook his head. "And I don't even know who that is. Something I should know. If you can just give me my phone back, I'll look it up and tell you his or her name. It's on the tip of my tongue."

"If the Director of the National Intelligence needs to report to *her* boss, *she* must go through me. Make no mistake, Mr. Langdon, I am in control of the FBI."

Langdon leaned back and looked at Saylor Ball, chief of staff to the president, more closely. She had auburn hair that cascaded just over her shoulders, parted in the middle, revealing a long face with wide light-blue eyes. She had a long neck and a slightly crooked nose.

Langdon said nothing. Waited.

"Have you not been told to cease and desist from investigating Judge Remington?"

He wondered if she knew about her assistant's continued involvement and the probes into the judge's background, as well as his current life. "I'm aware that the official inquiries of Remington have been halted."

"Why were you found in his office this past evening?"

Langdon assumed that this meant they had indeed passed from the night of one day to the morning of the next. "I went to pay him a visit. The door was open. I was afraid that there might've been some foul play going on."

"Five minutes to pick that lock? You should be ashamed of yourself."

Langdon knew that Fort Andross did not have cameras in the hallways. He knew this because Jimmy 4 by Four complained about this lack of security. Just to be safe, he'd carefully looked for one, in case there'd been some change to policy. There had been nothing. He surmised that this meant there'd been a hidden, private, camera pointed at the judge's door, being monitored by… the FBI?

"I trust that you found nothing incriminating?" Saylor gave her tight-lipped smile that was really just a baring of the teeth.

Langdon remained silent.

"So far your investigation has turned up nothing," Saylor said. "It has gotten you bashed on the head, taken you for a swim, which, by the way, I recently heard a rumor, that you almost had another swim with a crocodile with an interesting moniker, and all for what?"

Langdon remained silent.

"It must be humbling to suck on so many levels."

And then he knew. Sometimes keeping one's mouth shut paid dividends. This last line from Saylor Ball was a quote from Sheldon Cooper of the *The Big Bang Theory*. The same as the one-word note in the lock box in the desk. Bazinga. This suggested that, not only was she a fan of the show and Sheldon, but that it was her that left the note knowing that he was going to find it. And the FBI had just been waiting to arrest him. He'd been set up.

"What do you want?" he asked.

"I want you to stop."

"Why?"

"Because you are a thorn in the side of democracy."

"Some would suggest that people being thorns is the primary principle of democracy."

"You are a thorn more in line with Sandy AOC than a citizen."

Langdon wasn't sure what was more offensive, calling AOC by her high school nickname, the way she said AOC, or the suggestion that this was some sort of insult to him. "What are you trying to hide?"

Saylor blew out a deep breath of disgust. "Hide? I'm trying to hide nothing. Neely has had an exhaustive background check on three occasions now. He has passed them with flying colors. The ABA has given him the highest possible recommendation in terms of suitability for being a justice. In the next couple of days, the Judiciary Committee will send it to the Senate floor for a vote with their unanimous approval. I consider myself a very smart woman. Don't you think that if there was something wrong with Neely that I'd know it?"

Langdon thought it interesting that she referred to Judge Remington as Neely. "You set me up."

"I'm willing to let you walk out of here if you agree to cease and desist harassing… Judge Remington."

Langdon went with silent.

"It's not just yourself you should worry about."

"What's that supposed to mean?"

"Your daughter recently marched in the Dyke Protest Parade in New York. People get arrested at that sort of thing all the time."

Langdon gripped the table hard with both hands in an effort to not wrap them around Saylor Ball's neck. That would extend his stay in jail. A sliver of clarity sliced through his rage. She was trying to provoke him, he realized, because once charged with breaking and entering, he would most likely be out on bail in a matter of hours. But not if he attacked the chief of staff to the President of the United States.

"Spend more time with your wife, Mr. Langdon. It is the least you could do after leading her into that horrible ordeal last year."

"I would like to speak with my lawyer."

"You haven't been charged with anything as of yet."

"I'd like a phone call."

"You have not been arrested, nor booked, Mr. Langdon, so you are not allowed that privilege."

Langdon leaned back in his chair and allowed the tension to dissipate from his body. Took a breath. Tried his best to look nonchalant. "You can't arrest me, can you? Because the media exposure would be horrible for… Neely. PI breaks into office of man about to be confirmed to the SCOTUS. Why? Reporters might ask me that. Hell, as soon as you charge me, the big guns from all the major networks will be flying into Brunswick. Asking me what I was doing?"

There was a knock at the door and then Royal Delgado, the FBI agent, came into the room. He whispered into the ear of Saylor.

Langdon distinctly heard the word lawyer, and then 4 by Four. He smiled. They'd tried to keep his detention a secret, but Bart must've heard about it and called Jimmy, and now his lawyer and friend was at the desk making a ruckus, if Langdon knew him at all. Especially if the phone call had jerked the man from the comforts of a woman in his bed.

Saylor abruptly stood up almost slamming her head into the FBI agent's chin. "Remember that actions have consequences, Mr. Langdon."

"That's what this is all about."

His words stopped her at the door. She stood with her back to them both. "Turn him loose."

Jimmy drove Langdon to pick up his Jeep and he filled him in on everything that had happened. When he got home, Bart was sitting with Chabal at the dining room table. He repeated everything one more time.

After Bart left, Langdon suggested he was going to take a shower to rinse the events of the past hours away.

Chabal looked at him with a deceptively guileless face. "You know, I always wondered about those women who fall in love with prison inmates. The bad boys. I never quite understood it, until now, that is. You are my sexy prison fellow, and you are looking just fine."

Langdon grinned. "Even if I reek of jail?"

"Especially because you reek of jail."

Chabal stood and stepped over to his chair and gave him a long kiss. That led to the bedroom and some canoodling. Which, in turn, led to several hours of sleep. It was eight the next morning before Langdon made it to the shower but not much later when he walked out the door to go see a woman.

Chapter 37

Before pulling out of the garage, Langdon texted Missouri to call him. The threat from Saylor Ball had to be treated delicately, but most certainly not adhered to. Langdon, family, and friends had been imperiled before by governors, rich landowners, environmentalists, Boston gangsters, Russian gangsters, powerful lobbyists, mercenaries, and most recently, a group so radical and menacing that they'd been expelled from the Church of Satan.

He was most certainly not going to back down because he'd been warned off by the chief of staff to the POTUS. Even if the weapons at her disposal might be more dangerous than any of the other enemies he'd ever faced. At the same time, he figured that she had to at least give the appearance of being law abiding. What was her game?

The obvious answer was to ensure that Cornelius Remington took a seat on the Bench of the highest court in the land. Why? She had slipped and several times called him Neely in a very familiar way, suggesting more than a working knowledge, and if he was correct, more intimate than just a friend.

What did she hope to gain by having an affair with a future Supreme Court justice? Perhaps to manipulate him once he was seated. Perhaps she'd been threatened in some way—blackmailed or intimidated. Maybe she was being bribed by powerful interest groups to make it happen. It was even possible that her anxiety of the future of the country was pushing her to seat the candidate she most strongly felt was right for the job. Power, fear, money, and angst were all powerful catalysts in determining individual actions. Or it could be that she was just wicked.

As he got on I-95 going south, his phone buzzed. He answered, hit speaker, and put the phone on his lap.

"Morning, Missouri Langdon."

"Hi, Dad. What's up? Is Chabal okay?"

He usually left phone calls to her discretion and what worked best for her, so a text message saying call me was, indeed, out of the ordinary. "She's fine. Actually, better than fine. Thanks to you and the others, Chabal seems to have finally put the wendigo behind her."

"That's great news, Dad."

"Yep."

"So, what's up?"

"You on your way to work?"

"Yes. You got five minutes and then I disappear into the subway tunnels. You just call to say you miss me?"

Langdon chuckled. "Yes. And…."

It was Missouri's turn to laugh. "And?"

"I had a conversation with Saylor Ball in the wee hours of this morning."

"Whoa, Dad, you hanging out with the chief of staff now?"

"I guess you could say that. She asked that I stop investigating Remington."

"In person, nonetheless. You run into her having drinks at Goldilocks?"

"It was a more intimate setting at the police station. Just me and her in a room."

"You going to tell me about it?"

Langdon gave her a thumbnail sketch of the events of the previous evening. "But the thing is, she brought your name up."

"My name?"

"Yes. She pointed out how you participated in the Dyke March back in June and mentioned that people get arrested in protests like that all the time."

"She was threatening to have me arrested for marching in the Dyke Parade?"

"That's the long and short of it."

"She doesn't have the balls." Missouri snickered. "Pun intended."

Langdon smiled, shook his head. "Just be careful, okay? She is the right hand of the most powerful person in the world."

"The red right hand, bringing divine vengeance upon us queers, I suppose. Thanks for the heads up, Dad. I'll do some looking into who Saylor Ball really is and get back to you. Got to go now, about to descend into the caverns of Brooklyn. Love you."

The call disconnected before Langdon could reply, the words *love you* slipping from his lips too late. He wasn't sure what he expected from his headstrong and socially active daughter. Exactly what he'd gotten, most likely, but at least she was aware of the peril now.

Forty-five minutes later, Langdon parked on the street outside of Shannon Undergrove's house in Ogunquit. It was now just past nine. He assumed this was where he would find her, seeing as she seemed to work later in the day and into the night. He was flying solo today, having sent dog to the bookshop with Chabal.

It took three separate episodes of heavy knocking before the door opened and a sleepy-eyed Shannon opened the door. No wig, just her short black hair. No make-up. She was wearing sweatpants, not yoga pants, and a T-shirt that had a tri-colored cat and butterflies on it, pink, yellow, and blue.

"I suppose you're not here to bring me donuts and coffee," she said.

"You set me up."

Shannon opened the door. "Come on in."

Langdon followed her to the kitchen. The small home was

tastefully decorated and comfortable looking. Shannon hit a button on the coffee maker, and it began to percolate.

"Why?" He sat down in a wooden chair at the table.

"You want a cup of coffee?"

"Sure."

"Just give me a minute. I need caffeine."

Langdon sat silently while the coffee finished brewing. Shannon poured a dollop of low-fat milk into one cup and looked at him with eyebrows arched and jug poised. He shook his head no and she set the milk down and poured the coffee, giving him the black one.

They sat for two more minutes sipping the coffee before Shannon spoke. "It was me that raped Tara James. Not Michael Levy."

Langdon nodded. "Tara recalls it differently. She said that you were both drunk and that she didn't blame you for what occurred. It was something that happened, no more. That she even told you this."

"Tara is truly a seraph. An angel in disguise here on earth. Yes, I was drinking that night. And yes, Neely pressured me to lie with her. Told me that she wanted it. That she'd confided that she wanted me. When I still refused, he called me horrible insults and slurs about me being gay. I was Chuckie then, and still refusing to accept my true identity, and it was these accusations on his part that forced me to sexually assault Tara. But that is on me and not anybody else."

"And Remington has threatened to expose your indiscretion if you don't do his bidding? He told you to give me the story about the fake tapes, knowing that I'd break into his office, and face arrest?"

"Arrests? I don't know anything about any of that." Shannon sighed. "Or it's just me hiding my head in the sand again. Yes. Neely paid me a visit. Told me to meet with you and pass on the thing about the tapes."

"You've been doing his bidding for some time now, haven't you?"

"It stopped when I changed my name and my gender and moved out of Brunswick. Until this last time, that is. I had a few years of reprieve while he lost sight of me."

A tightening of her eyes suggested to Langdon this was not entirely accurate, but he let it go for now. "It was thirty-five years ago, and Tara doesn't hold you responsible for what happened. Why don't you just tell Remington to go fuck himself?"

Shannon sighed. Took a sip of coffee. Stared at the cup. Took another sip. "Before my transition, I was too weak. I am stronger now. But even if Tara doesn't blame me, I blame myself. And the community of people within which I now live? My actions would make me a pariah. It is indefensible."

"I imagine you know it'll never stop. Remington will be your puppet master for the rest of your life if you allow it."

"I know. But I don't see any other options."

"Who killed Michael Levy? Was it you?"

Shannon made a noise between a grunt and a sigh. "I don't know."

"You told me you thought it was Tara. Because it was him who raped her. But now we know that's not true."

"Mikey knew everything."

"What do you mean?"

Shannon shook her head.

"Tell me. Was there actual video? Or was that just a fabrication to get me in hot water?"

"Would it be so bad if Neely became a justice?"

Langdon sighed. "It sounds like he is a terribly immoral person."

"And who isn't?"

~ ~ ~ ~ ~

Judge Remington was feeling very pleased with himself. Once again, he'd proven that a superior intellectual capacity was more valuable than resorting to violence. He chuckled loudly as he sat at his desk in his office, the very same place Langdon had been the night before. Right before he'd been taken off to jail.

The poor sap had fallen hook line and sinker for the load of crap that he had Chuckie deliver. Or Shannon. Whatever he or she was called now. The thought of them stirred something in him, an urge that he tried to ignore, but it was wired into him by the genetic master who'd created him, and the best he could do was damp it down.

Now, the last obstacle in his path in becoming a justice of the Supreme Court had been removed. He rubbed his hands together and considered a diabolical laugh like the evil villains in cartoons emitted when a plan came together. Justice Remington. It had a ring to it.

His phone buzzed with a text. Just a single number. 9.

The number of justices. The code that said he should answer the next phone call from an unknown number. He could barely wait to share with Saylor the reference that he'd used in wiping the smirk from Langdon's face. If he had indeed gotten so far as to open the empty metal box in the bottom drawer. *The Big Bang Theory* was their show, Neely and Saylor, what they watched after fornicating. The big bang.

It buzzed with a call. "Hello, Sugar Pie."

"Were you behind setting Langdon up?" It was Saylor Ball.

"Why, yes, I was." Remington flushed with pleasure.

"Are you a fucking idiot?"

"What?"

"If he gets arrested the media will be all over it. He will tell his suspicions to the national news. Goddammit Neely, what were you thinking?

"First of all, don't talk to me like that. I will not tolerate being treated like some… some… misbehaving miscreant." Remington's flush of pleasure had quickly gone hot with anger, again reminding him of the close parallels of elation and fury, no, intertwined emotions, really. "But it is too late to second guess. The deed is done."

"I let him go."

"What… you…."

"Agent Parker notified me last night and I immediately took a jet into Brunswick."

"You're in Brunswick?"

"I tried to intimidate Langdon into keeping quiet, but I don't think I was successful."

"You spoke with Langdon?"

"I turned him loose, Neely. If we formally arrested the man, it would be a shit show of epic proportions. And the president would most definitely rescind his nomination before the judiciary committee even deemed you unfit for the position."

"On the say so of some bookstore owner?"

"Do you want the top news investigators in the world digging into your life? What you've done to Tara James? The radical left would have a hay day. What you've done with Shannon Undergrove? The conservatives would crucify you for that. We must muzzle this before anybody gets wind of it."

Remington nodded, his temper cooling, if not his irritation. "The man won't stop."

"I will deal with it. There are ways to stop people without allowing them the limelight."

Remington realized this was one of the moments to not pry further, endowing him with plausible deniability at a later time if necessary. "You are in town still?"

"Wheels up at noon."

"That's almost three hours from now."

"I am currently in our normal spot in room 122. Naked. In bed. I have left a key to the room over the right front tire of your car. As usual."

Saylor hung up and Remington stared for just a moment at the phone. From elation at hearing her voice to fury at the way she spoke to him and on to full-blown lust. The perfect trifecta of emotions like a Molotov cocktail ready to be ignited.

The door opened and his wife came into the office. "We have to talk," she said.

"I have an appointment and was just about to leave."

"This won't take long."

Looking at his comely wife and thinking about luscious Saylor Ball was an odd combination of angst roiling in his stomach. It brought a tightness to his chest and a prickling sensation in the center of his forehead. "What is it?"

"I have been a good wife."

"Yes." He could at least give her that.

"I have been at your side as your career has risen, raised our children, kept our home, and been the dutiful and doting wife."

"Toots, I really have to get going." He stood up.

"Sit."

"Toots—"

"I have looked the other way as you share your ding-a-ling with other women."

He sat.

"Quite frankly, I don't care if you indulge your needs with other women. But you know that I don't like it when your affairs become more than just a tingle you want to itch."

"Toots—"

"I want you to stop screwing Saylor Ball."

Remington tried to conceal the wave of emotions washing across his face. His perfect trifecta of emotions, his Molotov cocktail of elation, fury, and lust had just been doused by an ice-cold bucket of Toots.

"Do you understand me?" she asked.

Remington nodded.

"Good. You may go now. I will walk you out."

He walked her to her car and held the door for her, leaned down, kissed her cheek, shut the door and then went to his own car and drove to the hotel where Saylor was lying naked in bed. One last time couldn't hurt. And what Toots didn't know.... How had she known, he wondered? How much did she know?

Then his thoughts filtered back to the nubile and exotic bare-skinned bod of Saylor and all else was banished from his being by his inflamed desire.

~ ~ ~ ~ ~

Toots was watering the plants when Cornelius came through the front door just before eleven in the morning. He didn't call a greeting but went straight up the stairs and a minute later she heard the shower start.

A strange time to take a shower, she thought. His jacket was tossed on the chair in the front hallway. He knew that she hated that sort of disorder. She went and picked it up, hanging it on the coat rack.

A thought struck her, and she paused, her eyes flickering to the stairs, the sound of the shower still running. Toots reached in the pocket of Cornelius' jacket. Pulled a plastic card out. It was one of those hotel keys.

A second morning shower and a hotel key in his pocket. Interesting. Infuriating.

Chapter 38

Langdon was in his office out back of the Coffee Dog Bookstore with his feet up on the desk, chair tipped back, and eyes closed. Back to his thinking pose.

The morning conversation with Shannon had been enlightening. The judge had been blackmailing her, and before that, him, for years. For an incident involving Tara James that Tara did not hold Shannon responsible for. Something did not quite add up. Shannon had deliberately set Langdon up to be arrested by sending him on a wild goose chase into Remington's office. There appeared to be missing piece to this particular puzzle, and he couldn't quite sort out what it was.

Michael Levy had been murdered. Bart had told him the case was officially reopened by the Major Crime Unit. Not that there were any leads. As far as Langdon was concerned, the most likely reason for his slaying and subsequent cover-up was to shut his mouth. He, like the others, knew of Remington's bad behavior.

It certainly seemed a possibility that Michael Levy had decided to come out with whatever secret he was hiding regarding the judge and therefore had been killed to quiet him.

Duffy and Boyle had dropped off the face of the earth, but they were the most likely suspects in the killing, in Langdon's mind anyway, after they'd clunked him in the head and left him attached to a mooring in the ocean.

The wife of Remington, Toots, had started a brawl with Marsha

Verhoeven about an affair the two had recently had, even though the judge had bullied Marsha back in their college days.

There was a knock at the door and then Starling poked his head in the door. "Tara James is her to see you."

Langdon stood in surprise as Starling stepped aside to let Tara enter the office.

"You might want to come in and hear this as well, Jonny," she said.

Langdon pursed his lips, confused for just a moment, before putting together that she was talking to Jonathan Starling. He'd always been Star, or Starling, possibly Jonathan, but Jonny just seemed like a completely different moniker for the man he knew.

"What brings you back to Maine?" he asked.

"Too damn hot in Florida." Tara sat in a chair and patted the seat next to her. "Join us, Jonny, won't you?"

Langdon sat back down. "Chabal and Raven both out there?"

Starling nodded.

"Well, then, have a seat. I think you two know each other?"

Tara snickered.

Starling blushed. He looked as if he'd rather have swum with Bloody Bill Anderson than sit down next to Tara, but he did.

"Where are you at with your investigation of Neely Remington?" Tara's blue eyes glittered like sapphires set in her thin-tan cheeks.

Langdon contemplated the question and what to share. "Well, for one, Shannon initially tried to deny it was her who slept with you on that drunken night but now admits that it was her. And… Remington has been using this against her to blackmail her."

Tara grinned. "It is odd how Chuckie is now a she who once had sex with me. I guess that would be my one curious college encounter."

"You were pretty upset about what happened the summer you interned with me." Starling's voice was gravel from a sand pit.

Tara touched his shoulder with her hand and let it rest there. "That was then. This is now."

"What are you saying?"

"Time has a way of either sharpening or sanding memories. At the end of that summer I spent with you, Jonny, I realized that sometimes things just happen. Chuckie and me? Not so different than you and me. Me an intern. You my boss. The times we had. If you'd pressured me into sex with you, well then, that'd be horrific. That would have Me Too all over it. But you didn't. It was mutual."

Starling squirmed a bit uncomfortably even though she was letting him off the hook for his transgressions thirty-five years prior. "I'm sorry. What I did was wrong. You were young and vulnerable and I took advantage."

Tara smiled, her eyes softening to the color of robin's eggs. "No, Jonny. I wasn't a kid. You were sweet and helped me get through a confusing time. And then we were done, and it was time for me to go back."

Starling sighed. Said nothing.

Tara looked back at Langdon. "I been asking around. Watching the news. It looks like Neely is a shoo-in to be confirmed."

Langdon shrugged. "I know at least one woman from college who was severely bullied by him, but she wants no part of testifying. Shannon has been blackmailed for years to keep quiet about… something? Something more than what happened between the two of you. But I don't know what and she claims that what she did to you would make her a pariah in her new community, much less whatever else he has on her. I have a woman who was paid to have sex with Neely, but she refuses to go public because, A, she thinks it would be useless, and B, she doesn't want her family and friends to know that she prostituted herself. Two former mates of yours who whacked me in the head and tried to kill me are on the lam and missing—"

"Who?"

"Fred Duffy and John Boyle."

"That's surprising."

Langdon rolled that response over in his mind. "What is

surprising?"

"Fred and John were not a bad sort. I can't imagine them trying to kill anybody."

"From my viewpoint, this whole thing stinks in the worst possible way." Langdon let his frustration and anger creep into his voice. An anger that was most usually buried deep, hidden beneath a calm demeanor. But once awakened, this ancient Viking blind rage known as *berserkergang* could not so easily be put back in the bottle. "And the indentation in my skull suggests they are not the nice young boys you remember."

"Things get so complicated." Tara's voice was so soft it could barely be heard. "Life."

"The Maine Men of Mayhem and you, Tara James, because you were basically one of them, weren't you, as Remington's girlfriend?"

"Neely was so goddamn charismatic." Tara took a deep breath. "It was inconceivable to say no to him. Impossible to break away from his web. Once you were in, there was no leaving. I fully understand the sway that cult leaders have over their groups. How preachers can stand at a pulpit and spit forth hate and diatribe against marginalized groups and have their congregations eat it up like candy corn on Halloween night."

Langdon let the last statement echo into silence. "Why are you here, Tara?"

"We tried to get away. We did. But he just keeps reeling us back in."

"And those who tried to slip the hook were killed."

"What? Who?"

"Have you not heard? The MCU at the state police has begun an investigation into the murder of Michael Levy."

Tara gave a small gasp. "You mean Mikey's death… it's true then? What you told me in Florida?"

"It looks like he was killed and then carried from elsewhere to the bathroom in his home."

"Why?"

"You tell me."

"I don't know."

"Why are you here?" Langdon could feel the ripples rising from the depths of his being with a deep ocean blackness that threatened to consume him if not controlled.

"To help make things right, I suppose. To stop him before the Senate confirms Neely to a position where he can pull a Jim Jones and force America to drink the Flavor Aid."

"How?"

A single tear seeped forth from Tara's left eye and began to creep its way down her cheek. "I was not one of his boys back in college. I don't really have any direct proof of any misdeeds bordering on criminal that would give pause to his unanimous confirmation to the SCOTUS."

"What then?"

"Even though he is liberal in many ways, his stance on abortion has given right wing conservatives hope. The Evangelicals. The Christian Right."

Langdon nodded. Remington had gone on record saying that his religion gave him serious cause for concern regarding abortion.

"And?"

Tara sighed. Suddenly looked over her shoulder like she might make a break for the door. Sighed again. Squared her shoulders and raised her chin and stared Langdon in the eye. "Back in college, he convinced me at the time, against my wishes, to have an abortion. I think that would put the brakes on with some of the senators in the confirmation process."

"I'm sorry, but I really don't think that will do the trick." Langdon didn't want to belittle this momentous decision made by a young Tara James so many years ago, but it was too little, too late.

"It will be a start. Others will follow."

That was a cryptic statement if he'd ever heard one, Langdon thought. *It will be a start. Others will follow.* But it might just be true. Shannon. Marsha. Maybe he could hunt down Duffy and Boyle. It was a start.

Starling cleared his throat. "When did you have the abortion?"

Tara turned from Langdon to Starling, her eyes softening again. She put her hand back on his shoulder. "November 22nd of my senior year. I was three months pregnant."

Chapter 39

Langdon was facing another hefty lunch bill at Hog Heaven. He made a mental note to not check in with Bart on updates around mealtimes, which was really, quite impossible, as it was always mealtime for the behemoth Bart. He was also tasked with bringing food back for Chabal and Raven. Dog had chosen to come along for the ride.

Jonathan Starling had requested the afternoon off, presumably to go home and ponder the significance of the news just shared by Tara James. That he might have been the father who never was. Three months before her abortion, to the day, on August 22nd, was the last time they had sex before she returned to college for her senior year.

Tara said that it was also possible that Cornelius Remington was the father, as she'd slept with him her first night back, before remembering all the reasons she'd broken it off with him in the first place. That was what prompted her to go and forgive Chuckie Taylor for the drunken sex they'd engaged in, an act that she held herself responsible for as much as him.

And then she'd missed her period. The test came back positive. The doctor confirmed it. Tara agonized over what to do. After a few weeks of deliberation, she decided that she would have the baby. Then Remington caught wind of it, she having shared the information with a friend, who blabbed to another, and so on, until it reached his ears.

Tara never told him about Starling. Remington assumed he was the father. She tried to let on that he might not be, that there existed another possibility, but he smirked away those suggestions as if she were trying to put one over on him. In his world, everything revolved around him. Tara considered telling him about the summer of sex with Starling, but in the end, as it was so often the wont with Remington, she bowed down and allowed him to dictate the terms.

And those terms were an abortion. No paternity test was performed, and nobody would ever know for certain whether the father was Starling or Remington. Langdon shook his head in wonder at the two men being unknowingly linked together for all those years. Starling took the news hard. At one point he'd had the world by the tail, a brilliant young lawyer on the rise, and the next he was in over his head and driven into a bottle of brown liquor that took ten years of his life. And now to know that he'd once flirted with being a father?

As far as Langdon knew, Starling had never once dated in the twenty-five years of sobriety following his dance with decoction and the devil. No chance at fatherhood. No legacy to follow his footsteps. And just this morning, he'd discovered how close he'd come to creating offspring. Langdon had a feeling that he knew what thoughts were going through his friend's head. If Tara had come to him, would everything be different? Would they have married, had a child, had more kids, bought a house, and avoided the dark spell of his life that had tainted everything since?

Bart was in an unmarked police car in the back corner of Hog Heaven and Langdon backed the Jeep in next to him in the shade of a tree. It was a tad on the hot side to be baking in the opened-up Jeep. Bart had a peculiar rule that accepting lunch from a citizen while sitting in a town car was bribery while it was not the case if he was in said bribers vehicle. Plus, dog preferred the airy Jeep.

After Bart climbed into the Jeep, they exchanged mundane pleasantries until the server, who was not Susie, took their order.

Then, Langdon updated the cop on how Shannon was being

blackmailed by Remington for her involvement with Tara James and had thus set Langdon up to be arrested per the judge's instructions. When he told Bart about the abortion, Langdon left out the details about Starling's affair with Tara and focused on how Remington had convinced her to terminate the pregnancy.

Bart had his arm into the backseat rubbing dog's head. "You been busy since getting hauled in last night and not being released until the wee hours of the morning."

"You got to get Susie to convince her friend Alice to share her story with the Judiciary Committee."

"Case is closed, my friend. Even if Alice wanted to come forward, who would she come forward to?"

"The hearing is still going on."

"Not with any new evidence."

The server came back with a second person carrying a tray overloaded with burgers, shakes, fries, onion rings, and baskets of various food items for Bart. Langdon had merely ordered a chicken salad roll, fries, and a bottled water. Once the food was delivered, he then put in the order for Chabal and Raven to take back to them. Bart's lunch was almost twice what the three of them had gotten combined.

Langdon waited until Bart had half of a McDonny burger in his mouth before resuming his train of thought. "Then we need to tie him to the murder of Michael Levy."

Bart snorted and talked around the mouthful. "You gonna have to take that up with your buddy, that dandy, Jackson Brooks, at the State Police. You know MCU handles all the murders in Maine. Got nothing to do with me."

"Thought you were going to ask the chief if you could work with the Staties."

"Yeah. I did. Got my ass chewed. The chief told me in rather colorful language to stay in my own lane. Something about the next time that goddamn Langdon, meaning you, not your lovely wife, steers me down one of those dark country roads it was going to be the road to retirement for me. Or something like that. Sounded better when he said it, to be honest."

Langdon took a bite of the chicken salad roll and chewed thoughtfully. "It's turned into a real pressure cooker."

"What's that?"

"Well, you said that Medicolegal Death Investigator, Dallas Barbeau, had some reservations about the accidental part of the death but was told by ole Floppy Bums to rule it a terrible tragedy and move on. Then Levy is cremated before anybody can even blink. Now, when you bring it up to the chief, he flips out on you. A bit of an overreaction, I'd say, for just wanting to further investigate an incredibly weird death."

"Well, the truth is, it's not ours anyway you look at it. Murder happened in Topsham."

Langdon nodded. "I don't have any friends in the Topsham PD."

"Thought maybe the chief would let me work with them and MCU on it, seeing as there seems to be such a connection to Brunswick, but, yeah, let's face it, the chief don't like you much. But this was a bit over the top for him." Bart gave him the side eye. "You gonna eat those fries?"

Langdon dumped most of his fries in the latest empty basket on Bart's lap. "He afraid I'm going to do his job for him again?"

Bart fiddled with his phone—the buttons tiny for his fingers that looked like full-size carrots attached to a cow hock. "I got you Barbeau's cell phone number. Texting it to you now. Leave my name out of it. My next demotion is going to be to bottle collector."

"Any luck tracking down Duffy and Boyle?" Langdon asked as his phone buzzed with the incoming text.

"Ya know how I said the chief don't like you much?" Bart belched. "Well, he ain't looked too hard for a couple of fellows who bonked you and tied you to a mooring. Heard him say the other day that they deserved a medal, if anything."

"Doesn't anybody care that this morally devoid dude who is possibly a murderer is about to become a Supreme Court justice?"

Bart opened the door, turned and looked at Langdon. "I don't think morals is any longer a part of the criteria for political office."

Langdon sighed as Bart squeezed forth from the Jeep and lumbered away toward his own vehicle. "What do you think, dog, is America in an ethical conundrum?"

The beautiful thing about dog was that enigmas like this didn't much bother him. He was more concerned about what food scraps Bart might have loosed into the passenger seat.

Langdon looked at the text message from Bart with the phone number. Called it. No answer. Texted. **Dallas. This is Langdon. I need to speak with you about the Levy murder. Call me.**

He went to start the Jeep and his phone buzzed. He was expecting a text back from Dallas Barbeau telling him to get lost. It was not. It was from Marsha. **I have information for you. Come to my house at two this afternoon.**

Langdon pondered that request. The first time he'd visited this woman, she'd tried to seduce him, and he'd been waylaid upon leaving and left tethered to a mooring in the ocean. Was she now planning on finishing the job?

An hour later, after Chabal ate her lunch and was ensconced in the passenger seat of the Jeep, dog banished to the back, Langdon was on the way to Marsha's home on the Princes Point Road.

His phone buzzed. It was from Dallas. **Meet me today at the Maquoit Bay Boat Launch. 4. Come alone.**

Langdon texted back at the Cook's Corner light. **K.**

"Who's that?" Chabal asked.

"The medical examiner who worked the Levy death. He seemed to think there were some suspicious pieces but was shut down from up high."

"Shut down? By Floppy Bum?" Chabal said with a wicked grin.

Gosh, he sure had missed that wicked grin, Langdon thought. "Yep. Chief Medical Examiner Doctor Martin Flockenham himself."

Chabal smirked. "Sounds like an Albert Brooks spoof name. Did he agree to speak with you?"

"Wants to meet out to the boat launch at Maquoit today at four."

"I'll come along."

Langdon looked sideways as he took the right onto the Princes Point Road. "He said come alone."

"What if it's a set up?"

"What?"

"They're trying to shut you up, Langdon. And the problem is, *they* could be anybody." Chabal reached inside her blouse to fondle the butt of her pistol in the side holster underneath. "And I thought I might like to keep you around for a bit longer. On this side of the ground and not in some prison or government dark site."

"I think you might be overreacting. Dr. Dallas Barbeau has been an upstanding man in the community for thirty years. Lives in Topsham. Has a private practice as well as working at Mid Coast."

"Yet you bring me along for backup with Marsha Verhoeven?"

"Marsha seems to use flirtation as a tool in her arsenal. I thought your presence might remove that complication."

"Complication? Flirtation?"

Langdon chuckled. "By complication, I just mean that I want to keep things focused on the case at hand."

Chabal smirked. "And you are so damn sexy that the woman can't but help be diverted by your smoking good looks."

Langdon nodded. "And my natural charisma."

Chabal hit him on the arm. "Well, if she comes onto you in front of me, I might just shoot her."

"That might be a bit drastic." Langdon pulled into the driveway. "But I do think that Marsha Verhoeven tries to manipulate her surroundings. To what purpose, I'm not quite sure."

Chabal snickered. "Wouldn't be the first time some lady has used Jimmy's appetence for her own purpose."

"First, rein in the big words, two, don't shoot anybody unless you have to, and three—"

"Gotcha. Let's skip the lecture and go see this Mata Hari."

Marsha opened the front door, wearing not a skimpy bikini, but an equally seductive summer sun dress.

"Langdon," she said. "And my dear Chabal. You look wonderfully better than that dreadful night at the campfire."

Chabal smiled. "Thank you. It was a turning point."

"I can't imagine what you must've gone through. That doctor was going to eat you?"

"So he said."

"One day, you'll have to tell me how you got yourself in such a predicament, honey."

"And maybe you can tell me how you pissed ole Toots off so bad that she attacked you in my bookshop."

Marsha grinned thinly at Chabal. "But… where are my manners? Come in. Come in."

She led them into the house that could've been a Pottery Barn showroom. Two sofas and two swivel armchairs of neutral shades of whites and light brown topped with throw pillows of bright colors were interspersed with tan and beige wooden tables. These were topped with little wicker baskets, frames, old books, candles, and several ornamental keys. Driftwood collections, signs, and prints of horses filled the walls. It was all meant to give a vintage, cottage-like feel to the place, but Langdon just felt crowded.

Once they were seated with matching ocean blue stoneware mugs, Langdon had opted for coffee, Chabal for tea—Langdon cut right to the chase. "You said that you had information?"

Marsha tsked, admonishing his lack of social graces. "I got a phone call from Freddy this morning."

"Fred Duffy?"

"That's the one."

Langdon let that settle for a few seconds. "I didn't know you kept up with him."

"Let's not get bogged down in details that don't really matter, now, shall we?"

Langdon thought this was a good time to say nothing and wait. He took a careful sip of the coffee. It was very good. He looked over at Chabal. Shook his head slightly. Smiled with his eyes. He saw that she got the tongue-in-cheek suggestion that this was not a good time to shoot Marsha. Chabal smiled back with her eyes.

"I wouldn't say we were exactly friends, Freddy and me," Marsha said. "But we've kept up some over the years."

Langdon nodded.

"I was able to convince him to speak with you."

This was one of the men who'd almost killed Langdon upon leaving Marsha's house and she was now admitting to being friends, well, at least acquaintances with the man. "Why would he do that?"

"He wants to tell you the truth."

"How he tried to kill me?"

"What do you mean?"

"He and Boyle were the two fellows who ambushed me after I left here a couple weeks back. Is he supposed to be telling me why he did that?"

"I don't know anything about that."

Langdon looked Marsha square in the eye and couldn't tell if she were lying or not.

Chapter 40

Langdon and Chabal were discussing the latest revelations from Marsha while driving home when the world erupted around them as if some cosmic invasion. Lights, sirens, screeching tires—it was like a B movie on steroids. Several police cars blocked the road a hundred yards before the lights to Cooks Corner. Instead of getting caught in the maelstrom, Langdon banged a left to take the back way home through Coastal Landing.

As if on cue, his phone buzzed with a call from Bart. "What's going on?" Langdon answered.

"Dead body in a motel out by Walmart."

Langdon pondered that. A lot of noise for a dead body. "Murder?"

"Seems likely."

"We just drove past. A lot of action. I wouldn't be surprised if the National Guard was there."

"They might be. It's a real shit show."

"Who got killed?" That was the million-dollar question Langdon had been wanting to ask, even if his mind was still preoccupied with Marsha's offer for Duffy and Boyle. That was to meet with them the next day, as long as he promised not to turn them in until a deal had been agreed upon. "Some celebrity?"

"You could say that."

Langdon grunted in exasperation. This was typical Bart. The man hated to part from juicy morsels of gossip. It was a currency he hoarded and shared only in the smallest of portions. "Look, I got some info on how to find Duffy and Boyle."

"You don't want to hear who just got greased?"

"Look, I got enough going on. I got a lead on the two dirtballs who tried to kill me."

"I think you're going to want to hear who the dead woman is at the motel."

"Okay, okay, Bart, spill it. Who got murdered?"

"It was Saylor Ball. The chief of staff to the POTUS."

At fifteen minutes before four, Langdon pulled the Jeep into the Maquoit Bay boat launch. He'd left messages for Cooper Walker regarding the death of his boss, but he didn't really expect to hear back from him anytime soon. The young man was most certainly in way over his head, with the death of his immediate boss and all.

There was a small dirt parking area for about five cars at the boat launch, a spot where people often came to sit, eat their lunch, drink a cup of coffee, and look at the water. During low tide it was a favorite spot of clamdiggers, who most often used the launch for their airboats.

At four on the dot, a BMW pulled in next to him. If the man was trying to be clandestine and keep things on the down low, he was failing miserably. Langdon thought back to his own lime green Mustang in the Florida Keys.

Dallas climbed out, looked both ways nervously, and then back to Langdon. He was a short man, maybe a few inches over five feet, very fit, with the looks of a serious runner to his lean frame. Ray Ban Wayfarers hid his eyes, and Langdon figured that the man probably thought he looked like Tom Cruise in *Risky Business*. Maybe if he was forty years younger, but at least his height was right.

"You Langdon?" the man asked.

"Yep. You Dallas Barbeau?"

Langdon looked in his rearview mirror. A woman with a light

scarf and dark glasses of her own was walking a brown chocolate Lab alongside the road. Chabal had refused to not provide backup, especially with the most-recent murder of Saylor Ball.

"What can I do for you?"

Langdon nodded his head. "Get in."

Dallas stepped back as if he were going to run. "What?"

"Listen, man, I just want to talk to you." Langdon spoke in his most soothing voice. This was not one of his strengths. "And you stick out like a sore thumb standing there."

Dallas hesitated, nodded, and walked around the back and then climbed into the passenger seat. "What do you want?"

Langdon shook his head slowly back and forth. "I'm not sure."

"This is about Michael Levy?"

"I was told that you had reasonable suspicion to believe his death was no accident."

"His neighbor called the police when he couldn't get ahold of him. The cops took another day to go into the home. He'd been dead alone in the bathroom for four days. Yet, it was still obvious that he had bruising on his wrists and ankles that suggested he'd been carried somewhere before his death."

"Was there anything else to suggest some sort of struggle? A knot on his head, bruising of his face, skin under his fingernails?"

Dallas looked around nervously. The only other presence was the lady down by the boat launch throwing a ball into the water for a chocolate Lab. Dog was not much of a retriever but did love swimming after the ball but then dropping it back in the shallow water so that Chabal had use a stick to get it back.

"Levy had two small red marks on his neck. It was hard to be certain, as the man had been dead for four days when I did the autopsy."

"Certain of what? That they were vampire teeth marks?"

Dallas didn't crack the smallest of smiles but rather shot Langdon an extremely disproving glance. "They were consistent with the marks left by the barbed prongs of a Taser."

Langdon nodded. He'd seen firsthand those same marks. Two round dots, similar to a double tick bite, small bullseyes imprinted into the skin. "And no other signs of altercation?"

"No. His nose was bloodied and there was bruising on his face, but he was found face down, so if he received an electric jolt that caused a heart attack while sitting on the toilet and fell forward?" Dallas shrugged.

"So, he could've been knocked out, carried into the bathroom, had his pants yanked down and sat on the toilet, Tased, had a heart attack—and boom—died."

"Or been Tased first. It took him several hours to die from the heart attack."

"And you shared this with…." Langdon almost said ole Floppy Bum but caught himself. "Chief Medical Examiner Martin Flockenham?"

"Yes. He wanted no part of it. Took a cursory look at Levy, said the two marks could've been caused by just about anything including a spider bite and told me to wrap it up and report it as a terrible accident. So I did. But it didn't sit right with me."

"Did you do anything about it?"

"No. But Bart told me you think that Judge Remington might have something to do with Levy's death. And that you were investigating some irregularities in the man's moral turpitude. So I shared what I knew with Bart, who I am sure shared it with you, and here we are."

"And the MCU has spoken with you? Now that the case has been reopened?"

"Yes. I took pictures of the marks of course, but with the body cremated? I get the sense they are just doing their cursory due diligence and will shuffle it off."

"Isn't that an oxymoron? Cursory and due diligence?"

This earned a tight grin from Dallas. "They are putting up a good show of being thorough."

They sat quiet for a moment, looking at the water, Mere Point across the way, and the woman throwing a ball for a dog.

"In your estimation, Michael Levy was murdered?" Langdon finally asked.

"Yes. And in your estimation, you believe that Judge Remington had something to do with his death?"

Langdon nodded. "Yes."

"Why?"

"I don't know exactly. But the judge has many repugnant characteristics. His history is littered with actions more in line with a slimeball than a Supreme Court justice. And it's quite likely that Michael Levy knew and was considering sharing some of these more egregious offenses."

"They knew each other?"

"Friends since college."

"You have any proof of his less than moral tendencies?"

"Nobody willing to come forward and make a statement."

"What are you going to do?"

"I don't know. It seems that nobody cares."

After Dallas drove off, Chabal came and opened the back gate and let dog jump in. He, of course, was soaking wet, and shook, drenching the back of Langdon's head and the interior of the Jeep. Chabal thought it quite funny as she had not yet gotten into the passenger seat. Until he leaped into her seat, that is, saturating it with sodden dog and salt water.

It was time for dog's dinner so they went home, Langdon thinking he might stop back into the bookshop afterward, but was surprised by a car in the driveway. Not just any car, he realized, but a Mercedes AMG E 63 S. He couldn't think of anybody who drove such an expensive vehicle, even if well suited for the Maine winters. Langdon was even more taken aback when Angela 'Toots'

Remington stepped out of the car.

Her dyed black hair appeared slightly ruffled on her head. Her face had aged in the few days since he'd last seen her wrestling with Marsha Verhoeven on the floor of the bookstore. Certainly, she'd aged since the first day they'd met at her house, when he'd been welcomed in along with Missouri. It would seem that being the wife of a judge under the scrutiny of the entire nation awaiting approval to the Supreme Court by the Senate was an aging experience.

"Mr. Langdon, I need to speak with you." Her thin eyebrows scrunched towards each other, and her lips were pressed in a perfectly straight line across her face.

"Hello, Mrs. Remington. Have you met my wife, Chabal?"

Toots cast an impatient glance at Chabal. "I need you to stop harassing my husband."

"I don't know what you mean by that," he said.

"I have been assured that the official aspect of your background check into my husband has been concluded. Yet, you persist."

Dog was a bit confused as to why they were standing in the driveway and not going inside to fill his bowl with dinner.

"When I first came to visit you, Mrs. Remington, you alluded to affairs that your husband has engaged in. More recently, you attacked a woman in my bookstore, presumably, because she had been one of those women you spoke bitterly about. It is your words and actions as much as anything that have kept me involved. I don't believe your husband has the moral integrity required of the position he is being considered for."

"Marsha Verhoeven did not have an affair with my husband. She spouted untrue lies about him to all who would listen. Because he turned down her advances. She has been obsessed with Neely since their college days."

"How so?"

"Phone calls. Emails. Text messages. Letters." Toots took an envelope and handed it to Langdon. "I brought you one example of hundreds."

Langdon took it from her, looked at the front addressed to Cornelius Remington, from Marsha Verhoeven, slid the single piece of stationary out, and unfolded it. It was beige in color and had the initials MAV at the top.

> *Dearest Neely,*
> *I am devastated by loneliness and wish that you could find it in your soul and your heart to be with me. I could make you so happy, much more than that cow of a wife of yours and would dedicate every day to pleasing you. I know that you only avoid me because you long to be with me as much as I do with you. Let's stop all the pretense and be together. I don't know what I'll do if I can't have you. Please. I love you. And I know that you love me.*
> *All my love,*
> *Marsha*

He read it through twice before handing it to Chabal to read.

"You are saying that your husband and Marsha Verhoeven never engaged in an affair?" he asked Toots.

"No, of course not. She has been fabricating stories about him as long as we've been together. Like I said, she has been infatuated with him since college. I've begged him to get a restraining order. We have no pets now, but I always worried back when we did, when the children were young, that we'd come home to one of them boiling in a pot. You know, like Glen Close did to the rabbit in that movie *Fatal Attraction*."

"Why?"

Toots fidgeted slightly, shifted her feet, and then looked at Langdon defiantly. "Neely told me that he played a prank on her in college. Something about some smelly sea water. Afterward, he felt bad about it, and went and apologized. She tried to kiss him and spent the next few months telling everybody that they were dating. She's whacko, is what she is."

"Where is your husband, Mrs. Remington?"

"He flew to D.C. this morning. He is being interviewed tomorrow on the Senate floor."

Chapter 41

Langdon was lying wide awake at 5:00 a.m. trying to process the latest curve ball thrown by none other than Toots Remington. Much of the case he'd constructed thus far had been at the direction of Marsha. Ever since being steered to meet with her by Jimmy who was hoping to reconnect with her.

It had been Marsha who told him about the mean-spirited pranks played by the Maine Men of Mayhem at Bowdoin College. It was her who pointed him to the whereabouts of Shannon Undergrove, previously known as Chuckie Taylor. Marsha, who tried to seduce Langdon at her home, and then immediately afterward, he was waylaid by Fred Duffy and John Boyle. Two men whom she had just arranged to meet with Langdon.

His thoughts were interrupted by a knocking at the front door. Dog erupted from a prone position on the floor to flat on all four feet in a split second and exited the room in a stampede of barks.

Langdon went to the safe and got his Glock. Maybe he was being paranoid, but Michael Levy had been killed, Langdon had been almost killed, and yesterday, Saylor Ball had been murdered. So, yes, he grabbed his pistol, clipped the magazine in, while Chabal did the same with her Smith & Wesson Shield. He lay the gun down, pulled sweatpants over his boxers, tied them tight, and put the Glock in the back waistband, before sliding a baggy T-shirt on.

With a nod, he followed dog to the front door. Chabal stayed at the end of the hallway with her pistol at the ready.

Through the glass panes of the door, Langdon could see Cooper Walker standing on the front porch. He waved an okay back to Chabal, pushed dog aside, and opened the door.

"Sorry about the early hour," Cooper said by way of greeting.

"Come on in."

Cooper looked as if he hadn't slept, his eyes red with black smudges, but his hair was still perfectly coiffed upon his head and his suit was unwrinkled.

Langdon had set the coffee to brew at six, so he now hit the go button, and it began to percolate. "Coffee?"

"Please."

Chabal came out of the bedroom with a sweatshirt over her pajamas. "Good morning."

Cooper's face broke into a thousand-watt smile. "Chabal Langdon. So good to finally meet you. I'm Cooper Walker." He looked at Langdon. "Acting chief of staff to the POTUS."

Langdon nodded. It seemed wrong to congratulate somebody on a promotion that occurred because another had died. "The details surrounding the death of Chief Ball have been securely guarded. My buddy with the police department couldn't even find out anything. He said the motel was locked up tighter than a gnat's ass."

"She was found with a plastic bag on her head with a plastic tie around her neck holding it in place. The initial report is she died of suffocation."

Langdon stood and grabbed a container from the fridge and three mugs. "Creamer? We do this gourmet stuff."

Cooper shook his head. "Black is fine."

Langdon handed him a steaming mug. "Why are you here?"

"You were one of the last people to see her alive. After you broke into the judge's office, were detained by the FBI, and interrogated by Chief Ball. Saylor never showed up back at her room in the Bernard." Cooper took a sip of the coffee. "Instead, she was found naked and suffocated in a motel out past Cook's Corner. Under a false name. I was wondering if you knew anything about it."

"When was the time of death?"

"Between ten yesterday morning and one in the afternoon. The ME determined the earlier time, and one is when the cleaning lady opened the door and found her. She was supposed to fly out at noon and never showed."

"You don't really think I had anything to do with her death, do you?"

"What did she say to you at the police station in the interrogation room?"

"She told me to lay off the investigation. Threatened my daughter. Disparaged AOC. And let slip that she set the whole thing up with two separate *Big Bang* references."

Cooper pursed his lips. "Big Bang?"

"The locked drawer I broke into had the single word, Bazinga, from Sheldon Cooper, written on a piece of paper. Meaning Gotcha. And then she told me that 'it must be humbling to suck on so many levels', which is another… huh, interesting. She's a Sheldon Cooper fan, and your name is Cooper. You suppose that's why you got hired?"

Cooper gave a thin-lipped smile. "Maybe. Just maybe. I've come to find that my views on many things are different than that of Chief Ball."

"Any marks of a struggle?"

"It looks like a Taser was used on her. One prong mark in her neck and one in her left breast. Probably shot from about five feet. The initial report is she might have been shocked repeatedly, and once incapacitated, had the bag placed upon her head, zip tied, and then shocked her again so she was unable to rip the bag free until she asphyxiated."

"Naked? At a motel under a false name? It sounds like she was having a secret rendezvous."

"That would be my thought."

"Find who she was sleeping with, and most likely you find her killer."

"The FBI is digging into it."

Langdon leaned back in his chair. "Why are you here? You don't really believe me to be a suspect, do you?"

"Only two people in Brunswick that Chief Ball knows, as far as I can tell."

"Between the hours of ten and one on that day I was in Ogunquit speaking with Shannon Undergrove."

Cooper nodded. "I can have that confirmed."

"Which leaves us one other person."

"It's my belief that Chief Ball and Judge Remington were engaged in an affair. That something went wrong. Maybe she told him she was going to get the president to rescind the nomination before these allegations came out." Cooper shrugged. "Or something like that."

"Wow. That's a pretty strong statement. What makes you think that?"

"A thousand little things. But, trust me, the two of them had some special accord."

"Okay. So you didn't come here to accuse me of murder. Let's be clear. What do you want?"

"What do you have on Judge Remington?"

"Officially or unofficially?"

"Both."

"There is a woman he bullied in college and supposedly had an affair with, but the veracity of that has recently been called into question. I've spoken with a woman who claims that he paid her on several occasions for sex. Another woman that says he pressured her to have an abortion in college. He is close friends with two men who tried to kill me. There is the suspicion that Michael Levy was killed to keep him quiet about something. That's about it. All pretty thin."

Langdon refrained from mentioning that he was going to meet

with Duffy and Boyle. He had, after all, promised to hear them out without having them immediately arrested.

Cooper drummed his fingers on the table. "Get me statements from all three women, recorded, as well as one from yourself. Have them written, notarized, and recorded."

"One of the women is an unreliable source at this point and the other two refuse to testify."

"I know. You said that the other day. But now I am acting chief of staff. And this is not for the Senate. This is for the president. If I can convince him that there is sufficient circumstantial evidence to call into question the judge's character and integrity, he might just rescind the nomination."

An hour after Cooper left to fly back to D.C., Langdon and Chabal were at the bike path. This time they didn't bother with the leash. Dog was down by the river chasing a squirrel when Alice came along with her little Yorkie, right on time for her 7:00 a.m. walk. Langdon knew she lived just around the corner and guessed that her three children were settled in front of the television with bowls of cereal while she walked the dog.

"Hello, Alice." Langdon felt like he was the streetwalker approaching the potential John, or did they call the customer a Jane when the roles were reversed? He wasn't sure. "Can we walk with you?"

Alice snorted. "I knew I should've changed my walk time. My half hour of alone time a day. But when? Midnight? Why won't you just leave me alone."

Langdon and Chabal fell into step with her, trusting that dog would catch up.

"What if we could protect your anonymity and still wreck Remington's nomination to the Supreme Court?" he asked.

"How you plan on doing that?"

Alice had long legs and seemed intent on leaving them in the dust. That and being twenty years younger was giving Chabal a run for her money and testing Langdon's wind.

"The chief of staff to the president would like your written account of what happened. He has agreed to take that, along with some other like evidence of the man's poor moral character, directly to his boss, the president."

"Wasn't that the chief of staff who got killed out to the Greenlander Motel yesterday? That's what I heard, anyway."

"Yep. And the replacement for her doesn't seem to have such a sparkle for Remington that she did."

"What happened to that lady, anyway?" Alice stopped walking and stared at Langdon. "Was she killed to keep her mouth shut or something?"

Langdon started to reply that it was nothing like that, but then reconsidered. It would not be fair to Alice to give her false assurances. "I don't know. She was murdered. Why? I don't have any idea."

"And I suppose you can't promise to keep my name out of this whole mess. If the president wants to throw me in front of a bunch of rich white men from the old boys' club posing as the Senate, then he will, and they will pick my life apart."

"No. No I can't." Langdon sighed. "I'm sorry to have bothered you."

He turned back the way they'd come, Chabal at his side. The woman had a point. And it was her decision.

They'd gone about five steps when Alice's voice, fearful but laced with determination, chased them down. "I'll do it."

Chapter 42

Langdon had rousted Jimmy 4 by Four from bed and convinced him to meet them at his Fort Andross legal office. The man did not often see south of 10:00 a.m. for arrival time to work, the perks of being the boss in a single attorney firm.

Chabal recorded Alice's story while Langdon typed it up. The initial advances that Remington made to the sultry thirty-four-year-old mother of three. Her rejections of him. And then how she'd been caught soliciting sex and gone in front of the judge and how the man had smiled wickedly at her, knowing that she was now in his web and would have to do what he said.

It had not been just once, as she originally claimed, but had now been nine times he'd requested favors from her, and had not paid five hundred, but merely a hundred for each disgusting encounter. He liked to role play, her being the defendant in his courtroom, which she was, and then exerting his power over her, which he was. And her name was always Tara.

Alice admitted that after Judge Remington had pushed her into prostituting herself, that she had done it with other men as well, almost as if the seal was broken. The money she received for her services helped immensely with paying the bills. But it had been the judge who'd pushed her into it in the first place, who underpaid her, and who she felt the most revulsion for.

They read through the transcript, amended a few pieces slightly, and then Alice signed, while Langdon and Chabal witnessed, and

Jimmy stamped it and signed, making it an official document for Cooper Walker to take to the president. Then they brought Alice home.

For the next visit, with Tara James, Starling accompanied Langdon while Chabal stayed to work the bookshop. Tara was staying with a cousin in Pownal. When Langdon knocked on the door of the farmhouse in the countryside of the rural community, he was quite grateful that the door was answered by a middle-aged woman who looked nothing like the Florida cousins who had accosted him and almost forced him to swim with a reptile named Bloody Bill.

"Yes?" she said.

"Hello. My name is Langdon, and this is Jonathan Starling. We need to speak with Tara."

"Come in. She's been expecting you."

Tara was in the kitchen sitting at a solid wooden table, and they joined her. The woman offered coffee or tea, and when declined, left.

The three of them sat silent for a moment. Tara had an FSU sweatshirt on, and her hair was back in a hairband. She was casual, but exuded elegance at the same time. Just like the opposing cousins from Florida and Maine appeared to be opposites.

Starling was the first to break the peace. "Why didn't you tell me before?"

Tara reached over and grasped his hand. "We were a summer fling. Nothing more. You knew it. I knew it. I didn't need to burden your mind with this."

"But you considered keeping the child?"

A reticence filled the air for almost a minute. "Yes."

"Why didn't you? And if you had, would you have told me then?"

"How about I answer the second question first. If the baby had not been Neely's, yes, I would've contacted you and given you the opportunity to be part of its life."

After a few moments, Starling nodded. His creased and weathered face was like an Easter Island statue. Stony, stoic, and secretive. "And the first question?"

"I spoke with three people. Neely, first, of course, who was adamant that I have an abortion. That a child would ruin our lives. That *he* had ambitions. And they did *not* include getting married and having a child in college, or rather, just as we graduated."

Langdon and Starling remained as quiet as church mice. Three tears chased each other down Tara's cheek.

"That was when I spoke to Chuckie and told him that I did not hold him responsible for having drunken sex with me. Truth be told," she looked at Starling, "I had quite a few partners in college and since. I've never been all that shy about rolling around in the hay with somebody. I suppose that's why I never got married."

After another long silence, Langdon thought it time to move the story forward. "And you told Chuckie about being pregnant?"

"Yes. And asked him what he thought I should do. He was all for me getting an abortion. Told me all the reasons why I should. Yada, yada, yada."

Langdon liked the *Seinfeld* reference. "So, he and Remington both urged you to get the abortion?"

"Yes."

"And who was the third person?"

"Mikey Levy. He was an adamant no, which I kind of figured. He was a staunch Catholic, Father Levy we used to call him. He was extremely opposed to me doing so. Had me convinced as a matter of fact to not do it. And then…." Tears started to cascade more freely down the angular cheeks of Tara.

Starling handed her a handkerchief. She wiped her eyes. Her face. Continued. "When I told Neely I was going to have the baby he blew a gasket. Told me he was going to tell everybody I was a whore and I slept around, and any number of people could be the father. He railed against me until he wore me down and I agreed to have the abortion. To his credit, he did pay for half."

"I understand it was a difficult decision to make," Starling said. "And I understand why you didn't tell me."

"Mikey called me, you know, three days before he died, and he told me that he was going to ruin Remington's career as an esteemed judge and member of the community. He said he just couldn't take the smug-faced smirking bastard any longer and was going to go public about the fact that he forced me to have an abortion back in college. Not quite true, by the way, as it was my decision, but he certainly influenced me. When I heard Mikey died, there was a part of me that was relieved, you know, because I didn't want the dark secrets of the past catching up to me. Does that make me a bad person?"

"No." Starling squeezed her hand. "We all carry enough guilt around without taking the weight of honest emotions and heaping it on our conscience. "

"Do you think Neely killed Mikey? To keep him quiet?" Tara's eyes blazed from sad to outrage in a nanosecond.

"I don't know," Langdon said. "Possibly. Did you keep up with him?"

"After… well, after… you know, I steered clear of Neely. Didn't see him, speak to him, or anything. But I kept up a bit with the others. They weren't a bad lot, just came under the sway of the charismatic headlights of Neely is all."

Langdon thought of mentioning that Duffy and Boyle had tried to kill him, or at least seriously injure him. But he had more pressing concerns to take care of at the moment. "Will you make a statement for the eyes of the president to what you just shared with us? I can't promise that it won't come out, become public, but I have been assured that it won't. Unless it has to."

"Yes. Yes I will. I am just as guilty as Neely. But he has refused to definitively say where he stands on abortion and maybe this will force his hand in the Senate hearings. And if he killed Mikey to keep him quiet? I don't even care if I must testify to the Senate, on national TV, and confess in church. I will do it."

Tara followed them back to Brunswick and Jimmy's office where they repeated the process of recording both in audio and written word her statement, only this time the second witness was Starling and not Chabal.

Star walked back to the Coffee Dog Bookstore and Jimmy went with Langdon to pay a visit to Marsha Verhoeven. She'd agreed to meet Jimmy at Sugar Magnolias for a late lunch.

It was one of those beautiful Maine summer days that reminded Langdon why he lived here, and not further south, the icy cold grip of winter a dim memory in the recesses of his mind. The humidity that sometimes plagued August had broken, the temperature a dry and crisp 78°. Sugar Magnolias was just off the main drag below Bowdoin College.

The mile between Fort Andross and the restaurant encompassed downtown. As Langdon drove the Jeep down the wide Maine Street, he took a moment to appreciate his town. Trees provided shade on the sidewalks in front of the local businesses, including his own bookshop. People he knew stood and chatted, walked, went into restaurants, returned to their jobs, and shopped. Intermingled with them were the tourists that sustained these small businesses for the course of the year.

There was a thriving writing, artist, and creative community in the town of Brunswick, balanced with white-collar professionals and blue-collar workers, making for a diversity of class. Bowdoin College and the previous Brunswick Naval Air Station had provided a bit of racial diversity to the town, more than many places, if not much at all, but as of late, an immigrant influx had begun to further bolster that potpourri of cultures that still lagged behind much of the nation but was certainly on the upswing.

This was his town and he'd supported it every step of the way, fighting when he had to, participating when he could, and feeling proud even when there were struggles. And what he most definitely did not want was to send an emissary from his town to be a national disgrace to the Supreme Court. It was crucial to stop the confirmation of Cornelius Remington before it was too late, and Brunswick became the place that the adulterating murdering SCOTUS came from.

Marsha was not yet there, and they grabbed a table on the outside patio. Langdon stepped inside to say hello to the owners, and their daughter, who worked as the bartender. When he came back out, Marsha was sitting across from Jimmy.

He took a moment to puzzle over who she really was before joining them at the table. She had the magnetic personality of a movie star. Marsha wore a yellow floral-print sundress that made her red hair all the more luminous, which in turn, revealed the snow-whiteness of her exposed skin, marked by the occasional freckle. She sat casually in her chair like she was posing in a model photo shoot.

But, Langdon mulled in his head, were movie stars and models ever really comfortable in their own skin? They spent so much time being somebody else, it would seem easy to lose track of themselves. Perhaps that confidence they projected was just acting and posing? Who was the real Marsha Verhoeven?

"Langdon, are you going to come join us, or just stand there and gawk?" she asked.

He grinned, caught like a schoolboy staring at the pretty girl in class. "Hello again, Marsha."

"I'm glad you're here. I heard back from Freddy."

Langdon sat down at the round table.

"He wants to come clean on everything."

"What does that mean?" Langdon asked.

Marsha gave the smallest twitch of her shoulder. "How would I know?"

The waitress came and took their drink orders. Langdon went with lemonade while Jimmy got a vodka on the rocks and Marsha had a glass of Chablis.

"What does Freddy have to say?" Langdon tried for nonchalant. He was talking with a woman he didn't trust about meeting with a man who'd tried to kill him.

"Him and John will meet you at six at the Town Commons."

"In the parking lot?"

"He said that you should take the path to the right and just start walking."

Langdon chuckled. "So they can finish the job they started and kill me?"

Again, the slightest twitch of Marsha's shoulder. "I am only the purveyor of news. Do what you will."

"Angela Remington came to my house yesterday evening." Langdon leaned forward and tried to bypass the green sunglasses Marsha used to conceal herself.

Marsha scoffed. "And what did *Toots* have to say?"

"She said that you never had an affair with Remington. That you were infatuated with the man and had been stalking him since college."

Anger or fear flared her nostrils. A muted red crept across her cheeks. Then, the slight twitch of the shoulders, and the moment passed. "Of course that is what Neely told her when she discovered our correspondences and broke it off with me. Toots is just a stork with her head stuck in the sand."

Chapter 43

Marsha had agreed to go on record about being bullied by Remington and having had a year-long affair with him. Back to Jimmy's office they had gone. This time the witness along with Langdon was Jimmy's receptionist. Langdon then sent what they had to Cooper Walker. There was more to come, but this was a good starting point.

When Marsha and Jimmy started talking syrupy about going to her place for a nap, Langdon vacated the premises and went back to the bookstore. He was waiting on a call back from Shannon Undergrove, had a meeting that might actually be an ambush with Duffy and Boyle in two hours, and a mountain of information to sift through.

It had been a fruitful day thus far. He'd gotten the green light from Cooper Walker to gather anonymous statements defiling the moral character of Judge Cornelius Remington that would be only for the ears of the president. And now, some nine hours later, he'd gathered notarized allegations from Alice Rehnquist, Tara James, and Marsha Verhoeven.

One had been paid for sex, another pushed into having an abortion, and the third bullied coupled with adultery. Three women who'd been used poorly by Remington. Yet to come, he wanted to gather a statement from a fourth woman, Shannon, and meet with two other original survivors of the Maine Men of Mayhem, Fred Duffy and John Boyle. Two men who had assaulted Langdon, most likely on orders from Remington.

By the end of the day, Langdon figured he'd be able to share enough information with Cooper that if it got to the ear of the POTUS, would ruin the career of Cornelius Remington.

Even if the only one of the lot who Langdon felt comfortable believing was Alice Rehnquist. She alone appeared to have no ulterior motive nor contradictory story, other than wanting to put food on the table for her kids.

Langdon gave the nod to the second most plausible being Tara James, even though her cousins had done a number on Langdon that almost ended with him being so much chum in a pond. If she hadn't interfered and saved his bacon that might be all she wrote for one Maine bookstore owner and PI. If he were a betting man, Langdon would place a wager that Tara had fled to Florida because she possessed information not yet shared that she feared might get her killed. But she had come back.

Shannon Undergrove had initially cast the blame on assaulting Tara upon the dead Michael Levy and had set Langdon up to be taken into custody after breaking into the judge's chambers under false pretenses. How reliable was her accusations of Remington that she was being blackmailed by the man?

There was something slippery about Marsha Verhoeven that was perhaps the most concerning to Langdon. One moment the professional businesswoman, the next dating a friend of his, and out-of-the-blue she transformed into Mata Hari, Cleopatra, and Marilyn Monroe all rolled into one as she tried to seduce Langdon. She was a friend of a bullied girl in college, and then she *was* the bullied girl. She hated the ground Remington walked on and then she had a purported affair with the man. An affair that Toots Remington said was a fabrication and that she was actually no more than a stalker.

Of course, Duffy and Boyle were guilty, because they had been the ones who bonked him on the head. The fact that they didn't kill him but left him in a position where life and death hung in the balance of his own volition was most certainly interesting, though. Why? And were they acting on their own or in accordance with another entity? The logical choice would be that they'd done it at the behest of Remington. But the fact remained that outside of Alice, the entire group had known each other since college.

Who had killed Michael Levy and why? Who had killed Saylor Ball? Who to believe?

These were the thoughts tumbling through his mind like socks in a commercial dryer at a laundromat as Langdon walked into the bookshop.

Starling was at the counter ringing up a woman purchasing a book. Raven was on the floor speaking with a potential customer. And Chabal was over by the coffee urns speaking with Shannon Undergrove.

Langdon ambled over, drawing the attention of both women. "Hello, Shannon."

"Hallo, Langdon. I was just speaking with your cute-as-a-button wife."

Cute-as-a-button? Langdon smirked, looked at Chabal. "Just like a puppy dog, she is."

Shannon fidgeted and gave a broad smile. "I got your message. Thought I'd come pay a visit in person."

"Let's go back to the office. Why don't you join us, Cutie-Pie."

Chabal eviscerated him with her glare but followed on back to the inner lair. Once they were settled, Langdon cut right to the chase. "We now have the ear of the president and should be able to curtail Remington's appointment to SCOTUS. Would you be willing to share that the judge has been blackmailing you?"

"You mean I wouldn't have to testify on the Senate Floor?"

"I can't promise that for sure, but I think we can convince the president to merely rescind his nomination, effectively taking Remington's name out of consideration."

"And the things I've, uh, participated in will not become public knowledge?"

"In a perfect world it will stay between the three of us, Cooper Walker, and the president."

Shannon sighed. "It's far from a perfect world, though, isn't it?"

"That it is."

"I saw on the news that Saylor Ball was killed. Did you know that Remington was sleeping with her?"

"Who has the man not had sex with?"

"He is a hard man to say no to."

There was a lot rolled into that reply, Langdon thought, a strange mix of puzzlement and astonishment flickering in his gut, sizzling, igniting, and rising up through to a flickering bewilderment in his mind. "You?"

"There is something magnetic about Neely. I hated what he did. How he treated others. His casual disdain of humanity. But, truth be told, I desired him. Wanted him. There were times when I thought the emotion was shared. Never while in college, but in the years since, we have verged on something more."

"More?"

"There was always a prickling sexual energy between the two of us. But when I transitioned to a woman, his interest heightened. One night, a few months back, he showed up at my place in Ogunquit. He'd been drinking. He made advances toward me."

Langdon's mind whirled with the implications of this latest revelation. "You had sex with him?"

Shannon laughed hoarsely. "No. I refused him. Threw him out. I'd grown stronger, you see, as a person, and realized what a horse's ass he was—how he abused others, no matter the relationship. I realized that it was my weakness he preyed upon, my confusion, my indecisions."

Langdon nodded. "It sounds like you were the first one to say no to the man."

"The thing is, he threatened to destroy me. He was so angry."

"What'd you do?"

"I went to visit Mikey. Told him everything."

"You remained friends with Michael Levy, the staunch Catholic?"

Shannon smiled sadly. "He'd gotten over that whole Catholicism thing years ago. He was actually the one who encouraged me to make my transition. Become who I really was. Like he had become who he really was when he left the Pope."

"Is Cornelius Remington really blackmailing you?"

Shannon sighed. Looked down. Then back up to meet Langdon's eyes. "No. He is threatening me."

"Threatening you?"

"I got a text message one day. It told me to keep my mouth shut or I'd be following Michael Levy to Hell."

Wow, Langdon thought. "From Remington?"

Shannon smiled. But it was more sad than happy. "I can't say for sure. It was from an unknown number. I figured it was probably one of those burner phones, you know, so that it couldn't be traced back to him. But, yeah, it had to be Neely. He ended it by saying that MAYHEM would be unleashed upon me if I didn't keep my mouth zipped tight."

"Are you willing to make an official statement of everything you have just shared?" Langdon asked. "For the president's ears?"

Shannon nodded.

Langdon texted Jimmy. He didn't expect a reply, knowing the man was probably in amorous congress with Marsha Verhoeven at the moment. He looked at the time. "I'm supposed to meet your buddies, Duffy and Boyle, in an hour. I can't get ahold of my lawyer who has been notarizing, recording, and collecting the allegations against Remington. How do you feel about hanging out at my house until we can get you on official record for what you know?"

They closed the bookshop down and Starling followed them home to keep Shannon company. Bart was waiting at the house when they arrived. The beauty of the spot that Duffy and Boyle had chosen to meet Langdon lay in the fact that the Town Commons backed up to the Langdon house.

The public entrance to the Town Commons was about a mile directly east, connected by a maze of trails. Bart and Chabal went on foot to lie in preparation for Langdon, who drove back around skirting Bowdoin College and coming back out Route 123 to the entrance. There were two vehicles parked in the small lot. A black Ford F-150 and a Toyota Camry.

Langdon checked his Glock. Slid the magazine out. Clicked it back in. Racked the slide. Put the pistol back in his shoulder holster. Took a breath. Got out of the Jeep. Dog had been left back with Starling and Shannon. It wouldn't be the first time that Langdon had walked into what was likely an ambush. He hoped that it was the last.

"I'm getting too old for this shit," he said. There was nobody but him to hear.

The main trail of the Town Commons was a large loop. He went to the right as directed. The sun was several hours from setting, but long shadows still cast their darkened portents written on the forest, harbingers of omens promised. He probably could've just gotten Bart to call in a dragnet of local and state police to surround the woods and flush Duffy and Boyle forth like hares on the hunt.

But they most likely had an escape plan for just such an eventuality. And Langdon wanted to get them talking. There were still too many unknowns on who had killed Michael Levy, much less Saylor Ball. Owning a mystery bookstore, he knew well the character of the unreliable narrator. In this particular case, Langdon had four such capricious yarn spinners. Marsha. Shannon. Tara. Cornelius. Who was to be believed if nobody was telling the truth?

Chapter 44

There was a rustle in the shadows of the woods off to Langdon's left. He tensed, ready to throw himself into the bushes, draw his pistol, be prepared to return fire. Defend himself. There was no gunshot. Nothing more.

He'd slowed his pace in preparation for whatever might come, but now he resumed walking. It could've been a deer, a raccoon, a porcupine, a branch falling, or a man setting up to kill him. Two figures came toward him down the path.

It was a man and a woman, holding hands, most likely from the Camry in the parking lot, Langdon figured. They passed with a nod, caught up in each other, their body language suggesting burgeoning passion. Langdon wondered if it was an illicit relationship, an affair in the woods, but then mentally kicked himself. The perfidiousness of Judge Remington had tarnished his thinking.

A bird fluttered overhead. They were close enough to Route 123 that Langdon could hear traffic going by. And then there he was.

Fred Duffy standing in the middle of the trail. A lone figure. His face was ridged with age past his years. He was stoop shouldered, gaunt, and had thinning hair. A rifle was crooked in his arm.

"Hi'ya, Fred. Where's your buddy?"

Duffy nodded behind Langdon. Boyle was about fifty feet behind him, making Langdon equally distant between the two men. He held a pistol loosely in both hands, down by his side. His feet were set in the Weaver Stance, his right leg forward, left leg staggered, his left finger on the trigger.

"Thought you boys just wanted to chat." Langdon turned sideways, left side to Boyle, right side to Duffy. If he was lucky, they'd miss and shoot each other.

"Just taking precautions." Duffy shifted his position slightly.

Langdon sidled with him, staying between the two men. "Why don't we put the weapons down, then. Guns have always made me nervous."

Duffy laughed. "As they should. We just want to make sure you didn't have any other ideas than just talking."

"Like getting payback for getting clonked on the head by you two bozos and tied to a mooring in the ocean?"

"We was supposed to kill you. Thought you deserved a fighting chance. And here you stand. Alive and well." It appeared that Duffy was the spokesperson of the duo.

"What do you mean you were supposed to kill me?"

"You had become irksome. Certain parties wanted you gone."

"Irksome? You mean by investigating Remington's past?"

Duffy nodded. "You need to just let well enough alone."

Langdon shifted his eyes to the indistinct murkiness of the darkening woods and wondered where Chabal and Bart were hidden. His back was to the roadside of the woods, just a narrow strip of trees that he doubted they would have chosen for concealment. Therefore, hopefully, they lay in wait somewhere in front of him, to the forest-side of the path.

"I can't do that," he said.

"How about we tell you what you want to know but you keep our names out of it?"

"Your names are already in it, Fred. There is an arrest warrant for your assault on me. There will be no way to sweep it under the rug."

"One year in jail. Max."

Langdon chuckled. "At the very least it will be a Class B, but I'm thinking Class A felony assault. Serious bodily injury, the use of a dangerous weapon, and conduct that manifests a depraved indifference to the value of my life. That's thirty years, Fred."

Duffy raised his rifle slightly, if still not quite pointed at Langdon. "Not if you drop the charges."

"Doesn't matter what I do, now. The police aren't going to let a felony assault go."

"What do you suggest? We're not going down for thirty years."

"I'm thinking you know things, Fred, things worth bargaining with. Things to get your sentence drastically reduced, if you play your cards right."

"What is it you want to know?"

"What was going on between Judge Remington and Saylor Ball?"

Duffy looked perplexed, visible even through the gloom. "Saylor Ball? You mean that broad that got killed out to the motel? She was connected to the White House somehow, wasn't she?"

Interesting, Langdon thought. "She was the one fast-tracking Remington to sitting on the SCOTUS Bench."

"Chief of staff. That's what she was." Duffy nodded. "Had the ear of the president."

"I think they were having an affair."

"Don't know nothing about that."

"The acting chief of staff is ready to put the clamps on Remington. If you agree to cooperate, I'm sure that we could get the two of you a deal."

"What kind of deal?"

"I'm thinking I can convince the police to drop the assault charges against me and then you can come clean on Mike Levy's murder."

"Come clean?"

"Oh, I don't think you killed him. But you did help move the body and orchestrate it to look like a terrible freak accident. Whose idea was it to stage it to look like he electrocuted himself on the toilet via his headphones and that triggered a heart attack with his questionable ticker? Remington couldn't come up with a simpler diversion?"

"You have no proof."

"If you don't come clean then we'll have to see what Remington has to say. You want to trust that he won't throw you under the bus?"

Duffy smirked. "You think you got it all figured out, don't you?"

The smirk gave Langdon pause. "It was Remington who killed Levy and *forced* the two of you to help out, wasn't it?"

This time Duffy laughed coarsely. "Yeah, it was *Remington*."

"We ain't taking no deal, Fred," Boyle said coldly.

Langdon turned his attention from Duffy. Boyle had his pistol up, arms crooked slightly, legs staggered, left finger on the trigger, a desperate look on his face.

"Police. Drop your weapons." Bart stepped from behind a tree about fifty feet in front of Langdon. He had his weapon out and trained on Boyle.

Langdon pulled his Glock from the shoulder holster and aimed it at Duffy who now had his rifle pointed at Bart. Somehow, even in this incredibly tense life-and-death moment, Langdon's mind flittered to the final scene of *Reservoir Dogs*. He supposed Chabal, still hidden, was Mr. Pink in this scenario.

"Put down the gun and we'll walk away," Duffy said.

"I'm going to plug him right here and now," Boyle yelled.

"Drop the weapon," Bart said.

Langdon looked at Bart. All of his attention was on Boyle. As his should be on Duffy. He swiveled his head back. Any indication that the man was going to pull the trigger meant that Langdon had to do so first.

"I ain't going to prison," Boyle said. "Not for no bitch."

Langdon risked a look back at the man. His eyes widened. Chabal had stepped from a tree behind Boyle and was only about five feet from him.

"Drop the weapon, Boyle, and put your hands up!" Bart raised his voice to a deep boom to cover her steps.

Langdon looked back to Duffy. His eyes were pinned on Bart. Then they shifted and realization flashed as he must've seen Chabal. His rifle wavered.

There was a thunk behind Langdon. A gun fired. Duffy dropped his rifle and turned and ran. Langdon spun back to look. Boyle was on the ground. Chabal over him with her M & P Shield in both hands pointed down at him.

Langdon rotated his eyes toward Bart who jerked his head toward the direction Duffy had disappeared and then moved forward to assist Chabal.

The shadows were deeper, hiding roots on the ground, twists in the trail, but Langdon had walked back here thousands of times with dog. He knew it like the back of his hand. Duffy had a head start but that wasn't going to do him any good. Langdon had largely recovered from being clunked in the head and knew the terrain.

The chase lasted all of thirty seconds before Duffy tripped, stumbled, and crashed into a pine tree. He went to his knees and then fell on his face. Langdon was on him in an instant, knee in his back, Glock pressed to the back of the man's head.

Chapter 45

While they were waiting for a squad car or two to arrive and take the two men into custody, Langdon's phone buzzed with a call. It was Cooper Walker.

"Hello," he said somewhat wearily as he answered.

"I just shared the information you sent over with the president."

Langdon shook his head, trying to put order to the events of the past week, past day, past few hours. "The statements from Alice Rehnquist, Tara James, and Marsha Verhoeven."

"That'd be the ones."

"There's more to add."

"No need. The president was outraged. Beside himself. Never seen him so angry. He's going to rescind the nomination of Cornelius Remington tonight on the eleven o'clock news."

Langdon looked at the time on the phone. It was not quite seven. "That'd probably be a good idea. The rest is going to blow the lid right off this thing. Be best if the administration was out ahead of it."

"What's the rest?"

"Still working out the details. Might have to come down your way and have a conversation with the honorable judge first."

"No need. The president got the hearings put on hold until Monday to buy him some time. I believe the honorable judge is on a plane back to Maine tonight."

"Private?"

Cooper laughed. "No. He is flying commercial."

"Anything more on Saylor Ball's murder?"

"There was no sign of forced entry. Looked like Chief Ball was just getting out of the shower when she was Tased and suffocated. The only thing of possible interest is that there was only one key card in the room and the motel front desk person is certain he gave her two. No other leads at this point."

Sirens could be heard in the distance.

"Okay. I gotta go, Cooper. I should have the rest for you very soon."

"You did good work, Langdon, stopping that sleazeball from becoming one of nine."

Langdon wasn't sure how to answer. It had been an ordeal, and it wasn't yet over. "Thanks."

"Is that sirens I hear?"

Langdon hung up.

Two patrol cars pulled into the lot. Duffy and Boyle were put into the back of one and taken away. Another car came up with a lieutenant who questioned Bart while Langdon and Chabal waited.

"Did you thunk that guy in the head with your pistol barrel?" he asked her.

"Thunk?" Chabal grinned wickedly at him.

"That was the sound it made. I looked back and you were standing over him like some ultimate badass. You were like Clarice Starling from *The Silence of the Lambs*."

"I might've given him a tap to the noggin. Jodie Foster, huh? High praise indeed."

Langdon grinned at her. It was good to have his wife back. "Been a busy few days. Or weeks, really."

"Good to have it all done. Think I heard that Remington is losing his nomination."

"Almost done."

"Almost?"

Langdon nodded, raised a finger, took out his phone and called

Cornelius Remington. It went straight to voice mail. He then called Starling who answered after one ring.

"What's going on, boss?" he asked.

Langdon wondered for a brief moment what *was* going on. "I need you to gather Jimmy, Marsha, and Tara over to the house."

"The first two are already here. Jimmy tried to call you, then me, and after I filled him in, he ran down to the office and got his official stampy thing and we got Shannon's statement with witnesses and notarized."

"Can you reach out to Tara? Get her to come over as well."

"Sure thing, boss."

"Make sure you keep them there. I'll be along in an hour or two."

"What's going on, boss? What happened with those two fellows you were going to meet?"

"They're on their way to Brunswick PD right now. Don't imagine they'll be there long. Just not sure if the State Police or the FBI will get jurisdiction."

"Everybody okay?"

"Chabal thunked the Boyle guy pretty good, but yeah, other than that, everybody is good." Langdon looked at his wife who was laughing at his description of her hitting Boyle.

"What should I say to get Tara here?"

"Tell her that I got the whole story and I'll be sharing it with everybody."

"Gotcha, boss."

"Star? One more thing. Can you get me the cell phone number for Angela Remington and text it to me?"

"Sure. Password on your computer still CoffeeMystery?"

"Yep. LocateNOW is right on the desktop."

"I'll get it right over to you."

An unmarked car pulled up and FBI agents Delgado and Parker got out. They made a beeline for Langdon and Chabal. He answered their questions mostly, withholding only a few nuances of what had happened and what was going on.

There was now a collection of five or six police vehicles and several unmarked cars. Two men even wore ICE windbreakers making Langdon wonder how that might connect, ultimately deciding that they were probably just bored and showed up for the fun.

Delgado and Parker went over to speak with the head of the State Police, Colonel something or other, and the Brunswick Police Chief. Langdon fished his phone back out. There was a text from Starling with a phone number for Angela Remington. He called it.

"Hello?" her voice was frail and worried.

"Angela? This is Langdon."

"What do you want now, Mr. Langdon?" There was a hint of hardness underlying the whining tone. A deepening of tone and intensity. "Haven't you harassed us enough?"

"Are you picking your husband up at the Jetport, Angela?"

"As a matter of fact, I am. How did you know that?"

"What time does he land?"

"8:20. I am sitting in the cell phone lot right now."

"Do you think that you could bring him to my house in Brunswick?"

Angela snorted. "Absolutely not."

"I believe I have information that will exonerate him on the charges of murder, Mrs. Remington."

"Murder? What are you talking about?"

"Just tell him that the police are going to be looking to question him about a murder and I can provide an alibi for him. His political career rests on it, Mrs. Remington. If he wants to become a Supreme Court justice, you must bring him to my house before the police and then the media get to him."

There was a long pause over the airways. "Where do you live?"

"I will text you the address."

"I will see what I can do, Mr. Langdon."

Chapter 46

Langdon and Chabal were grilled for two more hours, first at the Town Commons, and then down at the police station, before being let go for the night. That made it close to nine when they got home to a full house. Everybody was in the living room. Marsha and Jimmy were on the loveseat, drinks in hand, whispering to each other. Tara and Starling were on the couch in animated conversation, catching up on more than thirty years of life stories. Dog was pressed up to the back of Starling getting head rubs. Shannon sat in an armchair scrolling through her phone.

There were two seats left for Langdon and Chabal, but he brought in an additional two chairs, with five sets of eyes pinned to him, six if you counted dog, who was the only one that got up to help.

As soon as Langdon and Chabal sat, Marsha plunged right in. "How'd the meet-up with Fred and John go?"

"It was interesting." Langdon went for evasive while he waited the arrival of the Remingtons.

"Are those chairs for them?" Tara asked. "It'll be just like old times. The gang all together."

"They won't be joining us as they have been… detained."

"Ha," Jimmy said. "Does that mean they need a lawyer?"

"You didn't have them arrested, did you?" Marsha's face flushed red in anger. "I set up a meeting between you and them in good faith."

"I wasn't planning on it until they decided that the best way to stay out of prison was to get rid of me."

"Who are those two chairs for if not Freddie and Johnny?" Shannon asked.

Langdon saw the flash of lights turning into their driveway. "I believe you're about to see."

He went to the door and opened it.

Judge Remington stepped from the passenger seat of the car and stormed up the three steps to the porch. "What bullshit are you playing at now, Langdon? Murder? As if? I don't know why Saylor let you out of jail in the first place, but you're about to go back."

"Won't you come in?" Langdon said in his best English butler speak. There was a tickle in his mind that this was unfolding like the end of an Agatha Christie book. "The other guests are already here."

"Other guests? What other guests? And we are not your guests."

"Right this way, Judge and Mrs. Remington. And to the right."

Langdon wished slightly that he was able to see the faces of the Remingtons when they saw their company gathered in the living room. He was privy to the expressions of those in the room, though, and that was interesting in itself.

Marsha's face was the most evocative. A shimmer of desire and excitement upon seeing the judge turned to enmity as she caught sight of Toots. Her face literally rippled with these emotions, the two strong proclivities of her base nature tussling across her face in an epic battle. Langdon wondered if Jimmy caught a flicker of her lust, and if so, whether he cared.

This raw craving of sensual hunger was mirrored in the face of Shannon, only without the opposing animosity for Toots. And, to a lesser degree, on the visage of Tara, suggesting that she was the one most over her crush and infatuation of the charismatic Judge Remington.

Langdon smirked as he thought of what a brilliant idea it was to gather these four women together in the same room with the judge and see what boiled out of the pot. The last encounter between

Marsha and Toots had led to a fist fight, with some slapping, hair pulling, and wrestling thrown into the mix.

Langdon cleared his throat. "May I present Judge and Mrs. Cornelius Remington."

The judge wheeled around, his face red, contorted in fury. "What sort of fiendish child's play are you up to?"

Langdon gestured at the two chairs he'd placed in front of the television. "Please, sit."

The judge looked like he was going to argue, perhaps try to storm out, but Langdon was not a small man. He was four inches over six feet and weighed in at twenty pounds over two bills. And right now, he was sharing his coldest stone face, with a suggestion of violence emanating from his eyes, and a promise of pain from his tight-lipped snarl.

The judge sat. Toots harrumphed and sat next to him.

"I believe everybody knows everybody," Langdon said. "It seemed like a good time to air out some dirty laundry and see if we can't clean it up and make it presentable again."

"What in God's green earth are you talking about?" Toots asked.

"Well, let me tell you, my dear Toots." Langdon sat back down next to Chabal. "We'll start with Tara James. Did you know that Tara was Neely's girlfriend in college and one night he encouraged a drunken buddy, Chuckie Taylor, to have sex with his drunken girlfriend? Or that when she got pregnant, possibly with Cornelius' child, he forced, well, strongly encouraged her to have an abortion? Otherwise, they might've married, and you never would have happened, Toots."

Tara's face was livid, but she remained quiet. Langdon regretted bringing up this old baggage, but it wasn't a secret from anybody in the room. And her cousins had almost made him swim with a crocodile named after one of the most notorious and most savage Confederate guerrilla leaders.

Toots' face was ashen with just two pinpricks of red on each cheek. She looked like she might speak and then pressed her lips firmly together, and then her need got the better of herself. "Neely told me about her. What a tart she was."

"And did you also know, Toots, that the person who assaulted Tara in college at your husband's urging is now a woman. And that woman is right there." Langdon nodded at Shannon. "And she is now Shannon Undergrove. And your dearest Neely has had sex with both Chuckie and Shannon."

Toot's mouth now opened in a perfect fish on a hook imitation.

"Yes," Langdon continued, "Neely had sex with Shannon before and after she transitioned into being a woman."

"I never told you that," Shannon snapped.

Langdon shrugged. "I have many failings as a person, as a PI, as a bookstore owner, but one of my true gifts is my ability to read between the pages. Often, that is where the real story is."

"That's a lie!" The judge went to stand up.

Langdon stood before he could, put a hand on his shoulder, and shoved him back into the chair. "Is it?"

"It's true," Shannon said. "Not something I'm proud of, but yes, it's true."

The carefully constructed façade of Toots began to peel back as if an onion. It was as if she was being reborn into something angrier and harder than the frail wallflower she normally presented.

"And Marsha." Langdon sat back down. "The fat girl that everybody picked on. Led by your husband. Publicly, he rode her hard, never letting an opportunity pass to make fun of her, ridicule her, and tear her down like breaking the will of a hostage. Privately, he snuck into her room and rode her equally hard. I would guess that a therapist might call this the Stockholm syndrome, or some variant of that. And yes, Toots, that sexual relationship has continued ever since college. All through the course of your marriage."

Toots cackled. "I put a stop to it two years ago."

Langdon looked at Marsha. "Is that true?"

Her face was mottled, her cheeks convulsing in hatred. "Neely told me that Toots demanded that we stop. That she was going to divorce him if we didn't. And he couldn't have that. Because he had ambitions."

Langdon nodded. "So that tells us two things. It tells us that Toots is well aware of the judge's sexual proclivities and is okay with them up to a point, but at that point, she has the power to stop them. Very interesting."

"Does this whole thing have a point?" Remington spoke in a hushed whisper. "I like sex. I have needs. My wife understands and accepts that. What business is it of anybody else?"

Langdon looked at him and then continued laying down what he was laying down, "Fred Duffy and John Boyle were arrested earlier this evening."

"What does that have to do with me?" Remington whispered.

"Well, to tell you the truth, I thought that you set them on me, to try and get me to back off of investigating your background and your current lifestyle. Because it was the two of them who assaulted me and tied me to a mooring in the ocean. That is what they were arrested for, but I have a feeling that they will break down and admit to being accomplices to murder."

"Duffy? Boyle? Who did they help murder?" Remington's voice was barely audible.

"It was really just the cover up of a murder. They carried Michael Levy up the stairs and into his bathroom and set it up to look like he'd given himself a bit of an electrical jolt that caused him to have a stroke and die. But the electrical jolt wasn't actually from a frayed wire on his ear buds as he sat on the toilet taking a shit, but rather, was the result of being Tased."

"Tased?" Remington mouthed rather than said the words.

"It turns out that Levy was going to come clean about a number of things he knew about you Cornelius, including an abortion, a homosexual relationship, a great deal of adultery, and being a rather boorish bully."

"How?"

Langdon turned to Toots. "I'm sure that you told yourself that it was a mistake, that you merely went to see Levy to encourage him to keep his mouth shut. That you shocked him with the Taser just so you could get his undivided attention. How were you supposed to know of his weak heart? You must've been in a tizzy when you realized he was dead. What had you done?"

The judge turned a confused look upon his wife.

"That's a lie," Toots snarled.

"I don't believe that's the story that Duffy and Boyle will be telling," Langdon said. "You see, I had a conversation with them. They thought it rather funny when I suggested it was Remington who killed Levy. They said that, yes, it had been *Remington* who'd killed Michael Levy. And the way they said it, along with a few other things, started to tickle my brain. Something to the tune of, that it was Mrs. Angela 'Toots' Remington who killed him and forced them to help cover up the murder. At the time, of course, I was thinking it was your husband. But then Boyle said he wasn't going to jail for no bitch. And then it clicked. You killed Levy, didn't you, Toots?"

Toots' face changed to defiant. The transformation from a frail housewife to something harder and more masculine was complete. "My name is Mayhem. Not Toots. Not Angela. I am not some floral embroidery to be put out like a decoration when guests come over. I am powerful. Strong. To be feared. I am the best of both genders." Her voice came out thicker and deeper and her eyes flickered wildly in their sockets. "Michael Levy deserved everything that he got. Some people don't understand that other people are chosen for a higher purpose and are not regulated by the laws as applied to the rest of humanity."

Langdon nodded as if in understanding. He said nothing about the metamorphosis of the docile Toots Remington into some androgynous creature of defiance. "They say that killing becomes easier. Is that true? Because it certainly seems that you had less trepidation when you killed Saylor Ball yesterday."

"Killed?" The judge stared in disbelief at Toots.

Toots glared back at him. Or was it Mayhem? "I told you to end it. Like I told you to end it with that whore over there. You promised me that you would. And then you got in your car and drove to the motel and fucked her. What else could I do?"

"What? How?"

Langdon smiled grimly. "I'm thinking that you came home, and Toots found the hotel key in your jacket pocket. Perhaps when you went to shower to cleanse the cheat off yourself. She took the key, went to the motel, let herself in, where Saylor had just finished washing the stink of you off herself in the shower, and Toots gave her two barbed prongs to the breasts. Or one anyway. But Saylor didn't have a bad heart, so Toots had to suffocate her. That sound about right, Toots?"

Toots face contorted. "Toots didn't kill her. Toots is weak. Fragile. Mayhem killed the slut. Mayhem put up with it while she was helping Neely get nominated and confirmed to the SCOTUS. But now that that is a done deal, she was no longer needed. So I told him to end it. But he lied to me. To me. To his wife. To Mayhem. And went and fucked the slut. What was I to do? Just take it?"

"Toots—" the judge began.

"Mayhem. My name is motherfucking Mayhem."

"What?"

Langdon looked at the grandfather clock in the corner of the room. "Just so you both," he looked at Toots, "all three of you know, the President is going to rescind his nomination from consideration in ten minutes."

Remington turned white. "You're lying." He looked as if he might fling himself to the floor and start blubbering.

Langdon smiled.

Toots, or Mayhem, turned her, or their, snarling face toward her, or their, husband. "Goddamn you. You are worthless. Just a cheating slimeball. I should've known. My mother told me that you were no good." She pulled a Taser from her purse, turned it on, and pointed it. A red dot appeared on the front of Judge Remington's pants, and she pulled the trigger. Two prongs propelled the few feet between them and buried their barbed points into his flesh.

"Toots Mayhem makes two good points," Langdon said with a smirk. "You are worthless, and you are a slimeball."

Judge Remington did not reply as he slowly slid from his chair to the floor, his body gyrating to its own rhythm, his eyes glassy, and his career over.

Epilogue

They sat upon the top of Bradbury Mountain in Pownal, about twenty minutes from home. At just 485 feet high, Langdon didn't believe it really qualified as a mountain. Nonetheless, from the summit, it had wide sweeping views of the surrounding area.

It being mid-September, mid-week, and overcast, they had the rock on the top to themselves. Too late for summer tourists, too early for leaf peepers, and not enough of a novelty for the locals, they'd only seen one other couple in the short trek to the top.

"Why are people like that?" Chabal asked.

Hm, Langdon wondered, what people and like what? The question could be aimed at the wendigo and his coven, or maybe at Langdon himself, or possibly… well, there was a myriad of people, not to mention characteristics to be like.

"Toots and Cornelius Remington, you mean?" he asked.

"That'd be a good place to start."

"For him, I think everything just came too easy, and it tarnished him. From an early age, both genders doted upon him, and he came to believe he was better than everybody else."

Chabal snickered. "Not anymore, he doesn't. Stripped of his robe, disbarred from the law, with a convict for a wife, and forced to wear the Scarlet A for Asshole around the rest of his life."

Langdon chuckled. "It would seem that Karma is a real thing."

"How about Toots? How does she go from being an upstanding and charitable member of the community to being on trial for multiple murders?"

Langdon didn't answer for a bit as he gazed out over the forests of Maine that led to the coast. He could see the factory building on Cousins Island, a light mark on the vastness before him. "I suppose it doesn't happen all of a sudden. It builds, and one thing leads to another. She realizes that her husband isn't a very nice man, then discovers his infidelity, just once at first, and then serial occurrences, and eventually a tidal wave of cheating that fills her nostrils with a stink that threatens to suffocate her. But by now, she has stature she's not willing to give up, she is the wife of a judge, a rising star in the legal field, and then the tantalizing baited hook of him becoming a Supreme Court justice."

Chabal waited for him to continue, but when he didn't, chimed in. "She'd sold her soul for that position of prestige and prominence, and when Michael Levy threatened to strip that away, she killed him."

"I think she meant to threaten him, but with his bad heart, yeah, she killed him."

"At what point do you think that Toots transitioned into Mayhem?"

Langdon shrugged. "I guess that'll be up to the shrinks. It couldn't have been easy being married to that pathetic prick for all those years."

"And you knew that Toots was the killer just because of how Duffy said the name Remington."

Langdon shrugged. "I wasn't certain. That's why I wanted to get everybody in the same room and see how things shook out."

Chabal chortled. "And boy did they shake out. Especially when she shocked him in the gonads. A fitting end to their story."

"Oh, their story continues. Just in prison and disgrace."

"How about Duffy and Boyle. College grads from good families, now on trial for being accomplices to murder."

"Not to mention the others. Shannon Undergrove, Marsha

Verhoeven, and Tara James. All tainted by the magnetism of Cornelius, haunted by his actions, floundering forward through life, victims of abuse."

Chabal sighed. "So many people, so much pain—and for what?"

Langdon pondered the reasons while enjoying the grandeur of the view. "It all comes down to a few basic things," he said. "Power. Fear. Money. Angst. And just plain wickedness."

Chabal snickered. "And together they all created Mayhem."

Acknowledgments

If you are reading this, I thank you, for without readers, writers would be obsolete.

I am grateful to my mother, Penelope McAlevey, and father, Charles Cost, who have always been my first readers and critics.

Much appreciation to the various friends and relatives who have also read my work and given helpful advice.

I'd like to offer a big hand to my wife, Deborah Harper Cost, and children, Brittany, Pearson, Miranda, and Ryan, who have always had my back.

Thank you to Encircle Publishing, Cynthia Bracket-Vincent and Eddie Vincent, and Chris and Deirdre Wait for giving me this opportunity to be published. Also, kudos to Deirdre Wait for the fantastic cover art.

About the Author

MATT COST is the highly acclaimed, award-winning author of the Mainely Mystery series. The first book, *Mainely Power*, was selected as the Maine Humanities Council Read ME Fiction Book of 2020. This was followed by *Mainely Fear*, *Mainely Money*, *Mainely Angst*, *Mainely Wicked*, and the newest, *Mainely Mayhem*. He is also the author of the Clay Wolfe / Port Essex Mysteries, *Wolfe Trap*, *Mind Trap*, *Mouse Trap*, *Cosmic Trap*, and the latest, *Pirate Trap*, was published by Encircle in March 2024.

I Am Cuba: Fidel Castro and the Cuban Revolution was his first traditionally published novel. His other historical fiction novels are *Love in a Time of Hate* (August 2021), and *At Every Hazard: Joshua Chamberlain and the Civil War* (August 2022). His love of histories and mysteries is combined in his 1920's Brooklyn 8 Ballo Mystery series, which begins with *Velma Gone Awry* (April 2023) and continues in *City Gone Askew* (July 2024).

Cost was a history major at Trinity College. He owned a mystery bookstore, a video store, and a gym before serving a ten-year sentence as a junior high school teacher. In 2014, he was released and he began writing. And that's what he does: he writes histories and mysteries. Cost now lives in Brunswick, Maine, with his wife, Harper. There are four grown children: Brittany, Pearson, Miranda, and Ryan. A chocolate Lab and a basset hound round out the mix. He now spends his days at the computer, writing.

If you enjoyed this book,
please consider writing your review
and sharing it with other readers.

Many of our Authors are happy to participate in
Book Club and Reader Group discussions.
For more information, contact us at info@encirclepub.com.

Thank you,
Encircle Publications

For news about more exciting new fiction, join us at:

Facebook: www.facebook.com/encirclepub

Instagram: www.instagram.com/encirclepublications

Sign up for the Encircle Publications newsletter:
eepurl.com/cs8taP